Death a

GEORGINA
CLARKE

DEATH
AND THE
HARLOT

CANELO

First published in the United Kingdom in 2019 by Canelo

This edition published in the United Kingdom in 2020 by

Canelo Digital Publishing Limited
Third Floor, 20 Mortimer Street
London W1T 3JW
United Kingdom

A CIP catalogue record for this book is available from the British Library.

Print ISBN 978 1 78863 791 6
Ebook ISBN 978 1 78863 453 3

Look for more great books at www.canelo.co

Printed and bound in Great Britain by Clays Ltd, Elcograf S.p.A.

To Tim

Chapter One

Soho, March 1759

There are few sights more ridiculous than a fat old man naked from the waist down.

Mr George Reed pulled off his wig and fumbled with his breeches. The most successful cloth merchant in Norwich — as he had told me more than once in the tavern — was struggling to reach his shoe buckles without grunting. His belly sagged under his vast shirt. At last, he stood triumphant and wiped a handkerchief across his brow to remove all signs of effort.

Ah, Mr Reed. Another respectable tradesman from the shires with time on his hands, money in his purse and a liking for pretty young women, who had found his way to the best bawdy house in London. In a moment, he would be clambering over me with all the excitement of a youth half his age. Unless his heart gave out first.

Nothing much was stirring below the shirt, mind. Mr Reed was going to need a helping hand. I shifted position on the bed, allowing a wisp of muslin to float away and expose a little more flesh. His eyes danced apologetically but little else twitched. I lay there, staring at a long and tedious evening.

Poor old goat, he really did want some help. I eased myself up onto an elbow and flashed him the famous

Lizzie Hardwicke smile, the smile that they speak of in taverns from Marylebone to Fleet Street – so I'm told – the smile that brings them running to throw gold into my lap.

'Well goodness me, Mr Reed, what have we here?' I leaned forward, so that he could see even more of me, and lifted the hem of his shirt.

He straightened his back.

'Upon my honour, I don't think I have seen the promise of such magnificence since I entertained the Duke of Rutland.'

His eyes widened. Every word a lie, of course. I have no honour; George Reed was not magnificent and nor was he going to be – and I would never question the fidelity of any duke to his duchess. But one thing that my career has taught me is that men will hear what they want to hear from the mouth of a beautiful woman, especially when she is nearly naked.

'The Duke of Rutland was here?'

I changed the angle of my leg, revealing the treasure for which he was paying so handsomely.

'His grace was right here. But he wasn't as splendid as you, Mr Reed.'

'Really?' He was, of course, susceptible to flattery.

'Hush now, sir, there's really no need for you to boast. Only bring yourself a little closer and keep me company.'

I patted the pillow next to me. Perhaps I could get this over with quickly. Polly, Emily and Lucy would be home soon with gossip to share, and Ma Farley was downstairs with a new girl. He didn't need to be invited twice, and strutted like a bloated peacock, ready to give me the benefit of his superior physique.

A full five minutes later I rolled him off and left him to doze. I couldn't leave the room until he was dressed – that was one of the rules of our house. There was little point dressing myself at this hour, so I left off my stays, shrugged a loose gown over my shoulders and tied it at the waist. I sat at the table to fasten up my hair with a blue ribbon. Blue was my colour; it set off my copper curls to their best advantage.

I scrutinised the girl in the mirror: nineteen years old, considered slightly built, and not yet showing the hardened face of a career on the town, I could still pass for much younger. I was respectably born, decently educated and, just six months ago, was living in the comfort of my father's house. Now I was here; one of a small number of girls in Berwick Street, earning a living on my back. It's strange, the way Fortune deals her hand.

Outside, the city was wallowing in darkness. The elegant streets of Soho had given up their nocturnal creatures. Girls walked slowly arm in arm with lovers more than twice their age; in windows, they lit lamps and sat in near nakedness. The night time was when the real business of London's day took place.

I closed my ribbon box, catching sight of the scars on my hand, shining in the light of the candle.

I did not choose to become a whore. Few of us do.

George Reed snuffled and snorted in my bed, turning over to face the wall. He hadn't been so bad after all, and splendidly quick – thank God. His handsome coat, sage green wool with gold buttons down the front edges and sleeves, was discarded on the floor. I laid it carefully over a chair. The tabby silk waistcoat, which I'd noticed earlier, was very fine; embroidered with exotic flowers. He would

3

need to be wealthy indeed to afford such a lovely piece. Did he pick it up in Spitalfields, or had it come from Paris? This Norwich cloth merchant had a good eye as well as a heavy purse. I stroked the needlework. Perhaps I could persuade him to visit again and part him from a few more guineas.

There was a soft thud. A brown paper parcel had fallen to the floor. I picked it up, feeling the weight of it.

'Leave that alone, girl.' Mr Reed was awake and sitting up in bed, frowning.

'It fell from a pocket as I was tidying your clothes.' No one wants to be thought a thief. 'I didn't want the silk to crease.' I handed him the parcel. 'Some important papers?'

He pulled at the hem of his shirt and cleared his throat. 'Yes. Papers.' He was embarrassed by his nakedness.

'You have a beautiful waistcoat, sir,' I gestured to it. 'Very fine embroidery. Perhaps I can assist you with it when you've dressed?' I handed him his breeches and turned away. A gentleman is happy enough to be watched and applauded when he's removing his clothes, but is generally shy when dressing.

I heard him huffing at the effort of tucking his shirt. After a minute, I held the waistcoat out, smoothing it over his shoulders and touching his neck softly once he had put it on.

'I hope that everything was satisfactory.'

'Yes, yes, very good,' he said, 'very good indeed.' His mind was still on the parcel.

I couldn't afford to lose this plump catch, however unappealing the thought of further transactions might be. I took his hand and held it flat against my breast, fluttering my breath with practised care as he squeezed.

'I wonder whether you are in London for business or... just for pleasure?' I might as well tease: he wouldn't be fresh for hours. He began to slobber at my neck, thoughts moving away from his papers and back to me. I risked a small moan to encourage him.

'Aside from the pleasure of you, it is all business. I've a few days left in town before I return home.'

'Then you might like to visit me again before you leave?'

He started biting my earlobe, which I tolerated. 'That would be most delightful.'

I pulled away, having secured the promise.

'Lovely,' I said. I held both of his hands firmly and gazed into his greedy eyes with as much cheeriness as I could.

'I'm sure that you could entertain me for a little longer, while I'm here,' he said, tugging me uncomfortably close again, 'I have the means to pay'. He started to grope inside my gown. I really didn't want this now, and he surely wasn't so vain as to think he would be capable?

'I'm not sure I'm available at this hour.'

He was a large man and quite strong and I didn't like the way he was pulling at my body. I had to get rid of him, promise him something.

'But we're having a party, a masked ball, here tomorrow night, as it happens. Would you care to join us?' As soon as the words left my mouth, I regretted my rashness. The girls would kill me.

'A masked ball?' His eyes bulged.

'Well, it's really nothing special at all, just some food and wine and a few friends.'

He licked his bottom lip and a sickly smile spread over his face.

'I've heard of such parties.' That wasn't a surprise. Mrs Farley's parties were the talk of the town. The combination of exclusivity and notoriety was enough of an enticement.

'I'll come. My friends at home will be green with envy when I tell them.'

I never should have asked him. In a little over a day he would be dead because of the party and I would be running from the magistrate and the hangman. If I had known that then, I would have given him every pleasure he wished that evening, every trick in my book, and then kicked him out for good. But I did not know.

I am a whore, not a fortune-teller.

Chapter Two

The noise coming from the parlour, when George Reed left, was extraordinary. Even for a house full of young women, it was loud, and it was a good thing we had finished for the night, as such a commotion would drive away all but the bravest of customers. Sydney, our ever-present doorman, tall, sleek and exotic, was perched on a stool in the hallway with his fingers rammed into his ears. He saw me and rolled his eyes; the disapproval of a sophisticated foreigner stretched over his dark face. I pushed open the door to the dimly lit room. Curiosity has long been my curse.

A young girl sat howling; arms flung across the table in front of her, a pile of fair curls on her head glimmering in the candle light. She was around fifteen or sixteen, possibly older. It was rather difficult to tell while she sobbed so extravagantly. Where had Ma found her?

Ma Farley was sitting across the other side of the table, arms folded under her enormous bosom. Lucy, elegant, poised, but blessed with a voice like a screech owl, was shouting something at Ma – I couldn't hear what it was. Emily, whose hatchet face had earlier been painted to perfection but now was smeared from the night's graft, was demanding answers. Ma was yelling back, ignoring the crying, and Polly was gently trying to hug and shush the girl. No wonder Sydney had closed the parlour door behind me.

I tugged off a shoe and banged the heel on the table. The room fell into shocked silence, as they turned to gawp at me.

'Thank you,' I said, brandishing the shoe. 'Now, who is our friend?'

The shoe, still in my hand, cracked down on the table again as they all began to speak at once.

'Sydney thinks he's gone deaf, you know. Ma, would you introduce me, please.'

Mrs Sarah Farley, Mother, or Ma to those who knew her well, stood up and straightened her soft cap, tucking a loose strand of greying hair behind an ear. Once, she had been a real beauty, but now, long past forty-five, her body was overused, overripe and overhanging. Her natural face had hardened with lines, so she filled in the cracks with powder and rouge. She pulled the young girl to her feet, not unkindly.

'Miss Lizzie Hardwicke, this is Miss Amelia Blackwood.'

The girl was nicely mannered. As we curtseyed I saw that her face – underneath the blotched cheeks and red eyes – was extremely pretty.

'Miss Blackwood,' I nodded my greeting and raised an eyebrow at Ma as the girl resumed her place at the table. 'A new companion?'

Amelia started bleating over Polly's shoulder again, but more quietly this time. Ma sighed and sat down heavily.

'It's not what you think, Lizzie.'

I hoped not. Brothel keepers, bawds like Ma, had a reputation for forcing innocent young girls into a life of sin and they were rightly hated for their procuring. There were plenty of stories: unblemished lambs arriving in London from the country, flattered or tricked into bawdy houses, their virginity sold to the highest bidder. Mrs Farley was not above such devices when it came to supplementing her funds, I was sure of it, but it wasn't her regular style. I waited for an explanation.

'She's been thrown out of her home,' Ma said. 'I found her at Charing Cross. Good job I was there; I'd just caught sight of her when Mrs Hamble and Mrs Bull came around the corner.'

Polly shivered. Miss Polly Young, our prettiest house-mate, had golden hair and the sort of countenance that fell into effortless smiles, but her own career in town had been launched by Mrs Hamble, and the memory still made her lip tremble. She had been fourteen at the time.

'What do you mean "she's been thrown out"?'

'Her father is an alderman. She fell in love with the local farrier's son and he caught them kissing in the yard. Threw her out on the streets.'

'That's a bit harsh for a fumble,' I said.

'He's got a reputation to maintain, apparently,' said Lucy, arching an immaculate eyebrow, 'although I'm quite sure I've never heard of him.' Lucy knew many men of reputation, as she was often fond of telling us.

'At least he gave her some money and allowed her to collect some clothes,' said Ma. 'Not all girls are so fortunate.'

Indeed, they are not.

'It's still a bit tough. She's barely fifteen by the look of it.'

'I'm seventeen.' Amelia raised her head from the table. 'And it wasn't a fumble; Tommy and I are in love. We want to marry.' She started to sob in great shaking coughs. 'I'll never see him again!' Her head flopped down and Polly stroked her shoulders gently. Eventually she stopped sobbing.

'So, what are we going to do with her?' Emily asked Ma. 'Is she staying here?'

If she was going to stay, she was going to be working.

'I think we can leave her for a little while,' Mrs Farley was not devoid of sympathy, even if she was running a business. 'Let's give her some food and a soft bed and see whether she wants to join us. It's quite clear that her father doesn't want her at home.'

'What about her beau? Thomas, is it?' Polly asked.

'Tommy,' came a newly muffled sob.

'Tommy. What about this Tommy? Do we know where he is? Does he really want to marry her?' I asked.

'He told me he loved me,' her little voice quivered.

Lucy's mouth puckered at such naivety.

'Of course he loves you,' Polly played with the girl's curls. 'But if he's not here to marry you, then that's not much use, is it?'

The girl looked at Polly. 'Not much use…?'

Polly spoke gently. 'If your father has disowned you then none of your friends or relatives will care for you. If Tommy is not going to marry you then you are alone.' The words were beginning to register somewhere in Amelia's mind as Polly went on. 'You have no home, no good name and no one to protect you. London is a dangerous place for a girl on her own.'

She looked at each of us in turn, trying to make sense of what Polly had told her. We all nodded at what was obviously true. Whatever respectability she had once possessed was gone.

'Can I stay here? Mrs Farley, you… you've all been very kind to me. Can I live with you?'

Eyes the colour of summer sky implored us. She was really very pretty; young and sweet, the way the rest of us were once. I could almost hear the coins jingling their way into Ma's strong box.

'I can work,' she said. 'I mean, I'm not very good, but I can do my best.'

She had no idea.

'Do you know what we do here, Amelia?' I asked.

'Why, you're milliners. That means you make hats.' She glowed at her cleverness.

We made hats. That's what the painted sign over the front door said. In a respectable street that was home to craftsmen and shopkeepers, we suggested that we too plied a decent trade. No one was fooled. Half of London's prostitutes said they were milliners – well, those who operated indoors, at least. Lucy began to shake her head in disbelief.

'You do make hats? That's what milliners do, isn't it?' Amelia's voice was high and anxious.

Poor sweet idiot. I laid a hand on her arm, catching Ma's warning glance. 'Well, even Lucy has been known to sew a feather onto straw once in a while.'

There was a silence.

Ma stood, took her by the shoulders and scooped her up into her welcoming bosom like a little child.

'Come now, dear one, let's go and find you a comfortable bed. There's no need to make a decision about the future just yet.'

There was no decision to make, as far as I could see. If she was truly on her own, then all she could do was hope to make a living from her beauty, live decently, escape the pox and save enough money to survive into her old age.

Amelia hobbled out of the room clutching at Ma.

'Poor little thing,' said Polly.

'I know,' I said. 'It's easy to forget how awful it is when you start.'

We were quiet, each of us with our own thoughts. Eventually Polly spoke, her voice deliberately cheery.

'But Lizzie, do tell us, how was your delightful companion this evening?'

I groaned.

'That good, eh?' She was laughing at me. 'I'm so glad that you took him out of the tavern. I thought I was going to faint at his tedious conversation.'

Lucy began to look interested. She had not been with us earlier, owing to an engagement in a gentleman's town house. Emily had been upstairs and busy all day from the hard look on her face.

'Who was it? Lizzie, do tell.'

'A cloth merchant from Norwich. He was fat and he grunted, and he struggled to get it up.' It was an accurate summary.

'Why on earth did you bring him home, though?' asked Polly. 'He was dreadful. He's been in the White Horse for the last four nights – you've not had to put up with him until now. Yesterday he spent at least half an hour telling me about a particular sort of weave, I forget

12

even what it was. And then there was the business with his handkerchief earlier.'

'His handkerchief?' Lucy's dark eyes sparkled with amusement now.

'Oh, he has an extremely large silk handkerchief with his initials embroidered in the corner,' I said, 'G. R. for George Reed. It's nothing special, except that he needed us to know most particularly that G. R. stood for George Reed, and that this kerchief did not belong to His Majesty. He insisted on pulling it out of his coat pocket and waving it under our noses for inspection.'

'You are teasing, Lizzie.'

'No, I'm not. He really was bone-numbingly dull.'

'I would have dropped him off with a streetwalker,' said Polly.

'Ah, but you didn't see his waistcoat, then,' I said quietly.

'What about his waistcoat?'

'I have rarely seen finer silk embroidery.'

'What of it?' Lucy was curious. She didn't understand the importance of my comment, even though she's normally such a grasping little minx.

'I guessed that if he could afford such quality then he was obviously carrying a very heavy purse. I thought that I might relieve him of some guineas while he is in town on business.' I grinned at them. 'I was right about the purse.'

I relished my moment of triumph as I saw their faces.

'Lizzie, I do wish I had your keen eye sometimes,' said Polly.

'I'm good,' I admitted with a smile. 'And for a few minutes grappling with that enormous belly I earned five guineas.' I had received more, but the remainder was stowed away in my secret store: my retirement fund.

'Five guineas,' Lucy gave a whistle. 'Not bad.' She examined the jewels on her fingers. 'Of course, not nearly as much as I earned this evening with Mr Gideon.'

No, it wasn't as much as Lucy earned. Miss Lucy Allingham, raven-haired and always impeccably dressed, was the serious talent, after all – even if she could whistle like a fishwife. She was setting her sights on a man who might keep her as his mistress, in the hope of gaining her own apartment, an easy life and a steady stream of income. She had several suitable candidates in her thrall and was working on each of them in careful rotation. Mr Gideon was one of the poor creatures; a wealthy but somewhat hesitant Jewish gentleman.

Polly bristled slightly, which suggested that her own evening had not been profitable.

'Good for you, Lucy,' I said. 'I hope he was as courteous as he was generous. But now, tell me, what has Ma got planned for tomorrow? Who is going to be here?' I drummed the table with pretended excitement.

Polly dived in immediately. 'Mr Stanford is coming. You know he adores you, Lizzie.'

'Charles Stanford? How lovely.' A young rake recently returned from the continent and keen to spend the sizable fortune he had lately inherited from his uncle. His lively wit and livelier body meant that his attentions were as pleasing as they were profitable. I had entertained him a few times.

'I hope you share him,' said Emily. 'He's more fun than most.' Miss Emily Greville, the oldest of us, has to work harder these days to make the money that once came easily. She has grey in her unimaginatively-mousy hair. She covers it in powder to hide it, but we all know it's there.

'He's bringing some new friends,' said Polly, clapping her hands. 'Two men, a Mr Herring and a Mr Winchcombe. They were in the White Horse yesterday, and I can report that they are both young and handsome.'

'Thank goodness,' I said. 'Last time we had a masked ball it was full of elderly men. Oh no!' I dropped my head in my hands, groaning.

'What's wrong?'

'I've just remembered that I invited Mr Reed.'

'George Reed? The man with the handkerchief and the wilting maypole?' Lucy looked aghast. 'Ma will kill you.'

I raised my hands in apology. 'I had to get him off me. I wanted him out of my room. Inviting him to the party seemed like a good distraction.'

'As long as none of us ends up with him. Lucy's right, Ma won't be happy,' said Polly. 'We can offer him to one of Mrs Hardy's girls. They're joining us for the evening.' We liked the Hardy girls. Mrs Hardy's establishment, though vastly inferior to ours, was nearby and we sometimes welcomed them to share our parties.

'Well for once I'm glad they are coming.' Lucy usually thought that inviting the Hardy girls was an unnecessary act of charity. 'They can take the weak and ancient and we can keep the young and the rich like Charles Stanford and his friends, Mr Herring and Mr Winchcombe.'

'I think that we had better get some beauty sleep before tomorrow's exertions,' said Polly, blowing out a candle.

'The masks will only cover our faces for a few brief minutes, after all.'

'And they do only cover our faces.' Lucy winked as she got up.

'Don't be lewd,' I said. 'Ma will get uppity.'

'She's too preoccupied with her little sparrow to worry about my lack of refinement.'

True. Somewhere upstairs Amelia Blackwood might just be realising that a new career on the town was calling her. If she had worked that out, then the comfortable bed would offer little sleep.

Chapter Three

Fingers of sunlight poked their way through the shutters of my room. I lay in bed, listening. The house was very still, which meant the girls were probably still asleep. Ma and the servants would be long gone, buying more food for the party. I strained to make out the different noises from outside. An oyster girl was on her way home, crying out to anyone who would listen that she had but a few left. I imagined the girl weaving her way, basket balanced on her head, shawl knotted around her shoulders to keep out the chill. It was the end of March, and the sun, although bright, would surely be weak. A church bell, somewhere, began to ring and then others took the hint and joined in. Noon.

I didn't fancy oysters, but bread and cheese would be welcome, or a pie. My stomach growled. The kitchen would be forbidden to anyone except those prepared to chop and cook, so there was nothing to be done except wander out to find something from the streets. It was probably wiser to leave for an hour or two, anyway. Very soon a predictable chaos would strike the house and suck me into a whirl of people wielding hair curlers, powder and gowns with all the energy of a wild storm. I wanted to avoid that for as long as possible.

There was a pitcher outside my door. The water had probably been hot a couple of hours ago, but now was decidedly cool. I washed my face, used my pot and dressed. Ma would have been horrified at how little attention I paid to my toilette, but hunger was tugging me outside. There was no need to make myself too attractive: I was searching for pies, not business.

—

Stepping out of the house and down the stairs onto Berwick Street I could hear a crowd in the distance, off to the left, towards Oxford Street. My favourite pie seller is usually in Thrift Street or Greek Street around midday, but, sufficiently intrigued, I turned and walked in the opposite direction to see what was going on. Oxford Street was filled with scores of people, many of them women. They were waiting for something, or someone, chattering with excitement, laughing and squealing. While they waited for whatever it was, local traders obligingly sold them food. Costermongers, oyster girls, pasty sellers, all moved in and out of the throng with baskets and carts full of tasty treats.

'What's happening?' I asked the thin-faced man who put down his pasty cart for a moment. 'A pie, please. Beef if you have it, mutton if not.' I reached for my purse.

'One beef pie left, sweetheart, just for you. Here you go!'

'Why the crowd?' I asked again before he moved off.

'They're bringing John Swann to Newgate today,' he said, nodding towards the west. 'It's why all the ladies are here. Didn't you know?'

I knew well enough who John Swann was. It had been difficult to hold an intimate or intelligent conversation in the taverns for the past week without my ears being assaulted by the latest ballads offered in his honour, or loud announcements of his capture. Highwaymen are no longer quite the scourge for travellers they once were, but the fascination for them has not dimmed. They attract a ridiculous amount of attention; much of it female. I've never seen the attraction myself but, apparently, they are extremely dashing, and usually handsome. John Swann was especially so, at least according to the musicians.

'Ah. Of course. I'd forgotten it was today. You must be doing brisk business.'

He was. I was talking to the back of his coat as he trundled off to find love-sick women in need of warm pies.

You can suffocate in crowds like this. Elbows rammed into my ribs and boots trod over my skirts, making it difficult to move, let alone breathe. Every so often a voice cried out ''Ere he is!' and the masses cheered and swelled forwards like a wave to catch a glimpse, only to ebb back with a sigh when they realised it was not him at all.

A few feet along the street there was a gap between the buildings. It was a place of assignation after dark, and normally to be avoided by the more decent working ladies, but there was a chance it would be empty. I pushed hard against the tide, head down and pie in hand, until finally I popped up like a cork. I was right: there was no one there. No wonder; it stank of the grime and waste of the previous occupants. There was a discarded box further into the cleft. It would be useful to stand on to see the procession. I held my breath and pulled in my skirts, still clutching the pie, and inched towards it. With my toe, I flipped it over. A rat bowled thorough my feet towards the crowd, twitched its tail and scurried off. The box was strong enough to hold my weight and, several inches taller, I leaned my back against the alley wall, watching the crowd, and eating the pie. It was no longer warm, and it had never been beef, but it wasn't bad, and it was good enough for breakfast. Where had these people come from? From across London and beyond, by the look of it. All bewitched by the myth of John Swann the highwayman.

The talk of the taverns was that he had been working the roads north of London with a small band of men, attacking carriages and robbing houses – taking money from terrified property-owners at pistol point. His weakness, of course, had been women, whom he had loved a little too widely. One disgruntled doxy, no doubt unhappy at sharing him, had decided to reveal his whereabouts to the law men. The means of his capture – naked, save for a bed sheet and his hat – had only added to his charm and notoriety.

There was a shout from somewhere west and then the noise began to build, steadily this time, a low hum becoming a full-throated cheer. Faces suddenly appeared in the windows of the houses opposite. Those who dwelt in this part of town knew the right moment to gaze upon criminals who journeyed up the road to face their trial or back down it to their doom. No disappointment this time: here came John Swann. Indeed, he was handsome; dark curls hanging about his shoulders, waving his hat to the people, behaving more like their newly-crowned monarch than a violent thief. No wonder the ladies had swooned. The constables in the cart remained seated, allowing him this moment in the sun, confident that he would be riding back down the road towards Tyburn before the summer.

The masses pushed forward, clamouring for his attention, his benediction. The cart struggled to move down the street, so the constables stood up and shooed away the people as if they were excitable dogs.

Behind the onlookers, one young girl threaded swiftly in and out of the crowd. She navigated her way easily in her rags, where I had been encumbered by my full skirts. I watched her, fascinated. She was tiny; limp-haired and thin from lack of food. As men and women swayed and stood on their toes to see the criminal, she moved with them, deftly sneaking her hands into bags and pockets. They were oblivious of her; their attention was fixed on their charismatic king riding off to court. The scrawny girl could not see, as I could from my vantage point, that the cart had nearly passed. In a moment, the company would disperse, and she would be caught loosening the strings of someone's purse.

We all play with fire in this city, but, on an impulse, I decided that this little one would not be burned today. I sprang from the crack in the wall and grabbed her wrist just as she was about to make another dive. Her head jolted up, eyes wide with panic.

'I wasn't doing nothin', miss, really.'

We needed to get away as quickly as possible. I held her wrist tighter and pulled her behind me.

'Don't struggle,' I turned and hissed in her face as she began to whine. 'And don't cry at me. I've probably just saved your life, stupid child. Come on.'

We marched firmly along until the crowd were far behind us. Some were only now beginning to feel for their purses and realising that, even as they cheered the great thief, a lesser one had relieved them of their goods.

I kept hold of her wrist but slowed the walk.

'How much have you lifted today?'

'I'm not a thief, miss. Honest.'

'Of course not. You accidentally fall into people's pockets.' I glared at her. 'That's what you'd tell the magistrate, obviously.'

Large globes of tears began to drop from her eyes. She would get no sympathy from me until I had heard the truth – although I could probably guess it.

'I mean, I'm not normally a thief. I don't take from people's pockets. It's just that…'

She sniffed back some of the snot that was now running along with the tears and wiped a grubby sleeve across her face.

'Well?'

'I've not had much luck with the gentlemen recently. I haven't eaten for days.'

One of us – except without the decent clothes, the good food and the bed. If she didn't have the pox she was certainly riddled with lice. I could see them in the lank strands of brown hair. She stank of stale drink. No wonder she wasn't making any money.

'Where have you been working?'

'I was on the Strand for a while, but some new girls moved in and took my regulars, so I moved out west. Covent Garden was too busy.'

You can hardly move for the whores around there, it's true.

'I just got hungry. And I saw the crowd and they were all watching the cart and I just, well I just had a go at it.'

'You've lifted purses before, though, surely? If a gentleman has had too much ale?'

She looked at her feet and then peeped up at me from under her lashes. The street girls all do it. Gives the rest of us a bad name.

I frowned, and then tucked her arm firmly under mine, releasing my hold on her wrist.

'I'll take you to a decent tavern and fill you up with food. Then you can use your stolen money for some new clothes and a pretty ribbon. Perhaps you'll have more luck with a better gown... and a wash. What's your name?'

'Sallie, miss.'

'How do you do, Sallie.' I turned, made a deep curtsey and winked at her. 'Delighted to make your acquaintance. I'm Lizzie Hardwicke, of Mrs Farley's establishment on Berwick Street.'

She tugged her arm from mine and looked me up and down, recognising me for what I was.

'Miss Lizzie Hardwicke, I am forever in your debt.'

'You are. You'd better learn to keep your hands out of other people's pockets, or you'll be following John Swann to Tyburn.'

Her face darkened with fear again.

'Cheer up, Sallie, there are taverns and bawdy houses opening further west every day. There's more than enough work to go around.' All the smart bawds, like Mrs Farley, were moving out of Covent Garden.

She had fallen too far for me to find her a respectable trade – any more than I could find one for myself – but

I could help her out as best I could. There, but for the grace of God, walked I, after all.

We turned off Wardour Street into Compton Street, stepped around the young lad grinding knives in his usual spot, and into the White Horse tavern, where there was always a warm welcome for Ma's girls – even in the early afternoon. Anne Bardwell, mistress of the tavern, was standing, hands on wide hips, watching over her domain with flinty eyes. Harry Bardwell, round-faced and equally portly, but jollier than his wife, was carrying a tray of beer to a group of customers. He saw us and hurried to set down the tray before bustling over to greet us.

'Lizzie! My favourite lady in the whole of London!'

Every woman was his favourite, especially if she was sitting in his tavern and attracting men through the doors. But he was decent and fair, and had not once, in the time I had known him, tried to shove his hand up my skirts. He wouldn't dare with a wife like his. I laughed back at him.

'Mr Harry Bardwell, allow me to present to you my newest friend, Miss Sallie... Sallie, do you have a name?'

'If I do, then I've forgotten it. I'm always just Sallie.'

He lifted her hand to his lips as if it belonged to the queen herself. As he did, I saw him take in her sparrow-thin arms and hollow cheeks.

'Well then, Just Sallie, as a friend of Miss Hardwicke you are most welcome here. I assume you would like a bite to eat?'

Sallie barely had time to nod before Harry swept her away to a corner table.

'I found her picking pockets in Oxford Street.' I stood next to Anne as we watched her husband bring out two pies and a jug.

'You're soft-hearted,' Anne folded her arms. The look on her face suggested that she had smelled something bad. 'Whoring is one thing; thieving is quite another.'

You can't argue with logic like Anne's.

'Thieves never stop, once they've got a taste for it,' she said, not to be interrupted. 'Take that John Swann, for instance. He started out as a diver, but he got too big for his boots, didn't he? Wanted more money, more jewels, and soon enough he was robbing the coaches.'

Anne was not charmed by looks and reputation.

'The only thing she's got a taste for is food,' I nodded over to Sallie, who was wolfing down the first pie. 'She was picking pockets because her usual trade had dried up.' I sighed. 'She wasn't much good at it, as far as I could see. If she'd done any more she would have been caught. I've told her that there's more work around here every day.'

She didn't look impressed.

'I don't want a thief in here. It's enough that Swann's men are roaming around, grabbing what they can.'

'Really? John Swann's men are here?' I scanned the room, wondering who they were. Most were regulars. A couple of respectable types were having a quiet drink and there was a young woman I didn't know cuddled up to an old gentleman in the far corner.

'Not in *here*.' She looked at me as though I were an idiot. 'Out on the streets. House-breaking. Everyone knows he has associates. It's only a matter of time before they kill again.'

His associates were cut-throats and hard-faced whores, most of whom operated in the dark, not in broad daylight. If they had, indeed, been drawn to Soho, they wouldn't be wandering at this hour.

'I don't think Sallie is one of his associates, Anne.'

'I'm just saying,' she hissed. 'We can't afford a bad reputation. This is a smart part of town. People won't come if it's full of criminals – like Covent Garden.'

I thought it best to indulge her.

'Don't fret Anne,' I put a hand on her meaty shoulder. 'Even when it's full of Ma's girls, even when we're dancing on the tables with barely a stitch on, even when everybody here is screaming drunk, this is still a respectable house.'

She looked at me sharply. 'It'll be quiet tonight, then. Aren't you all supposed to be polishing yourselves up for a party?'

God's teeth! I'd forgotten about it. Ma would be furious if I didn't get home soon.

'Thank you for reminding me,' I said, rolling my eyes and pulling some coins from my pocket.

I went and sat next to Sallie, who was now finishing off the beer. She gave a large belch, giggled, and wiped the heel of her hand across her mouth. I laid the coins on the table by her pot.

'This should cover whatever you eat and drink here, Sallie. You'll do as I suggested, though? Put what you've taken to good use and have a bath?'

She looked at the coins and then up at me. Her face, I saw, was covered with a film of dust. She had been out on the streets for a long time.

'I had a sister like you – always telling what to do and how to do it.' She slid the coins off the table and into her lap. 'Not as pretty as you, though. Nor as fancy.'

I had brothers once.

'You can earn well if you look as fancy as I do.' I shrugged, pointing to the purses on the seat next to her. 'You can buy some clothes, or you can blow the money on gin and die in the gutter. It's your choice, sister.'

There was nothing more I could do for her. She was on her own.

Mr Bardwell landed another pot of beer in front of Sallie.

'How was your young man last night, then?' He nudged my shoulder and laughed.

'Old and incapable,' I said, getting to my feet, rolling my eyes, but laughing with him. 'I think I nearly killed him.'

'Better luck at the party tonight, then.' He chortled in his amiable way as he carried his tray to another table.

'No luck for me,' I called after him. 'He's coming back for more. The least I can do is finish him off and put him out of his misery.' I was still laughing as I fell out of the door; one of very few occasions when I had left that tavern both sober and alone.

Chapter Four

Sydney opened the door with an air so unruffled that it gave me no clue as to the level of noise and chaos I was about to find. This was his job: to present a dignified welcome to our guests.

I winked at him.

'How bad is it? I stayed away as long as I dared.'

His face remained impassive for a moment before he frowned, raised a long finger and wagged it at me.

'Miss Lizzie, where 'av you been? Mrs Farlee, she 'as been looking for you, bad girl!'

That was not a good sign. Sydney's accent becomes more French the more agitated he is.

'I was caught up in something at the Bardwell's.'

'*Vite*,' he said, flapping his hands at me. 'Get upstairs now. Mrs Farlee is in the parlour giving the wishes to the maids.' He looked at me with a disappointed expression. 'She will not be pleased to see you dressed as this.'

Sydney wasn't pleased either. He, always immaculate, preferred us to leave the house in our Sunday best. He would never have understood how hunger had outweighed my desire to be beautiful. Even now I was captivated by the delicious smells that were wafting from the kitchen.

I scurried up to my room and found a gown laid on the bed. The pale blue with silver thread embroidery would show my blue eyes to good advantage and there was a velvet mask in a similar shade. I would be elegant and mysterious; at least for a few minutes.

I heard the sound of feet shuffling heavily on the landing outside my door and smiled. There was a gentle tap and Meg, one of our servants, peeped in.

'Would you like a hand with your dressing yet, miss?'

'Thank you. I would.' I am happy to dress myself, but Ma expected perfection – and I really cannot be trusted to manage that alone.

Meg was a slight creature, a cripple with deformed legs who hauled herself up and down our stairs and shared our lives, but not our trade. She was a hard-working girl, with a keen eye for fashion. Had it not been for her deformity she would have been an elegant lady of the town. Had it not been for Mrs Farley, she would be selling her twisted body for a shilling on the streets. At some point in her life, and with a wisdom beyond her years, she had decided that being a servant in a comfortable bawdy house was preferable to the alternative; at least here she was warm, fed, unbothered by men and surrounded by silks and lace – even if others wore the pretty clothes.

She was also a gossip, and a gossip with opinions. While she helped me into petticoats and gown and combed and fixed my curls into a high dome, she gave her own account of the afternoon's events. Lucy had been sent the wrong hairdresser and taken an hour to calm down – which was hardly news. Of greater interest was the arrival of Amelia's love, Tommy.

'He turned up at the house and was banging on the door. Sydney wouldn't let him in and he caused a real commotion.'

'Her young man? He came here? Is he handsome?'

Meg, world-weary at fifteen, laughed.

'You can judge for yourself. In the end, he was making such a nuisance in the street that Ma let him in. Sydney was furious.' She gestured towards the attic. 'He's still here.'

'What? On a party night?' Ma really had gone soft in her old age.

She pressed a small beauty spot to my cheek.

'Miss Blackwood's been told to stay in the attic and keep out of the way. And the boy, Tommy Bridgewater, is to leave before the guests arrive.' Naturally. Ma would be very keen to keep her little lamb as white as possible, even if she wasn't entirely pure.

The fussing was near enough complete to Meg's satis-faction, and I was ready to entertain our guests. It had taken a while, but eventually, Lizzie the eater of London's pies and frequenter of its taverns became Miss Lizzie Hardwicke of Mrs Farley's Berwick Street establishment, resplendent in her finery and ready for the evening's sport. The thought of good food, plenty of wine and the delightful Charles Stanford was raising my enthusiasm for the evening ahead. This was my career now; and even if much of it was disagreeable, there were sometimes compensations.

Still, I wanted to catch a glimpse of Amelia's Tommy.

'I haven't quite finished your hair! There's no powder in it.' Too late. I was out of my room and skipping down the stairs to our little parlour – peeping into the best salon to catch a glimpse of the glorious table beginning to be set with treats by servants hired especially for the evening. The room was full of candles. I could already see the dishes of biscuits and pickles and plates of oysters, and space for so much more.

I found Amelia sitting at the same place as yesterday with Polly and Lucy. She was still weeping, too, but her tears were fresh. Here was a new drama. Ma was nowhere to be seen: she would be directing the servants' operations on the floor above with all the comprehensiveness of a general preparing for battle. Emily was standing, hand on hip, near to the fire. She watched with a look of disdain as Polly stroked Amelia's hand.

I didn't notice him immediately, but with his back to the company, gazing out of the window, was a brown-haired man whom I took to be Tommy.

'Lizzie! Where have you been?' Emily was always keen to know my whereabouts. I think she worried that I was stealing her custom.

'What a lovely gown,' said Polly.

'Meg thinks it does wonders for my complexion,' I ignored Emily. 'I'm going to try and keep it on for the whole evening.'

'Hush,' said Polly, nodding her head towards Amelia.

I gestured towards the young man.

'Will you introduce me? I assume he isn't a guest for tonight?'

Lucy stood and led me to the man. He had the strong shoulders and arms of a blacksmith, but, barely more than a boy, his cheeks were still soft and he had eyes like a kindly-treated puppy. Another innocent in this den of corruption. I sank into a polite curtsey.

'Mr Bridgewater, I am delighted to meet you in the flesh, having heard so much of your good character from our new friend Amelia.'

He blushed a little and bowed. The serious expression he wore didn't suit him at all. This was a young man more used to smiling.

'Miss Hardwicke, I am grateful to you and these other ladies for your hospitality, but I hope to take Amelia away from this house very soon. Very soon indeed.'

'What a shame, when we were only just making her acquaintance. I take it that you have found employment?'

His lovely eyes betrayed the truth.

'I am well on my way to securing a new post, Miss Hardwicke. A good farrier is always welcome where gentlemen keep horses. Horses always need shoeing.'

'I am very pleased to hear that, Mr Bridgewater. And your lodgings? They are nearby?'

His was too easy a countenance to read.

'I hope to come by something very soon, miss.'

I hoped so too. Amelia's future would be only slightly better than Sallie's otherwise. Indeed, it would look like mine – and I didn't wish that on her.

The door opened, and Ma swept in. There are some who believe that Mrs Farley is still a handsome woman when she wears her finest clothes. Mrs Farley certainly believes it, and she had dressed accordingly. Her silk gown was blood red, her hair was powdered and immaculate, and around her neck and in her ears sumptuous jewels sparkled – gifts from the wealthy lovers of her golden years. The face, however, was that of a woman who had drunk sour milk.

'Why are you still here?' She was looking at Tommy. 'I told you to get out of my house. Guests will be arriving at any moment and your presence is not required.' She surveyed the rest of the room with displeasure.

'All of you: upstairs at once. And Amelia, you are not to come down from your room until tomorrow morning. You must not be in the way.'

'Unless she fancies joining in,' Emily whispered to me with a wink.

I snatched up my mask and pushed Amelia out of the door towards the stairs.

Chapter Five

We sat in silence as we had been trained to do by Ma. We were elegant ladies, hands gently clasped in laps, backs straight, eyes demurely cast down until our friends from Mrs Hardy's and our other evening guests arrived. Only the masks, the flimsy gowns cut so low that we spilled from them with very little exertion, and the thoughts racing around our heads would have betrayed us.

This was our best and largest room, filled with the sort of fashionable furniture that marked Mrs Farley as a woman of good taste. The fire blazed merrily and its golden flames, along with the smaller candle lights all about the room, made the place glow with warmth. The table was now piled with food: soups, jellies, a veal escalope girded with lemons, roast beef and stewed venison. The scent was delicious; making my stomach gurgle. Card tables waited for players. And here and there lay couches and comfortable chairs for reclining and conversation. It looked lovely; serene, even. I wondered how long it would take for the scene in front of my eyes to transform into the swaying, writhing mass of bodies that it inevitably would.

I heard Sydney answering the door and Ma taking entrance fees, and my heart began to knock inside my chest. The evening would bring her a substantial amount, but it would also confirm the reputation of our house as a place of delight for the more discerning. She had been planning for weeks and was anticipating that this party would be even livelier than the last one; it was little wonder that she had been so annoyed by Tommy Bridgewater's presence earlier. Everything must be perfect for our guests. We must be perfect.

I was always anxious just before the gentlemen arrived. I knew what I would have to do tonight, and I had grown used to it, but that didn't stop the tremor in my soul that preceded every encounter. We were the real delicacies of the evening, the meat, waiting to be selected and devoured. Lucy, Polly and Emily sat as still as I did. It was difficult to tell what they thought or felt at this moment.

We never spoke of the fear.

Our guests were, as they usually were, gentlemen of quality, ready for an evening of drinking, gambling and what they might politely describe as pretty company and entertainment. What they were really here to enjoy would not be spoken about in polite company, of course.

I was grateful to notice Charles Stanford as soon as he entered the room, distinguished by his vigorous manner as much as his looks – his face being partly obscured by a black mask. He had a fine figure, tall and neat with broad shoulders, encased in a coat of rich midnight blue embroidered with exquisite flowers. A freshly-powdered wig covered his light brown hair. He looked magnificent – and he undoubtedly knew it. It didn't take him long to make his way over to me. He pulled me up from my seat and made a bow.

'Miss Hardwicke, how lovely to see you.'

'Mr Stanford.'

Brown eyes sparkled with mischief at the holes of his mask.

'Well, I assume it's you, Lizzie. It's rather difficult to tell.'

'It is certainly me, Mr Stanford. Rather diverting, though, don't you think? Not being able to see people's faces? And I do believe that the Hardy girls look prettier than usual.'

He tugged the ribbon at my cleavage to undo my gown, and his hand found a breast. He was quick this evening and, despite my veneer of reserve, I was excited by his directness.

'I'm more interested in what's under here,' he said. 'Damn it, Lizzie, I'm in great need of a fuck.'

He always was.

'I think that Mrs Farley would like us to pretend restraint for a while longer.' I giggled and removed his hand. 'You've only just walked in and there's so much food to eat.'

'Don't tease me, please. Oh, what I'm going to do to you tonight... shall I tell you?'

He didn't have the opportunity. The all-seeing Mrs Farley moved across the room and bade him good evening, turning him away from me and steering him towards Lucy. That would cool him down for a while. I rearranged my dress a little and went to greet the other gentlemen.

Polly called me to meet Mr Herring and Mr Winchcombe, Charles' friends. Both wore soft black masks, as all the gentlemen did this evening, making them seem like disorientated highwaymen who had found their way into Berwick Street by accident. John Herring was a little haughty for my taste, a man in his mid-twenties with pale skin, translucent eyelashes and a sharply-pointed nose. His plum-coloured coat was well-cut, and he wore an expensive scent. Joshua Winchcombe was more engaging; large-limbed, with dark eyes. A curl of black hair was trying to escape from under his wig. He was a similar age to Mr Herring, but he had none of the other man's affected airs. I found his voice a little loud as he bellowed into my ear, but he had an energy about him that was attractive.

I heard the door open again downstairs. More guests were ushered in, men and women similarly masked and all in a jolly mood and I moved around to bid them welcome. Gradually, the room began to fill with people; flirtatious women wanting money, and wealthy men, happy to be flirted with. One man stood apart. Large and jowly – eyes flicking about under his mask in a mix of shock and wonder – it was George Reed. He moved towards Mr Herring and Mr Winchcombe, as if seeking out something, or someone, to ease his disorientation. The three men exchanged a few words before the younger two moved away towards Polly, leaving him quite alone.

I watched Emily swim across the room to greet him. She was always able to make a nervous gentleman feel welcome in our house: those who wore expensive clothing at least. She knew that I had relieved this one of several guineas. She could have him to herself, as far as I was concerned.

That was not Emily's intention. Her aim became clear almost immediately. She ushered Mr Reed towards me and laid my hand on his arm. She wanted me to deal with him while she entertained the younger men. I knew that she didn't much care for me, but this seemed like particular cruelty. Nevertheless, she pretended courtesy.

'Here you are, Mr Reed, a familiar face for you beneath the mask. Miss Hardwicke was only telling us earlier how much she had enjoyed your company yesterday. I am sure that she will take care of you – for the whole evening, should you wish it.'

I did not wish it. I was looking forward to spending time with Charles. Even one of the other men might be preferable. Joshua Winchcombe, perhaps.

Mrs Farley was at the table ladling soup, encouraging the company to eat and Mr Reed, who hardly needed a meal, took me by the hand and led me to the table. I could see Charles in a dark corner of the room with his hands under someone's skirts; one of the Hardy girls. He had no intention of sitting for dinner.

In the meantime, I had a job to do. Emily had unkindly made sure that I sat down with Mr Reed, which meant that I was unable to leave him easily. I kept my feelings to myself, tucking away my thoughts about Charles and, instead, attending to the man I was with, heaping beef on to his plate and pouring his burgundy in as bright a fashion as possible.

In between mouthfuls of drink and food, George Reed decided to entertain me with stories of Norwich, of his business transactions from earlier that day in the city and of his journey to our home.

'D' you know, Miss Hardwicke, that it is possible to take a carriage all the way out to Kensington now? There are new houses being built far and away to the west. You ladies may yet need to move to keep up with the fashionable people.'

A good hostess, I confessed myself astonished by his information – as if it had never occurred to me that houses might be built as the population of London grew larger.

From the other side of the table, Polly threw me a sympathetic look as Reed leaned across to help himself to more food. Her own companion was Mr Herring, who sat stroking her delicate collarbone, entranced, as she nibbled a pastry.

Mr Reed, delving into a mountain of syllabub, was still talking loudly about house building an hour later, even as others were engaging themselves in more amorous adventures. Quarters of the room around us seemed to be shuddering and grunting. Polly had disappeared. I tried to ignore the sight of Charles' backside heaving into a pile of petticoats.

Mrs Farley laid a hand on my shoulder. Putting her mouth to my ear she spoke quietly.

'Why don't you take Mr Reed to the side room, Lizzie? I think that his conversation would be better elsewhere.'

It was an instruction rather than a suggestion. He was out of place and she wished me to take him away. This was my punishment for inviting him in the first place. I guessed that Emily would have told her.

I nodded. I understood my duty to the other guests, as well as to Mr Reed. When he paused to take a breath, I took his sweaty hand and spoke urgently.

'Mr Reed, dear sir, I made you a promise yesterday evening and I think that it's time I honoured it.'

He looked at his hand and then up at me.

'Miss Hardwicke, I would be delighted.' He suddenly became aware of the rest of the room – and what was

39

taking place in it. I couldn't understand why he hadn't noticed it before.

'My goodness. All of this. My word.' He wiped his mouth; a troubled look on his face. 'Are we to exert ourselves here?'

I shook my head gently.

'No Mr Reed, for our very special guests we have other rooms. Something more private. Come.'

Chapter Six

The floorboards creaked as I led him along the landing, but not loudly enough to cover the sound of him belching.

I hoped with passion that he would spend most of the evening asleep once I was done.

The smaller room was lit softly with candles. Dim light usually makes even the ugliest man bearable, but in this case, I thought the room still far too bright.

He slumped into a chair that barely contained his frame, pulled off his mask and unbuttoned his waistcoat. His belly, until now contained in the finely-embroidered fabric, sank into a great mound over his thighs. I began to undress slowly – close enough for him to see, but far enough away to make it impossible for him to grab me. Not that he looked capable of getting out of the chair.

The sounds of satisfied lust could be heard not too far away. Someone was having a pleasant time. He heard it too.

I was down to my shift and could put off the dreadful prospect no longer.

'Would you like to stay in your chair, sir, or shall we move to the couch?'

He gestured that he would remain where he was, so I moved to him and straddled his knees. His breathing became laboured.

'I can't.' He was barely audible. 'I really don't think I can.' Despite yesterday's faith in his capabilities, his face was a picture of embarrassment. 'I think, I really think that... it is the wine, you know.'

'Don't worry, sir, I'm certain I can help. It happens to a lot of gentlemen, you know, especially when they have drunk and eaten well.'

I did my best for a good amount of time, but not the sound of fornication elsewhere nor the sight of me stretched across his lap was going to arouse this old man who had over-filled his belly. We both knew it.

He looked at my breasts, barely inches from his nose. He touched one, sadly.

'Miss Hardwicke, you are a beautiful young lady, but I regret I'm not quite in the mood to enjoy you again.'

'Hush, sir, do not distress yourself.' I was beginning to feel a little sorry for him.

'You may dress again, if you wish.'

I did, and then sat at the end of the couch, wondering what to do. I waited for what seemed like a very long time. Perhaps he was asleep. I heard him clear his throat, snort and swallow, and tried not to shudder.

Mrs Farley had taken payment from the guests already. She would have made a good profit before they were halfway into the hallway. It was up to us to earn our own money from the evening. If I was going to make anything at all, I had to entertain him in some way.

'We could have a game of cards?'

'That would be pleasant.' He pulled a handkerchief from his pocket and wiped the sweat from his forehead. 'But I would be very grateful, Miss Hardwicke, if you didn't mention this situation to your friends. There are many fine young gentlemen in the other room. I would be very distressed if any of them knew about my... weakness.'

The appearance of manly vigour was essential to this self-important merchant. He did not wish to be sniggered at for his inadequacy.

I nodded. I might, after all, be able to part him from some coin at another opportunity, if I behaved with kindness now.

'What weakness would that be, sir?'

He opened his mouth to clarify, but then shut it and smiled.

'Good girl. Thank you.'

I stood up and rubbed my hands together; affecting a breeziness I didn't feel. 'We have a card table in here, Mr Reed. Now let's see what we'd like to play.'

There was, indeed, a table, and four chairs, but there were no cards. I hunted around but couldn't find any. Muttering in annoyance, I took a candle and left the room to find some. This was not the evening I had hoped for. I wondered how Amelia was faring in the attic – and what she could hear from the floors below.

Trying to ignore the sights that greeted me in the brighter, livelier room I plucked a pack of cards from a side table and turned to leave. Even Mrs Farley was engaged, I could see. No one else would need a deck of cards tonight.

A wide-eyed girl, who should have been safely tucked up in her room, stood in the doorway.

I tried to shoo her out, but she was fixed to the spot; fascination, horror, incredulity over her face. I pulled her aside, but she broke away to stand staring at them all. Amelia Blackwood's mouth began to open and close like a landed fish and soundless questions emerged like bubbles.

'Lizzie? What...? Who...?'

She was in grave danger of upsetting the whole evening.

I tugged her away again, hissing in her ear.

'Don't. Don't say a word. Come with me.'

I pushed her along the landing forgetting for a moment that George Reed was waiting for me.

'Get back upstairs, you silly cat. Pay no heed to what you saw. Just go away and keep out of sight.'

'Lizzie, does this happen often? Is this what you do all day, all night?'

'Of course it's what we do. There's no money in hat-making. You're living in a brothel.'

I took her by the shoulders.

'It's not so bad really. We look out for each other. We're warm and well fed. It's better than being on the street.'

She shook her head.

'Is this what I will be expected to do?'

It was time to be honest.

'Well, if you stay here then yes, it is. We have servants. We don't need another maid, but a pretty young girl is always welcome at Mrs Farley's parties.'

'I can't. I really cannot.' She began to sob – quietly at first, but then in deep, loud gulps of noise.

'No one will force you, Amelia, but you have limited choices.'

We might have continued our conversation quietly, perhaps in her room at a later hour, without causing a commotion or interrupting the evening's entertainment. But Mr Reed, who was obviously wondering by now what had happened to me, had stumbled out onto the landing. Perhaps the rest had refreshed him, because, despite his earlier embarrassment with me, the sight of a tearful Amelia was having an all-too-obviously arousing effect.

'Miss Hardwicke, who is your very pretty friend?' Amelia's sobbing was more appealing than my nakedness? I tried not to be affronted.

'This is Miss Blackwood, Mr Reed, and she is a temporary guest in our house. I apologise for the disturbance. I will escort her back to her room and then return.' I brandished the deck of cards. 'I'll be ready to play in a just few minutes, sir.'

But Mr Reed was far more interested in Amelia than in cards, even as she was shrinking further and further into my shoulder. His eyes danced over her slender body, as if she were a morsel at the table. There are some men – I have met them – who become over-excited by the scent of fresh meat. Mr Reed, I realised with alarm, was one of them. And whatever had happened with Tommy Bridgewater in the barn, Amelia Blackwood was, without doubt, the nearest to virginal that we had under our roof. I had to get her away from him.

'No, don't take her away. I would very much like her company.'

'Mr Reed, I am afraid that Miss Blackwood is not available this evening.' I pulled her behind me.

'Oh, come, Miss Hardwicke, surely for the right price she is, else why is she here?' He barged me out of the way, a big man, powered by newly-awakened lust. Amelia began to scream. I pummelled Reed about the shoulders, but this had little effect as he took hold of her.

Ma appeared on the landing, hair dishevelled but with her skirts and petticoats in order, as Mr Reed tried to claim his prize. I couldn't tell whether she was angrier with him, with me or Amelia. The other guests, unhooked from one another and in various states of undress, joined her to see what the commotion was about.

Gentlemen do not, as a rule, behave rudely or loudly in our house, but the other men, already upset at having to halt their passion, now began to upbraid him for his appalling manners. Amelia's feelings were not considered, of course.

Mr Reed, still holding her hand, began appealing to Mrs Farley's basest financial instinct. None of us saw Tommy until he was suddenly there.

'Let go of that lady, sir.'

'Tommy!' Amelia seemed as surprised as the rest of us to see him.

Where had he been hiding? Had he stolen into the attic, disobeying Mrs Farley's orders? Or had one of the servants taken pity on him and offered him a floor for the night? Whichever it was, he was now standing, shaking with fury in our midst.

'I said, let go of the lady, sir.'

'I will not. Who are you to come in the way of my business?'

'She has no business with you, that's all I know!' Tommy launched himself at Mr Reed and began beating him about the head and shoulders while Amelia shrieked for him to stop. Reed's wig fell off. The gentlemen, some with their breeches flapping open, ran to pull him away and all was a turmoil of yelling and punching until Mrs Farley's voice of authority prevailed.

'Get that man out of my house. Now!'

She may have meant Tommy, but the young men were happier to eject Mr Reed and pushed and carried him off downstairs, some of them, incredibly, still in masks. I ran down with them, Mrs Farley was galloping behind, bellowing to Sydney to open the front door.

There was a pause on the step. A moment of calm. Reed was laughing. He was actually laughing as he stood, about to be ejected on to the street, as if it were all a huge joke.

'I know who you are, Tommy boy,' he laughed. 'I know!'

They threw him out and closed the door. We could hear him shouting for a time, about Tommy, about the disgraceful depravity of our house, about the injury to his dignity.

Sydney opened the door and threw his wig and hat into the road, before closing the door firmly again.

Mrs Farley looked at me with murder in her eyes. I had brought disgrace to her house and I would not be allowed to forget it.

The party was over. The girls had dressed themselves and were bidding Mrs Hardy's ladies a good night in subdued tones. Amelia and Tommy had escaped upstairs – rightly judging that we had seen too much of them for one evening. The gentlemen kissed the ladies but made it clear that they were now stirring themselves for beer or gaming houses and they begged their leave of us.

'I'll deal with you in the morning,' was all that Mrs Farley said to me. I only hoped that I would not find myself homeless and friendless come dawn. I was certainly not going to be paid for my efforts.

Chapter Seven

'I fear two consequences of last night's upset.' Mrs Farley sipped from her new porcelain teacup, the picture of severity and refinement and a world away from the old whore I had seen last night with her skirts around her neck. 'The first is that I will be accused of keeping a disorderly house and we will have to close. The second is that the fine gentlemen such as we entertained here will stay away.'

I stood before her, contrite. The girls, I knew, would be eavesdropping at one door or another. Mrs Farley probably knew it too, but she didn't mince her words. The teacup made a delicate chink as it touched the saucer. It was a very fine set.

'Frankly, I don't know which is the worse of those two evils. If you were not such a hardworking girl and so good for my business I would throw you on to the street for inviting Mr Reed here without permission.'

I held my tongue. I wished I hadn't invited him either.

She smoothed her gown over her knees and looked up at me with a hard face. Mrs Farley was a generous landlady and the rules of her house were fair and, compared to many, she exercised remarkably little control over her girls. In some places they were little more than slaves; we enjoyed great freedom in our choices. But she was, first and foremost, a business woman and would decide my fate based on her pecuniary interests.

'I will not have the reputation of this house besmirched. Any man you bring home must have my approval before he enters your room. And any man I choose for you must be entertained with courtesy.'

I nodded. I could hardly be accused of ever displaying discourtesy, but I knew that she needed to wield some power over me now.

'Yes, Mrs Farley.'

She fretted with a strand of hair that had worked its way loose, trying to tuck it back into her cap.

'Mr Reed's outburst on the street last night may have done us a great harm among our neighbours, Lizzie. Only time will tell, but I fear that some will see this as an opportunity to call in the law.'

'We have good neighbours, Mrs Farley. They know us and watch out for us, as a rule.'

'The tides are turning. Some people in London would prefer it if our way of life came to a complete end. I heard of a house in Covent Garden only last week that was closed down for being disorderly. I once thought it one of the most genteel in that part of town.'

Covent Garden was a pit of vice. The only thing genteel about the bawdy houses was that the girls condescended to wear clothes when they left their front doors. It was different here in Soho, but I could sense that she was anxious.

'The gentlemen will still come, Mrs Farley. The decent gentlemen come here for soft voices and conversation as well as for anything else. What happened last night was a shock – for which I am, madam, truly sorry and ashamed.'

She sniffed and pulled herself upright, nodding at me. My ordeal was over, at least for now.

'What will happen to Amelia?'

Her face softened. She wasn't without heart. The girl had been offended and frightened.

'I have given her until the end of the week to make up her mind. I can't keep her for any longer if she is not prepared to pay her dues. Her young man is still out looking for work.'

There was a sharp rap at the door. One of the servants came in — even before being bid. Her eyes were wide as the porcelain saucer. Mrs Farley stood up sharply, about to reprimand her.

'Mrs Farley, Sydney has just brought news.' Old Sarah was breathless.

Were we to be closed down already?

'There's a dead body been found at the White Horse, Mrs Farley. Mr Stanford is there...'

'Charles? Is he injured?'

'No, Miss Hardwicke. It was he that got word to Sydney. They think it's that man from last night, Mr Reed.'

Mrs Farley put a hand to her mouth and sank back onto her chair. Sarah rushed to her as I, ignoring everything that Ma had just said to me, dashed off to the Bardwell's to see what was going on.

Chapter Eight

It was less chaotic inside the White Horse than I had expected. Men and women, who only recently had been pleasantly drunk were now sobering up quickly. One, still intoxicated, was barking for the magistrate, the landowner, the undertaker; in fact, anyone who could tell him exactly what had happened. His companion called for the same because he swore he knew the answer. Anne Bardwell was shooing them towards the door, even as I was trying to enter. A serving girl moved quietly, collecting the empty tankards.

Harry Bardwell was engaged in close conversation with Charles and two other men I did not know. Charles saw me and raised a hand to call me over. His face was sombre.

'Lizzie! You've heard?'

'News came to us only this hour. What happened? Who is it?'

He rubbed a hand across his brow. One of the other men cleared his throat. Mr Bardwell was apologetic.

'Where are my manners?' he said. 'Mr Davenport, this is Miss Hardwicke.' I turned to the stranger and met a pair of intelligent eyes.

'We're here on behalf of the magistrate, Mr Fielding,' he said. 'William Davenport of Bow Street.' He bowed politely and gestured to the other man. 'This is Jack Grimshaw.'

Mr Davenport was dark-eyed, not quite as tall as Charles, but lean. Most constables were built like bulldogs. Mr Grimshaw was a bulldog, with a neck so thick and so short it was difficult to tell where his head started and his shoulders ceased. He scowled at me and said nothing.

'You're a long way from Bow Street,' I bobbed back a curtsey.

'Our business takes us further afield every day.'

Mr Davenport flicked a glance over me, making his own judgements, even as I assessed him.

'What brings you here, Miss Hardwicke?'

I decided to be vague. It was common knowledge that Mr Fielding wanted to keep a check on London's brothels. I would need to warn Ma if Fielding's men were in the neighbourhood.

'My home is not far from here and I know the Bardwells. I heard that a man had been found dead and I was concerned.' I put a hand out to Harry's shoulder and squeezed it.

'Thank you, Lizzie.' He patted my hand.

The men said nothing.

'So, what happened?' I really did want to know.

'We think it's George Reed who's dead,' said Charles. 'After we left your house we ended up here. Reed followed us, still shouting after Tommy, but he didn't come in. Tommy Bridgewater wasn't with us, in any case. I found the body when I went out the back to piss.' He looked at Anne, who had ejected enough of her customers and now had her arm looped through Harry's. The back yard of the White Horse was a mound of mildewed barrels, last month's chicken bones and dead dogs; it stank of piss. There was a privy out there, but most people just used the rubbish heap – unless it was raining, and they felt the need of a roof.

'It was starting to get light by then. That's how I saw it – the body, I mean. I saw a hand reaching out from under a sack, all white and shiny, so went to look. I couldn't see his face, but it looked like Mr Reed from the size of him. I didn't want to get too close. He's lying very still, and awkwardly. I'm sure he's dead. I didn't see him earlier when I used the yard – when it was dark.'

He didn't say it, but plenty of others must have failed to see the man as they pissed over the rat-infested pile.

Mrs Bardwell put a hand to her mouth; the same thought occurring to her.

'You were the one who found him, then?' I said. Poor Charles.

'You had been out in the yard earlier that night, Mr Stanford?' William Davenport cut across me, making it clear that he oversaw the questions.

'Once or twice I think. But I didn't see him then.'

'And what about this Tommy Bridgewater? Who is he?'

'He's a young man. I met him earlier in the evening.' He paused and glanced at me. 'As I've already told you, there was a jolly party in Berwick Street. Bridgewater was there.'

Mr Davenport turned back to me.

'I'm here to ask questions about a dead man, Miss Hardwicke, nothing more. But I'm going to assume, for the sake of argument, that you were also at the same party in Berwick Street last night.'

I nodded.

'With some other ladies of the town and a few gentlemen in high spirits?'

I nodded again. There was little use pretending.

'I'll need to speak to them all later.'

Ma would not be happy; she didn't like the law men, but if I managed to get home before this Mr Davenport, I could at least forewarn her.

'Had Mr Reed been at the party?'

'He was there, yes.'

'Then, he was known to you?'

That was a complicated question to answer.

'We met the day before yesterday. I spent time in his company again last night but would have to say that I knew him only very briefly.'

The faintest hint of a smile crossed Davenport's mouth as he caught my meaning.

'But I wonder, Miss Hardwicke, if you knew him intimately enough to tell me if the man in the yard is truly George Reed?'

Charles cut in.

'I don't think that's necessary. Miss Hardwicke doesn't need to see a dead man and I've already told you that it is Reed.'

Davenport looked at him.

'You said you *think* it's Reed, but you also said that you had only made his acquaintance yesterday evening. I don't think Miss Hardwicke is the sort of lady to faint at such a sight, are you?' He turned back to me. 'I would be happy to have a confirmation from you.'

I'm not afraid of dead men; the dead can do you no harm. But I am ridiculously squeamish about blood.

'Is there much blood?'

He shook his head. 'I've no idea until I can turn him over.'

I didn't want him to think me weak. I stood a little taller. 'I will take a look.'

Harry Bardwell shifted from one foot to another.

'Sorry Lizzie, Mr Stanford says the gentleman's been drinking in here, but I can't say I knew him well.'

'It's all right, Harry. If I am the only person who knows Mr Reed's body as well as his face, then I must tell if it is him. If there's not much blood, I shall be fine.'

'Thank you, Miss Hardwicke, that is most helpful,' said Davenport.

Mr Grimshaw led the way to the back of the tavern. We followed in serious procession, Anne Bardwell at the back, clutching a cleaning cloth.

Davenport hesitated as we reached the door.

'Before we see the body, Miss Hardwicke, perhaps you could describe the man you knew, even briefly, as George Reed.'

That sounded like a test of sorts. I could only be honest.

'He was a cloth merchant from Norwich,' I said. 'Around medium height but very large around the belly. I would imagine that he was older than fifty, but not very aged.'

'Go on.'

'There's not much more to say,' I said. 'He had the sort of complexion to suggest that he ate and drank far too much, and he had gout. I worried about his heart when he came to visit me. Oh, but he dressed very well.'

'Can you describe what he wore last night?'

'He had a green coat. Sage green, with gold embroidery and buttons down the front and sleeves. It was well made, but nothing fancy. The waistcoat on the other hand was very pretty. Tabby silk with embroidered flowers. It looked as though it might have been French.'

Davenport was staring at me.

'You have a keen eye for fancy details, Miss Hardwicke.'

I glowed at the compliment.

'But I understand that this is often the way with whores.'

I disliked him immediately.

Chapter Nine

It was the stench that hit me first: the warm smell of rotting vegetables and the sharper tang of human waste. I took a deep sniff at the inside of my elbow; as if perfumed fabric and living skin could protect me against the stink of vile decay.

The Bardwells rather grandly described this small walled courtyard as a storage area. Everyone knew, though, that it was a giant rubbish pile, and that they were too tight to pay the soil men to cart it all away regularly. Staff simply threw the old cartons and barrels into a corner at the back, safe in the knowledge that it was all hidden from the sight and smell of the tavern customers – except when those same customers came outside to relieve themselves of the beer that had gone through them. Occasionally, when the pile grew too large, Mr Bardwell would bring the stored goods inside, set the little hill alight and burn the waste away, cabbage leaves, rats and all, watching over it just in case a spark set the whole tavern ablaze. It was a time-consuming, smelly, and fretful business. I knew this because he complained every time Anne nagged him to get on with it. I couldn't understand why they didn't just pay up and get it removed, like everyone else.

Looking at the heap of old sacks and mouldy boxes, I guessed that she had been encouraging him to 'get on' with the task for a few weeks. In the meantime, tavern customers being as they are, it had been well-watered with piss, making it even less pleasant – and even less likely to burn.

The body was lying face down towards the back of this disgusting mound. All that was immediately visible was a fat white hand, poking out from a coat sleeve. Someone was going to have to climb up and turn him over before I could see his face. I was not going anywhere near the rotten stuff.

Davenport, who didn't appear to be affected by the smell, issued instructions.

'Mr Stanford, Mr Bardwell, a hand if you will. You too, Jack. We need to roll him down.'

Charles was repulsed at the idea and hesitated. Harry, probably feeling guilty at the size his rubbish mound had grown to, stepped from foot to foot, muttering 'poor, poor man' to himself. Even Jack Grimshaw looked unhappy. They shuffled forward.

Davenport took a well-placed step on to a wooden crate. It held his weight and he jumped from it to the back of the pile.

'I think I can push him over from here by myself. But I'll need you men to pull him from the front.'

Davenport was strong. He braced himself against the dead man's right shoulder and then tipped the whole body. A rat scuttled over a broken barrel stave and dived out of sight. Grimshaw and Harry sprang forward and steadied the man as he tumbled, easing him on to the ground.

It was George Reed. He was definitely dead.

'Well?' Davenport was suddenly next to me, flicking dirt from his sleeve.

Mr Reed was still in his embroidered waistcoat. His coat was wide open, so I could see it in all its loveliness. His shirt had come untucked from his breeches; possibly there had been a struggle. It was his neck, though, that drew my eyes. For around it, pulled excessively tight, was his own handkerchief: the one we girls had mocked. I could even make out the embroidered 'G.R.' on the corner. Someone had garrotted the man with his own ludicrous handkerchief. His face bulged over the top of it, eyes staring into nothingness. I took a deep breath.

'This is Mr George Reed. It is the man who visited me the day before yesterday and who attended our party. A cloth merchant from Norwich.'

Anne Bardwell stifled a sob with her cloth, and then ran back into the tavern.

'Poor Mr Reed,' said Charles. 'No man deserves to be strangled while he's relieving himself.'

'I don't think he came out here for that reason,' I said.

'Of course he did, Lizzie. Why else would anyone come out here?'

William Davenport was kneeling on the ground, feeling around the dead man's head, and inspecting the red weal underneath the handkerchief. He stopped and squinted up at me.

'Why do you say that?' he said.

I hesitated. Surely, they must see what I saw? Or was I being foolish?

'It's his breeches, Mr Davenport. They are firmly done up. Surely, if he had been attacked while he was at his business they would have been undone?'

Davenport looked to where I pointed and then back at me.

'You're quite right, Miss Hardwicke. I hadn't noticed.'

'That still doesn't mean that he didn't come out here for that purpose,' said Charles. 'This place is known enough to customers at the tavern. Anyone could have told him – or followed him.'

Mr Bardwell groaned.

'But the surrounding wall isn't so high, either,' Charles went on. 'Someone could have climbed over and attacked him. There are a lot of John Swann's men in town, people are saying.' He peered over the body. 'I'll bet he's been robbed as well as strangled.'

Davenport stood up and wiped his hands.

'Well, he has neither purse nor pocket watch,' he said. 'So, I would say that he was robbed – although whether he was killed first or robbed first, I cannot tell.'

Something wasn't entirely right about Mr Reed. As Harry Bardwell worried aloud to Charles and Mr Grimshaw about thieves and murderers climbing his wall and drinking in his tavern, I squatted down to the body. Something else was missing.

'What do you see?' Davenport's voice was sharp.

'It's more what I don't see,' I said.

'What?'

'Something is missing. Have you gone through all of his inside pockets?'

'Yes. He has nothing with him.'

I bent down and patted Reed's coat. It was definitely missing.

'He had a packet with him. A parcel full of papers. He was very careful with it and I think it was important to him.'

'They'll have been after a purse, not papers,' Jack Grimshaw said.

'That would be the most likely explanation,' Davenport agreed.

People were robbed often enough in London, and on the roads. John Swann had been brought to town only yesterday and other gangs might well be nearby. Grimshaw was probably right: but Mr Reed struck me as the sort of man who would carry a small amount in his purse but keep important documents close about his person at all times. He had, after all, brought them to Berwick Street.

'I suggest that you and your fellow runners start asking after Swann's men,' Charles said to Davenport, sounding like a man issuing instructions to his staff. 'You'll find some of the more decent thieves ready to point you in the right direction in exchange for their liberty.'

'Thank you for your advice, Mr Stanford,' said Davenport in a measured voice, 'I'll be sure to follow it as soon as I've completed my own investigations.'

'Well, don't leave it too long. We don't want too many innocent men murdered in the taverns, do we?' Charles threw an arm over Mr Bardwell's shoulder and grinned. 'It won't be good for business if we're all too afraid to relieve ourselves.'

Harry laughed, but his eyes were worried.

'People are saying the gang is around Soho. Our customers'll go elsewhere if they know a man's been murdered.'

'Don't be ridiculous,' I said quickly, 'I'll bet Mrs Bardwell is hoping a murder will bring plenty of revenue. There's nothing like a scandal to draw in the gawpers.'

I nodded to the doorway. 'I expect you'll find that she's already scrubbing tables in preparation.'

Mr Bardwell scuttled back inside and then poked his head out to call to us.

'You're right about the cleaning. She's humming to herself.'

His face fell again when he saw the body on the ground.

'May I ask someone to take him away?' He addressed Mr Davenport.

Davenport nodded.

'I think I've seen enough,' he said. 'We'll make enquiries about relatives, but he'll need to be buried soon. If you can see to it, we'll make sure that you're not left short.'

Harry went back inside.

'I'll see you home if you like, Lizzie.' Charles was suddenly protective, even though it was daylight. Still, I wasn't going to miss an opportunity to walk the streets with my arm through his.

'That would be very kind.'

'I'm sorry, Mr Stanford, but she's going nowhere until I've asked her some questions,' said Davenport, lifting his eyes from the corpse to us. 'You may go, sir, if you wish.' He turned back and began poking the heap of rubbish with his toe, flipping over a broken box.

Charles, a gentleman of wealth and breeding, was free to leave. I was a whore with an eye for fancy details – like watches and purses. George Reed had, after all, been one of my customers. I could see how Davenport's mind was working and it made me nervous.

Charles took my hand.

'I can stay with you, Lizzie, if you want.'

The concern in his face made me smile. I didn't want to be alone with Davenport and Grimshaw, but I needed to warn Ma that Fielding's men would be making their way to her house very soon. After her lecture this morning, I thought it wise.

I pulled Charles inside the tavern and spoke as clearly and quickly as I could.

'Charles, never mind the business here. Davenport and Grimshaw are Mr Fielding's men. I need you to hurry to Mrs Farley and tell her that they're on their way. I'll try to keep them talking here long enough to give her a chance to make the house look respectable.'

He nodded. He understood.

'If you're sure...'

I gave him a gentle push.

By the time Davenport and Grimshaw came in from the yard, Charles had already gone.

I flashed them my best smile, ready to keep them close to me for as long as possible.

Chapter Ten

'You can save your charming smile, Miss Hardwicke; it won't work on me.'

William Davenport scowled, as if to emphasise that he was immune to any feminine magic I might employ, and gestured me towards a table by the wall, set with benches either side. Jack Grimshaw scowled too, although that seemed to be his only expression. He left the tavern after a few quiet words at the door from Davenport and sloped off up the street. I imagined him kicking a dog or a small child on the way back to Bow Street – he looked the sort.

Davenport threw his legs over the bench opposite me and wrapped his hands around the pot of beer Harry Bardwell had brought him. Harry had brought one for me too. I examined the liquid, not knowing what to say or how best to behave. The beer in the White Horse is good; not overly strong, but helpful for calming your nerves if you're being questioned about a murder.

'So how did you meet Mr Reed?'

I cleared my throat. 'He found me in here two days ago and accompanied me home. He told me that he had business in town for a few more days and then he was returning to Norwich.'

'You had some business with him yourself?'

'He paid generously to spend time in my company, yes sir.'

'Was he a decent man? Kind towards you?'

'You mean, did he treat me so badly that I might have wanted to kill him?'

Davenport regarded me in silence. I couldn't work out whether he was trying to imagine me strangling George Reed or grappling with him in my bed.

'Honestly, he was a man of small wit. He talked loudly and at length about the people of rank that he knew and told me a lot about the cloth trade in Norwich.'

He knew the type; I saw it in his smirk.

'But he visited your house for the party as well? Did you invite him or was he known to the woman who runs your house?'

'I invited him.' I ignored the question about Ma. 'I was trying to get him to leave, that first evening, and I suggested the party just to get him out of my room.' I took a mouthful of the beer; the taste of it calmed my growing agitation. 'I didn't think he would come, but he turned up and was very rude to some of our guests.'

'In what way?'

'He became overly familiar with a young girl in the house. Miss Blackwood is staying with us... just until her young man has found work and they can marry.'

Davenport snorted.

'Until you can put her to work, you mean!'

'No. She's not the working sort. She has no business in this city. Tommy is hoping to find honest employment.' You need to be hard to earn a living here, and Amelia was as soft as kitten fur.

'Ah yes, Tommy. I was coming to him. Mr Stanford said that George Reed was "still shouting about Tommy" when he arrived here.'

'Tommy, Tommy Bridgewater, intervened when George Reed was trying his luck with Miss Blackwood. There was a bit of pushing and shoving with the other men and then Mr Reed was asked to leave.'

'I imagine he didn't leave quietly.'

'He made a terrible row about it. He was shouting in the street, much to our disgust. Berwick Street is a decent place and we live quietly among our neighbours.'

The beer was stirring a memory.

'What?' Davenport was alert to my expression. 'What is it? Out with it, girl, it may be important.'

Was it important? I closed my eyes and tried to remember what George Reed had said as he was leaving. It wasn't even a memory of what was said; it was more of a feeling, something that didn't fit with the rest of the evening. I frowned.

'Mr Reed was shouting a lot. But as he was in the doorway he said something quietly – almost under his breath. He said: "I know who you are Tommy, I know who you are" and then he laughed. It was as though he knew Tommy Bridgewater from somewhere else. Then he carried on roaring as he fell into the street.'

'He already knew Tommy Bridgewater?'

'That's the strange thing. His words suggested that he did, but I had formed the impression that they met for the first time yesterday. How odd. Maybe he did know Tommy.'

I met his eyes.

'I'm sorry, sir. I don't think I'm being much help.'

'Well, Miss Hardwicke, so far you are the one person who knew anything about George Reed at all. That makes you helpful – and of interest.'

'What about his papers? Are you going to look for them?'

'Do you know what they were?'

'He told me they were important documents.'

'Then I expect that they will be at his lodgings.'

'And will you be hunting down John Swann's men, as Mr Stanford suggested?'

He raised an eyebrow.

'By myself? Do you think a man like me would be a match for a gang of cutthroats?'

I had seen him balance on a wooden box and jump over the rubbish heap in the yard without too much trouble. He was as agile as a cat. Indeed, his dark brown coat was cut generously around the shoulders, rather than being fashionably tight, suggesting that he was ready to chase or climb. He might not threaten a larger man by his physical presence, but I imagined he would know how to use the sword he carried.

I studied him properly for the first time. He had the air of a gentleman in the way that he spoke and carried himself. His wig was simple; pulled into a pigtail with a black ribbon. His clothes were sober but clean and of good quality. The pale waistcoat with small amounts of embroidery and the unfussy shirt gave the appearance of neatness or frugality. He wasn't above thirty years, but his face was melancholy – as if he were an older man. I spend hours cheering up men like him.

'Well, Miss Hardwicke, would I deal well with John Swann's gang?'

I saw no reason to compliment his physique, and his sharp words did not encourage me to flattery.

'Perhaps you should take Mr Grimshaw with you.'

His mouth puckered at the slight. 'Well, he's handy with his fists,' he said. 'And he carries the pistols.'

I had drunk my fill. I stood up as Harry ambled past.

'Do I need to settle with you for Sallie?' I asked him. 'The girl I brought in yesterday.'

'That little diver? No, Lizzie, she didn't eat or drink any more that I saw. You've paid already.' He patted my shoulder, collecting our tankards and the coins Davenport placed on the table.

'She wasn't really picking pockets,' I said to Davenport as Harry wandered off. 'Well, she was, but she wasn't very good at it and she was just hungry, so I brought her in and fed her.' The words tumbled out a little too quickly. I shrugged. 'Thank you for the beer, but I need to be getting home, if you'll excuse me, sir.'

His eyes narrowed.

'Sit down. I haven't finished yet.'

I obeyed, uncomfortable at the hardness of his tone.

'Mrs Bardwell reports that, when you were here yesterday afternoon, you suggested your evening with Mr Reed nearly killed him.'

I sighed and rolled my eyes. It was typical of Anne to turn my joke into a serious matter.

'It was a figure of speech. He was a fat old man who struggled to spend five minutes with me.' I giggled, to make light of it, but Davenport's mouth remained in a fixed line.

'This isn't a laughing matter. I have a man lying stran-gled on a soil heap. His attacker could just as easily be a strong young woman as a man.'

I swallowed hard. He leaned forward, his voice low.

'You snigger about a dead man, even having seen his strangled body. You've made light of a friendship with a common street thief and may, for all I know, be holding stolen items for this woman, who may, in turn, be working for any of the gangs we know of who operate between here and St Giles.' He held up his hand as I tried to interrupt. 'You, more than anyone else, were intimately acquainted with Mr Reed and you have already commented on his fine clothes and his wealth. You tell me about a parcel which you suggest that no one else will know about and yet his purse and watch are missing.'

He laid a hand on my arm.

'You don't know their whereabouts, do you?'

I shook my head, ashamed of my disrespect for George Reed, and suddenly afraid.

'I am neither a thief nor a murderer, sir.'

His hand gripped my arm for a moment before he let go and sat back.

'But you do see my dilemma?'

'I see that I am an easy target for your suspicions.' Fear melted as anger began to fill my body. It sharpened my wits. 'If you believed I had anything to do with Mr Reed's death, then we would be out of this place and on the way to the magistrate.'

He sucked his teeth and looked away. I had guessed correctly. I was a free woman and he had very little to connect me to the murder. I could walk out of the tavern now.

But my curiosity had been roused. I heard myself say:

'I can't prove to you that I didn't thieve or kill, but I can make it my own business to find out for you who did kill George Reed.'

'Really?' He was scornful. 'You pit yourself above Mr Fielding's men?'

'I can go where you cannot, Mr Davenport. I can walk in places, ask questions, I can flirt and wheedle in ways that you could not imagine. I will hear things on the streets that you will never hear, and the people who see things in bedrooms and alleyways will confide in me because they will trust me. They may fear or respect one of Mr Fielding's men, but such people will not trust them.' I almost believed all that myself.

There was a long pause. He held out a hand.

'Then I look forward to seeing the results of your investigations.'

I shook his hand; the face above it was grave.

'This is a serious business, Miss Hardwicke. You won't find me easy to deal with, if I come to believe that you're guilty.'

'I will be most earnest in my search for Mr Reed's killer, sir. Not least because in finding him, I prove my own innocence.'

'Don't try to leave London. I, and others, will hunt you down and find you. That's what we do.' He smiled pleasantly enough, swung his legs off the bench and stood to offer me a hand up. The smile disappeared as his fingers gripped me hard. 'I mean it: if you're conning me, and

I've been played for a fool by a murderous whore, then I'll drive your cart to the gallows myself.'

I stumbled through the door of the tavern, lurched around the corner and threw up the contents of my stomach.

Chapter Eleven

The house was alive with conversation.

Charles, who had hardly been allowed across the threshold before being pumped for news, was giving an account of Mr Reed's demise to a noisy audience. Mrs Farley kept interrupting him, wanting details. Polly, Lucy and Emily were on the stairs, leaning over the rail with Meg and Sarah. Sydney was in his usual place by the front door, but he was so keen to hear what had happened that he didn't notice me come in. Mr Winchcombe and Mr Herring were also in the hall – I wondered how they had heard of it so soon.

Charles saw me.

'So, how was the constable, Lizzie?'

They all turned to stare.

'Mr Davenport thinks I killed George Reed.'

My head started to spin and Sydney, who by now was not only aware that I had come in, but that I was not fully myself, leapt from his stool and offered it to me.

'What nonsense! How can he possibly think that?' Mr Winchcombe said, his loud voice prevailing as they all fired questions at me. I waited for the noise to die down a little before stating the obvious.

'I'm a harlot with a dead customer. Look at it from his point of view.'

'How ridiculous. Reed's death doesn't make you a murderer,' Winchcombe responded.

'I said as much to Mr Davenport.'

Charles cut in.

'But if he thinks you murdered Reed, then why are you here and not in front of the magistrate?'

He was cleverer than his friend.

'I would love to tell you that I charmed him, but the truth is, he has nothing to incriminate me other than supposition.'

'I'm very glad to hear it.' He pushed past the others and wound an arm about my waist.

'As am I,' Ma stood with her hands on her hips, scowling. 'And now Mr Stanford says that we're to expect a visit from your constable.'

I nodded, wearily.

'He's looking for a killer, Ma. And unless we're hiding one here, I'm sure he'll leave us alone.' I hoped, rather than knew this to be the case. 'This is a respectable house – like you said.'

Her lips pinched together. 'Well, we had better make it so before he arrives.' She began to issue orders and the small crowd drifted away to get on with transforming a brothel into nothing more than a milliners' shop which, from time to time, offered tea and polite conversation to well-bred gentlemen. Davenport would not be fooled in the slightest.

The three gentlemen who were currently in our hallway – none of whom was interested in hats, tea or even much conversation – made to leave. Mrs Farley had not given them any instructions, after all.

I tugged at Charles' coat.

'Wait – I need you to help me find who really did kill George Reed.'

'I will be very happy to help you.' He still had an arm around my waist. He decided that trying to put a hand in my gown was the most helpful thing to do. I shoved him away.

'Charles, I'm serious. I've told Davenport that I want to ask questions and form my own ideas as to who killed Mr Reed.'

The three men found this amusing.

'Mr Fielding is recruiting whores to Bow Street now?' Charles' voice was full of laughter.

'Don't be dismissive. I want to make sure that I'm not hanging for a murder I didn't commit, that's all.'

'The runner has agreed to let you hunt for Reed's killer?' Mr Herring asked, equally incredulous.

I nodded. 'Do you want to hunt with me?'

'Well, I think Stanford has it right,' he said. 'Reed was probably done over by John Swann's fellows. It is rumoured that they are here in London now, on their way towards St Giles or Seven Dials, like as not, and thieving as they go.'

'My father used to tell me of a man near Harrow who was robbed of tuppence and all his clothes when he was a boy,' Winchcombe joined in. 'The footpads were caught trying to sell the clothes in a tavern. Men like that would think nothing of grabbing a man's purse while he was taking a piss.'

'Mr Reed didn't go to the yard for that purpose. His breeches were secure – didn't Charles tell you?'

He had ignored my observation in favour of his own opinion, it seemed. I decided to appeal to their sense of adventure; make an investigation sound daring but not too dangerous.

'We could go and see the place where it happened? Take a look? Charles and I have just come from the White Horse, and, if the undertakers haven't arrived yet, there'll be a body. We could search the yard. Besides, you might recall something important if we talk over a drink; something to help catch a killer.'

The truth was, I wanted to go back there, to see if there was anything that would tell me what had happened. And one of the men might just recall something of interest.

It took a fraction of a second for them to agree to this new excitement. It was broad daylight after all, so we were unlikely to be set upon by the dangerous associates of a highwayman. I slipped my arm through Charles' as the four of us set off down the street.

'Why were your friends in the house?' I asked him, as we walked slowly behind the other two. 'I was surprised to see them so early in the day.'

He laughed. 'It's not early, as far as they're concerned; it's late. I passed them on the way, rolling out of a gaming house. Winchcombe's an extremely committed gambler – not a very good one – and Herring was with him.'

Now I looked, I could see that both men were in the same clothes as last night. They looked a little dishevelled. Mr Winchcombe needed to straighten his wig.

'They were out all night?'

'Herring said that Winchcombe disappeared off from the tavern by himself. He asked around the other drinkers and discovered that a new gaming hell had opened up recently. He decided to take a look and found Winchcombe there, losing heavily. He said that the wine and the company were very bright, though, so they both stayed until morning.'

'What about you? Weren't you with Herring?'

'I didn't fancy going, so I stayed at the White Horse.'

'Alone?' That was unlikely.

He pinched my arm and gave me his most appealing grin. Not alone.

'I hope she was kind to you,' I said in my haughtiest tone. I hoped she was deserving of his attention, the lucky trollop.

'She wasn't as charming as you, of course.' He dodged as I punched his shoulder – not entirely in jest.

'She can't have been without charm, if Anne Bardwell let you have a room.' Anne was picky about who she allowed upstairs. I wondered who he had found.

He didn't say anything. I pulled his arm, curious. 'Who was it? I want to know?'

He shrugged me off and shoved his hands in his pockets, walking ahead. 'Didn't ask her name. We had a few drinks and then left.'

'You went back to her lodgings?'

He turned to scowl at me, annoyed that I'd pressed him. 'An alley, if you really must know. Very brief. I paid her and went back to the White Horse. The other two had both disappeared by then, so I had another drink on my own. By that point it was nearly dawn, I think.'

How delightful men are. They have an itch; they scratch it and carry on with life. I hoped he hadn't caught anything nasty. But I'm hardly in a position to question his morals.

Herring and Winchcombe had reached the tavern ahead of us and were arguing with Anne Bardwell in the doorway. When Charles and I arrived, it was clear that the White Horse was closed. Anne stood, jaw set squarely, arms folded over her belly.

'No, you're not coming in. I've only just got rid of the constable and we've still got a dead man to move because the undertakers are in no hurry.'

We tried for several minutes, but Anne was having none of it.

'Perhaps we might talk to you and Mr Bardwell about what happened last night,' I said, peering into the empty tavern, hoping to catch a glimpse of the landlord.

'It's no good you looking about for Harry. He's helping the men carry Mr Reed away to their cart. That unfortunate gentleman's too heavy for the little shrimps the undertakers finally sent us.'

Anne Bardwell would probably have managed to carry out George Reed by herself, such was the width of her shoulders. She was no shrimp.

'Are you sure we can't come in and wait for him?' I knew that he would be more willing to talk than his wife. 'And have a drink and a bite to eat?'

'Your wheedling won't work on me, hussy. I have work to do and no time for idle chatter. No one is allowed into this tavern until a decent time has passed.'

It is difficult to argue with decency, even when you know that the real motives are less honourable.

I sighed.

'Well, gentlemen, we must sadly leave Mrs Bardwell to her cleaning and polishing. This tavern will be the talk of London very soon and the customers will expect the very best when they come to gawp. I only hope,' I said loudly, sweeping my skirts in exaggerated disdain, 'that there is still a welcome for Mrs Farley's girls once the fashionably curious have moved on. We do, after all, attract a good custom in the ordinary times.'

Chapter Twelve

The men grumbled at me as they trailed behind. I had suggested the tavern and it was closed. The murdered man was being removed. There was no body, no adventure, no drink and no food. We reached the corner of Wardour Street and I stopped.

'Well, if we can't poke about inside the White Horse, then perhaps we might ask people outside if they saw anything?' I said, hoping to encourage a little enthusiasm, but their hope of a daring escapade had dwindled.

Winchcombe declared that he was off to bed, or perhaps he would find supper first. 'Or is it breakfast now?' Herring, too, was yawning.

'What about you?' I said to Charles, expecting that he would also want to find a bed – possibly even his own. To my surprise, he agreed to join me.

'I'll come, although you know my thoughts. But if there are cutthroats roaming the streets, even in daylight, I can offer my protection.'

When the other two had said farewell, we stood and watched the street sellers. An oyster girl sat in a doorway, picking beards from the shells she had yet to sell, and a man heaving a cart of salted pork exchanged a few words with her as he stopped to rearrange his wares.

Three women turned into Compton Street and passed the time of day together in such a way as suggested they were friendly with one another. Their clothes were clean enough, if a little shabby. Kindred spirits. I raised a hand to them and one waved back. It was Just Sallie.

'Sallie! How delightful to see you.' I curtseyed to her and she shrieked with laughter. I could smell the gin at five paces.

'Well, if isn't my big sister Lizzie!' She seemed impossibly pleased to see me and quickly introduced her new friends Bess and Kitty. Kitty was no more than sixteen, tight blond curls peeping from under her bonnet, a saucy expression and plump lips. Bess, on the other hand, was a plain thing, square-faced and with eyes as small as raisins. She could not have been much over twenty, not much older than me, but already she looked worn out. I wondered at their existence, but knew better than to pry.

'You found a new gown, I see.' Sallie was in pale pink sprigged cotton with a matching bonnet. It wasn't a good fit – second-hand clothes rarely are – but it made her skin look less sallow.

'I had a bath, too. What do you think?' She twirled, and for a moment she was a giggling child.

'It's charming. You look like a rose bud. I hope that it was a good business investment.'

She gave me a toothy smile.

'It was the best use of other people's money that I have ever made, Lizzie. I haven't been back to Covent Garden in two days.'

'I'm very glad to hear it.'

'Is that your gentleman?' Kitty nodded over to Charles, who was in deep conversation with the pork man.

'For now, he is,' I said. Although Charles would be happy to spend an hour or two with a pretty little nymph like her, I was in no doubt.

'Were any of you ladies out in this street yesterday?' I wasn't standing in the street for an idle conversation. 'In the hours before midnight.'

Kitty shook her head.

'I was in Thrift Street and then I went to the Bull's Head until nearly dawn.'

Bess shrugged.

'I wasn't in this street at all. I decided to try nearer to Oxford Street and met a couple of culls in the alleys before heading back to wait for Kitty.' She smiled at her friend. 'We look out for one another.' That was kind, but I thought that Kitty wouldn't look back for Bess if she were snapped up by a decent bawdy house.

'What about you, Sallie? Were you on this street last night?'

'I may have been. I think I was, but I can't rightly remember. I'm still trying to work out where places are.'

The drink would not help her memory.

'I want to find someone, anyone, who may have seen a large gentleman in this street last night. He was wearing a dark green coat and probably had a full wig with a plain hat. An old man with a large stomach.'

'Why are you looking for a man like that when you have such a handsome one already?' Kitty smirked at me.

'Because this gentleman was killed last night, and I am trying to find out what happened to him.' That took the wind from her sails. 'He was lately a companion of mine and I was rather shocked to hear that he had died.'

'He died in this street?' said Bess. Her mouth hung open in horror. 'I didn't hear about it.'

'He died in the back yard of the White Horse. He was strangled with his own handkerchief.'

Sallie swayed a little and steadied herself on Kitty's arm.

'Lizzie! That's terrible! And he was a customer of yours?'

'You didn't kill him, then?' Kitty was very sharp.

'Of course not, otherwise why would I still be out on the street? I'd be in hiding, surely.'

She nodded slowly – as if thinking through what she would be doing, had she just murdered a man.

'Sallie, are you sure you can't recall seeing him? Or anything suspicious, or anyone acting strangely around the White Horse last night?'

'Sorry, Lizzie. I might have had a mouthful of purl – just to keep me warm. I'll be sure to let you know if I do remember something.'

I wouldn't drink purl if I was freezing to death. A disgusting mixture of milk and rancid gin – or whatever else they put in it. It was cheap, and it got you drunk, though. A lot of the street girls drank it just to get through the night's work.

'Your gentleman is calling for you,' said Bess. Charles was beckoning me over to the man with the cart.

'Well, I'd better go, then,' I said, rolling my eyes. 'I'll see you soon Sallie, if you're staying around here. And very pleased to make your acquaintance,' I said to the other two, as the three of them danced off along the street. Charles looked up as they went by him and touched his hat. He said something to them and they burst into squeals of laughter. Sallie and Kitty looked with longing at the

82

man who was both handsome and wealthy, presumably offering him their charms, until Bess tugged them away and they skipped off arm in arm.

I sighed and walked over to him. The oyster girl got up from her step, put the basket on her head and wandered away.

'Lovely ladies,' he said, watching them go. 'Friends of yours?'

'We're in the same line of business, but I wouldn't say we're close.'

He laughed.

'The little one had rather pretty curls.'

'Kitty? Is she the girl you met last night?'

'No, I think I would have remembered her.'

I wasn't going to give him the satisfaction of my jealousy.

'What did you find out?' I asked. 'I hope your conversation was more fruitful than mine.'

'The girls didn't see anything, then?' He was still watching them as they pushed and pulled each other, pausing now and again to glance back at him and giggle.

'It seems not. Kitty and Bess were elsewhere last night and if Sallie did see anything at all she now cannot remember it because, as far as I can tell, aside from that badly-made pink gown, she has spent most of her money on gin and purl.'

'I think I may have fared better, then.' He pointed over to the pork seller, who was tugging his cart down towards St Anne's.

'He saw something?'

'No, but he's heard people saying that Swann's men are around.'

John Swann again.

'Charles, I really don't think…'

He cut my words off with a wave of his hand.

'I know you don't agree, Lizzie, but it's obvious. These men think nothing of stabbing and shooting carriage drivers or cutting the throats of the rich. A man like Reed, flaunting his wealth in taverns, rolling out of decent establishments like Mrs Farley's, a man like that would be an easy target.'

He kissed me on the nose and declared that he needed a rest, having been awake for two days. I watched him go and made my way home. It made sense to assume that Reed had been an unlucky victim of a robbery, but Reed had not been stabbed, or shot, or surprised even. It was possible, the more I thought about it, that he had gone out to the yard to meet someone.

Chapter Thirteen

When I reached the house, it was Meg who answered the door and not Sydney, which was odd. She pulled me in quickly and put a finger to her lips before I could ask what was happening.

Davenport was here, then.

The door of the parlour was flung open and there he was, casually leaning on the doorpost, as if he owned the house.

'Miss Hardwicke, how good to see you again. Do come in.'

Mr Grimshaw's fat head poked through the doorway, the look on his face suggesting that I had little option but to do as I was bid.

The girls would all be out, I guessed. Lucy would be with one of her rich men, tucked up in a mansion for the rest of the afternoon. Polly and Emily would have found a tavern and be entertaining company. Now that I was stuck with Davenport, my own prospects of a lucrative or enjoyable afternoon were diminishing.

Mrs Farley sat bold, proud, and resolute at the table. Tommy and Amelia were with her. Amelia was not crying, but she looked tiny and pale. Tommy was subdued. Davenport pulled up a chair for me, while Grimshaw leant against a wall.

Davenport sat down next to me and laid his hands carefully on the table.

'You've been back to the White Horse with three gentlemen from the party, I hear. Did you discover anything to your advantage, or to mine?'

'Mr Bardwell was out assisting the undertakers and Mrs Bardwell was reluctant to let us in. She's keen to polish and clean the tavern before crowds of morbid-minded drinkers begin to visit.'

A flicker of amusement crossed his face.

'Is that what she told you?'

'Of course not. She talked about keeping the place closed out of respect for Mr Reed, but she was wiping down the tables even when you were there and, by the look of her, she's not stopped scrubbing since then.'

He nodded solemnly.

'Your excellent powers of observation failed to find anything beyond the fact that the White Horse is now very clean?'

Was he mocking me?

I frowned back at him. 'I spoke to three very foolish young ladies, two of whom were elsewhere last night and one of whom might have been in Compton Street, but was too drunk to remember.' I sighed. 'Mr Stanford had a conversation with a man selling pork who told him that John Swann's men were, indeed, hiding in many of the corners of the capital. How he came by this information Mr Stanford didn't say.'

'Well I imagine that Mr Stanford was more interested in the young ladies anyway.' He had the measure of Charles.

'Still,' he turned to the other people in the room, 'at least I have had the opportunity to meet the famous Tommy.'

Mr Bridgewater's eyes were anxious. Had Davenport found his murderer? I hoped not, for Amelia's sake as well as Tommy's.

'Are you all right, Amelia?' She was gazing dreamily over my shoulder, eyes not focussing.

'I've given her some brandy,' said Ma.

That would explain it. It would also mean that Davenport would have difficulty pressing her for worthwhile answers to his questions. Clever old Ma. She nudged a wedge of bread and a plate of meat and cheese towards me, guessing that I was hungry. I hadn't eaten all day; so much had happened that I had barely noticed. It's why Ma is so good at her profession: she supplies what people need before they even know they need it.

Davenport turned his attention to Tommy while I began to fill my empty stomach in as delicate a way as possible.

'Tommy was just telling me that he is struggling to find any honest work in London, Miss Hardwicke. Why is that, I wonder?'

'I've told you, Mr Davenport, there isn't so much work for a farrier as I thought at first. At least, no one needs help in the places that I've asked,' said Tommy.

'Have you asked widely?' I cut across Davenport, mouth still full of bread.

Tommy's eyes met mine.

'Not really, Miss Hardwicke, I wanted to be with Amelia, to make sure that she was safe and well before I started to look for work in all seriousness.'

He was a sweet boy. I poured myself a glass of wine from the jug on the table.

'There you are, Mr Davenport, he hasn't found any work because he hasn't really looked for it yet. I'm sure that someone will want a strong and willing young man to assist him,' I said, knocking back the drink and pouring another.

Davenport didn't look convinced.

'You haven't explained to me why you are both in this part of London in the first place; why Miss Blackwood is in a bawdy house rather than in her own home. Where is her father? Why hasn't he come to take her away from this place of sin?'

'Mr Davenport!' Mrs Farley put on her most affronted expression. 'I have a decent home here. Why shouldn't she come and lodge with me?'

Davenport raised a hand from the table.

'There's no need to be theatrical, Mrs Farley. I am here to ask questions about the murder of a gentleman who was lately known to one of your so-called lodgers, but I could just as easily make life difficult for you with Mr Fielding.'

The mention of the dreaded name quietened her down at once. Davenport was right: he was doing her a favour by ignoring her business.

'Mr Bridgewater? Where is her father and why is she not with him tonight?'

Tommy took Amelia's hand under the table.

'We wished to be wed, sir, that's the truth of it. But he disapproved. A stable boy is not good enough for his daughter.'

'He is an alderman, Mr Davenport. Alderman Black-wood.' Amelia spoke softly. 'He thinks that he is very fine, but he was once a mere apprentice himself. He has forgotten that. He wants his daughter to marry one of his new grand friends – as befits his station.'

So, Alderman Blackwood was a respectable tradesman who wanted to move up in the world and was prepared to sacrifice his daughter for the privilege. I find such men odious. Give me the dissolute aristocracy or the feckless poor any day; at least when they sell off their children it's for good reason – to pay off gambling debts or avoid starvation. To pimp your daughter to raise your social status is, frankly, objectionable.

Tommy banged a fist on the table, causing us all to jump – and spilling some of my wine.

'An old man, Mr Davenport! Think of that. My dearest girl wed to a man three times her age.' There was a temper inside him. Davenport saw it too.

'You have a real passion there, boy. It might be better to learn to tame it before you confront her father again.'

Tommy and Amelia exchanged a swift glance.

'Is that why you were forced to leave?' Davenport leaned forward, catching the scent of a truth.

'Amelia told us that Mr Blackwood caught you together and threw her out.' I wanted to know the truth as well.

Tommy's shoulders sank a little.

'That is the truth, Miss Hardwicke,' he looked at Davenport. 'Her father threw her out on the street because she loved me. But it's not the whole story.'

He ran a hand nervously through his hair.

'I'll give you the truth, I swear it, sir. When Mr Black-wood had dealt so harshly with his daughter, I went to find him, to plead with him to take her back and bless our marriage.'

'I imagine he was not keen to hear you.'

'No sir, he was not. He was, I must say it, most unpleasant. He wasn't concerned for Amelia. He told me that I had lost him the chance to marry into quality. Quality! The man he intended for her is downright ugly and riddled with gout.' Tommy took a breath and calmed his voice. 'Then he threatened me. He told me that he would have me whipped, or worse, if I didn't leave his house.'

'Go on.'

'I, well, I hit him. I couldn't help it,' he appealed to Amelia, 'he was shouting and raging at me and my hand screwed itself up into a fist and I punched him on the chin. Like this.' He showed us an impressive looking swipe.

'And then I ran.'

'You didn't check to see whether you had killed him?'

'No sir, I ran as far and as fast as I could, and I am sorry for that. But I am not sorry for punching him.'

'Do we know yet the health of Alderman Blackwood?'

Amelia nodded.

'He is very much alive, Mr Davenport. I was packing my bag to leave when I heard the commotion. One of the servants told me that Tommy had hit him and that he was shouting like the devil. I didn't stay to find out any more, but he was certainly alive, and very angry, when I left.' She beamed lopsidedly at Tommy. The brandy was still working.

'You could still marry, Amelia,' I said to her. 'Even if your father has disowned you, why are you waiting?'

She made a hopeless shrug with her little shoulders. 'I suppose I still hope that he might love Tommy as I do.'

I narrowed my eyes at her, realising that there were practical as well as romantic concerns. 'And I imagine there's your fortune to consider.'

She blushed. 'My father was prepared to set aside a considerable sum when I married, Lizzie. Even half of it would be plenty for us to live on. We have nothing, at present.'

'And then, of course, you have no work, Mr Bridge-water', said Davenport. 'And no prospect of work without a decent letter for a new employer.'

Tommy groaned and rested his forehead on the table. I snatched up my glass, not wanting the wine spilled again.

Davenport watched him. Tommy was a young man with a temper. He was also, now, a man without means. Could he have killed Reed for his purse? Would he be prepared to have Amelia working instead?

I didn't see him as Reed's murderer. He might be passionate and quick with his fists, but everything about Reed's death suggested someone had lured him there. Reed had no reason to meet Tommy in the back yard of the White Horse. Unless...

Davenport was there before me.

'How did you come to know Mr Reed? Had you known him long?'

Tommy raised his head.

'I didn't know him at all until last night.'

That was odd, because Mr Reed certainly knew him.

'But the people I've spoken to already tell me that he left this house saying he knew who you were,' said Davenport, echoing my thought. 'How did he know you?'

91

'I'm telling you the truth, I didn't know the man until last night. He tried to shove his hands into Amelia's gown and I pulled him off her. I called to some other men to help me. There was a bit of pushing and he shouted a lot.'

'Mr Reed was asked to leave,' said Ma, smoothing her skirt. 'We don't like loud people in this house. They upset the girls and the other guests.'

Davenport ignored her. 'But as he was leaving he said that he knew who you were. What do you suppose he meant by that?'

'I don't know, sir, I really don't. I didn't know him at all. I didn't mean him any harm, really I did not. I only wanted to protect Amelia.'

She laid a tired head on his shoulder and he put an arm around her.

Davenport was not convinced.

'I'm on the hunt for a purse and a watch, Bridgewater. George Reed was robbed as well as murdered. A man without money and without the prospect of employment might be tempted to kill for such a purse.'

'Not me, Mr Davenport. I would not kill a man for his purse. Never.'

'Even though you've tried to injure two men with your fists.'

'For the woman I love. Not for money.'

'You won't live on love for ever,' said Ma with a laugh.

'We will manage, Mrs Farley,' said Tommy, 'we will find honest work and get by.'

I really hoped that they would, but the world did not treat such innocents with kindness.

'I would like to have a look for Mr Reed's belongings in your room, Miss Blackwood. I assume that will be acceptable with you, Mrs Farley?' Davenport stood up.

She could not refuse.

'Certainly. I will take you up. It's starting to get a little dark, though, you may prefer to visit tomorrow morning...' She wanted him out of the house before the evening's business began. The girls would be coming home with men to entertain.

'It's quite light enough. I'll look now.' He cocked his head to Grimshaw, who rolled himself away from the wall. Ma, resigned to having Fielding's men around for a while longer, led the way. I followed, with Tommy and Amelia in my wake.

Chapter Fourteen

They stamped all the way up to the attic: the heavy tread of the law, rather than the delicate skip of Soho ladies.

There were precious few belongings for them to search through. Amelia had packed a bag, but Tommy had left in a hurry and had barely anything to his name. For all the Blackwoods' recent prosperity, Amelia had made herself as poor as a washerwoman, pinning her hopes on Tommy's employment, or a thaw in her father's heart. It was oversight – or stupidity – that she had not packed a few jewels or items of silver to pawn. I had.

It was Grimshaw who was searching through the cupboards, drawers and shelves of the room. I could only assume that Davenport had deliberately decided to let him get on with the task in order to intimidate the young lovers. He stood watching, face severe, as Grimshaw scattered garments over the bed. Ma looked as if she were half-expecting him to find something. Tommy and Amelia clung to each other in the corner, visibly terrified by the sight of the giant-fisted man wreaking havoc on their possessions. For all his courage in the face of Mr Blackwood, Tommy was helpless when dealing with men like this. I, however, was less afraid, and bullies make me angry.

'How dare you do this to their things!' I grabbed Grimshaw by the arm, to prevent him from tearing a shawl.

He shook me off as if I were an irritating fly and got on with his task.

'Mr Davenport, is this necessary? This destruction?'

He blinked at me.

'Destruction, Miss Hardwicke? Mr Grimshaw is searching for a purse.'

'He can search well enough without tearing clothes and throwing everything about,' I was shouting, the anger burning hot behind my eyes. 'Miss Blackwood has little enough as it is, without him ruining her property.'

Davenport shrugged. Then, after a moment, he called Grimshaw away from his task.

'My apologies, Miss Blackwood, Mr Bridgewater. Mr Grimshaw, here, is used to dealing with rougher folk.'

Grimshaw was rough enough himself. Amelia would want to wash her shifts now his grubby fingers had handled them.

'Did you see anything, Jack?'

Grimshaw shook his head. 'Nothing here, Will.'

Davenport bowed to Amelia.

'Then we'll be on our way for now.'

The men left the room and descended the stairs. I pushed past Grimshaw on the landing, caught Davenport by the arm and shook him.

'What was that about?'

'Not that it's any business of yours, Miss Hardwicke, but I wanted to see how Tommy reacted.

'Well, he was obviously terrified.'

'He was. Which rather suggests that he isn't a murderer – or even a thief.'

We paused on the landing as Grimshaw made his way down ahead of us.

'You don't think he killed Mr Reed?'

'Well, if he did, it wasn't for his purse. But he might have been defending Miss Blackwood, and he's got a quick temper.'

We were outside my own room. I put a protective hand to the door – a mistake.

'Is this your room?' My hesitation was all that he needed. He called his friend back. 'Jack, in here.'

I growled at him. He was playing a part in front of Grimshaw, I could tell.

'You can drop the hard man act with me,' I said, hissing at Davenport as he pushed past. 'I don't want my petticoats torn or my hats battered.'

Grimshaw started opening drawers and pulling out clothing.

'Go easy, Jack,' said Davenport, gesturing to the garments. 'Miss Hardwicke's outfits are worth more than your wages, so try not to rip them.'

I followed behind Grimshaw. Where he emptied, I re-folded and re-packed.

I suspected that Grimshaw was getting his own peculiar pleasure from rummaging through my small clothes. Although having a man under my skirts is a daily occupation, watching him running his hands through my stockings and shifts was making me uncomfortable. If he'd been in Emily's room, rigged out with birch rods and chains for those who sought their pleasure in pain, it would have been he who was embarrassed. I was half-inclined to send them down to her room. It would certainly amuse Emily – but Ma would have kittens about it.

Once the room had been thoroughly turned over, Davenport put a hand on Grimshaw's shoulder and called him off the search. There was, as he had probably expected, no sign of Reed's purse or watch, but every sign of an irate woman.

The two men skulked out. I kicked Davenport's ankle as he passed me. Hard enough to make him aware of my fury.

'You deserved that.' I said, as he looked at me in surprise.

'Probably,' he said, evenly, 'but you entertained Mr Reed here, and Mr Reed is now dead.'

I watched, hands on hips, as they tramped down the stairs and out of the house, waiting for my anger to subside before following them out of the front door.

Chapter Fifteen

Afternoon was tipping into evening. The air was chilly, but this did not deter people who were seeking pleasure. It never did. Gentlemen and ladies will walk the streets hunting for a warm body, a warm pie or a warm beer whatever the weather. I was searching for none of these – although I had offers of all of them. I was looking for answers. And proof of my innocence.

My customary saunter became a more purposeful stride towards the corner of Wardour and Compton streets, and to the White Horse. It was still in darkness, but a crowd had gathered around the doorway, where Anne stood illuminated by several lamps, making her look like an actress from Drury Lane. She was telling the sorry tale of poor Mr Reed to a captivated audience. There were some small embellishments here and there: how he had spent the evening being lured into sin by wicked whores (that would be me) before showing himself a fine and most generous patron of that very tavern. He had drunk plenty of ale and praised the good order of the establishment, according to Anne. He must have gone to drink there when Charles was off with his twopenny whore. Apparently, passers-by had told of howls and blood curdling screams as he was strangled to death even as he went to relieve himself. It was strange that none of these passers-by had seen fit to answer Reed's cries for help.

I needed to work quickly. If Anne was telling her own version of events, then very soon it would become gospel truth and the more ignorant would be prepared to swear to its accuracy.

The streets were busier now and filling with more of the people who might have seen something last night. It was the street walkers, link boys and gin sellers I wanted.

The little oyster girl was still out, at the back of the tavern, and near to Milk Alley. She was without her basket, so probably selling something other than oysters now, to make ends meet. Near to a brazier, a man in an oversized hat stood with his gingerbread cart, laughing with a girl in a pretty pink gown.

'You didn't get very far tonight, then, Sallie?' I said, catching her by the arm as she swayed.

'One or two uprights in an alley, sis.' Her words were slurred.

The gingerbread man laughed.

'She's a sweet one, this girl,' he said, 'spends more time drinking her money than earning it, I reckon.'

Sallie would be running out of coins and picking pockets again soon.

I bought us both a slab of gingerbread. It was hot and sweet.

She wasn't capable of conversation, so I chatted to the gingerbread man instead, while she leaned on the handle of his cart. He had a friendly face under the hat, and he was plump and cheerful — as would seem only right for his trade. Who would buy gingerbread from a thin-ribbed man, after all? He was happy to talk.

'Were you here last night?' The warm spices filled my mouth. He nodded.

'I'm here most nights, moving down Wardour Street.'

'Why this spot?'

'This is my pitch. Has been for a couple of years now.'

'A good place to sell, then?'

'Not bad at all. I moved here when the better people did. Where they lead, those who want to be like them will follow. And they are the ones who love my gingerbread.'

Clever man. It was the same with bawdy houses. If you wanted a better quality of customer, you moved nearer to the people of quality. Those who aspired to wealth and decency required a better sort of establishment and there were we – ready to provide it for them. That had been Mrs Farley's shrewd assessment when she set up her business, and she had been right. Soho was developing quickly and fine new houses were being built at a rapid rate.

'Take the man I saw last night, for instance,' he went on. 'Told me that he was about to become very rich. He was on the way to making a deal, he said. He was a man who looked like he enjoyed the finer things of life.'

'Mmm.'

'He took three pieces of gingerbread from me. Large belly to fill.'

'A large man? He wasn't wearing a green coat, was he? Big saggy face?'

'That's him. Friend of yours?'

'Someone I knew. He died last night.'

'Wasn't the gingerbread as killed him?' His face had an anxious grin.

'Definitely not. This is good stuff, you know. I can't imagine three pieces would kill a man – although a cartful might make him ill. No, this man was strangled. Just over there.' I pointed down the alley to the back of the White Horse.

'I would have seen a man being strangled, I'm sure of it.'

'No, I mean behind the wall. In the back yard of the White Horse.'

'Bardwell's place? I wondered why it was closed tonight.'

'I think they are keeping it closed tonight out of respect for the deceased.' That was what Anne was telling the crowds. 'It'll be full of people again tomorrow.'

'There's some villains abroad, that's for sure.' He tutted and rearranged his wares. 'And him just about to come into money, too. Poor devil.'

'Did he tell you how he had come by this deal?' It was news to me. Mr Reed had given no indication that he was going to be rich − and he was the sort of man who had otherwise boasted about his wealth.

'He seemed keener to eat his gingerbread than talk about his business, but he said something about Paris.'

'Paris?'

'I don't like the Frenchies so I didn't take to well to that. A good Englishman doesn't need money from the French.' He puffed out his substantial chest and stood a little taller, as if he spent his life eating roast beef.

I murmured agreement at his concern, although I'll take coins from any man, whatever his country, and Soho is full of French.

'True. But did he say any more about Paris?'

'Not really. What was it, then? Something about meeting someone in London who he had known in Paris.

This man was going to pay him a lot of money. That's what he said. A man from Paris was going to pay him a lot of money.'

'Lucky Mr Reed.'

'Well I wished him luck and Godspeed and he rubbed his hands together and went off that way — back towards the Bardwell's.' He sighed. 'He was killed you say? I wish I had told him not to take money from a Frenchman. No good ever comes of dealing with foreigners.' He shook his head.

Could this be something? A man from Paris was going to make him rich? Maybe he was killed for his purse after all. Reed had made some sort of deal with a Frenchman, was carrying extra gold and someone had overheard or seen the gold and killed him for it.

Sallie had finished her gingerbread.

'I'm so tired. I need to sit down.' She hobbled to a doorway and sank down on to the step.

I went and shook her.

'Sallie! Wake up. You can't stay here all night. Where are your lodgings?'

She didn't answer. She was sleepy and half-cut. Anything could happen to her in this state.

'Don't worry, miss,' called the gingerbread man, 'I think her other friend is just around the corner. She might know where to take her.'

'Thank you. I'll go and look.'

'I'll keep an eye on her, don't you worry. Not that she's got anything worth stealing, by the look of her.'

I walked back toward the White Horse and saw Bess, standing listening to Anne's latest tale. She raised a hand when she saw me.

'Is this the man you were talking about earlier? The man who was strangled? They say his screams could be heard as far as St James's.'

I snorted.

'Don't be ridiculous. Anne Bardwell tells a good story but if his screams were so loud then how come nobody heard them?'

'Oh, yes, I see your point... what's the matter?'

I had pulled her away from the crowd.

'It's Sallie. She's lying bowsy in a doorway. She needs to get back to where she's living. Do you know where that is?'

Bess rolled her eyes.

'She's lodging with me and Kitty until she can find her own place, although the way she drinks she'll never have any money for rent.'

'The way she drinks she'll be dead by Christmas.'

'Truth be told, she's not the best of companions. Kitty and I are looking for a better sort of gentleman these days. Sallie's happy enough with thruppence or even just a beer and a pie.'

There were far too many girls on the streets who were the same. Drunk, poxed, full of lice and ready to lift their skirts just to eat.

'Good evening ladies.' It was a man's voice that interrupted, just as I was about to encourage Bess to take Sallie home. I wasn't sure I had the energy for a customer, and I didn't make a habit of picking up from the street. When I turned around, it was William Davenport tipping his hat.

'Why, Mr Davenport! Good evening to you, too. It can't be more than an hour since we parted, and now here you are, looking for me again.' I thought he had been heading home. 'Are you looking for some sport, after all? An hour of pleasure in the arms of a beautiful lady?'

He frowned at me.

'I'm trying to catch a killer, Miss Hardwicke.'

I put my hands on my hips, swaggered and leered at him like a common bunter. 'That's a cryin' shame, sir, cos I can offer very reasonable rates, to a handsome gent'man like you.' He opened his mouth to respond but then closed it, recognising that I was teasing him. His face relaxed a little.

I laughed at him. 'But would you buy me a nip of ale, though? I might have some news for you about Mr Reed.'

There was a moment of hesitation. He still thought that I was offering something else.

'Really, I do mean just a drink.'

He offered me his arm and we walked, leaving Bess to deal with Sallie, away from the White Horse. He didn't speak, but walked with purpose to a tavern on Peter Street and ushered me politely through its door.

Chapter Sixteen

I told Davenport of my words with the gingerbread man and he listened carefully, head on one side. We must have looked a very serious pair. Around us, life was less complicated: men of every age and condition were buying drinks for women in the hope of passion. A couple of musicians kept the room entertained with a familiar tune and the staff danced along as they carried trays of food to well-watered customers.

I tried to keep the report as clear as possible, but even as I told it my own questions kept tumbling out.

'I don't understand why Mr Reed was making money from a Frenchman. And were the missing papers related to the transaction with this person?'

Davenport rubbed his temples.

'I'm not sure, Miss Hardwicke, I'm not even sure that we'll ever find out.'

'I thought that his waistcoat might have been from Paris. Would this business have concerned sales of cloth, perhaps?'

'Tell me again, tell me what the man said about Paris. Precisely, if you can.'

I closed my eyes and tried to shut out the noise of the people around us.

'He said that Mr Reed had met someone in London whom he had known in Paris and that this person was going to give him, no pay him, a lot of money.'

I opened my eyes and he was smiling.

'What is it?' I said.

'Is that exactly what he said?'

'Yes.'

'Then the person Mr Reed was meeting was not French. Or not necessarily so.'

'I don't understand.'

'Mr Reed had met someone in London whom he had known in Paris. If he had travelled to Paris as an Englishman, then so have many others. People do travel to France, you know.'

'I know that.' I, like the gingerbread man, had assumed Mr Reed was meeting a Frenchman, someone from Paris. But what if we had it wrong? Perhaps he was meeting a fellow traveller? Another thought struck me.

'He said person. Not man, but person. Mr Reed might have been meeting a woman who was paying him money.'

'True.' He took a mouthful of beer. 'Tell me more about the other people at the party. I've met Bridgewater – or Tommy as he's known – but who were the others?'

I hesitated. 'We don't normally like to talk about our guests.'

'I'm not interested in their tastes. I only want to know who was there. And what about the women? Might any of them, for example, have been to Paris?'

For all I knew any of them could have been.

'There were four of us from the Berwick Street house. I have never been to Paris, and I doubt if any of the others have. Except Sydney.'

'Sydney?'

'Our doorman. He wasn't in the house earlier, which was unusual. You didn't meet him, but he's French.'

'Is he now?' He was interested.

'But I don't think Mr Reed would have had dealings with Sydney. Why would he?'

'Why indeed? Who knows what a cloth merchant and a brothel bully would have in common — apart from a shared acquaintance with your house?'

'He's not a bully,' I said, frowning at him. 'At least, not like the usual ones. Mrs Farley insists on calling him a doorman. He's tall and strong and he's perfectly capable of throwing out violent men and blacking someone's eye if needs be, but he's not aggressive. I can't see him strangling a man, either. Oh…!'

'What?'

'I've just remembered, Mrs Farley lived in Paris once. With the late Mr Farley — if there ever really was a Mr Farley. She models her house on those she saw there. That's why we've got such an elegant and exotic doorman. It's why we are all so very respectable compared with other establishments.'

He dismissed this comment.

'So, there's one woman who's been to Paris, at least. And your so-called doorman. What of the others at the party?'

'I have no idea about the girls who came from Mrs Hardy's. I could ask them. And there were about a dozen men, of whom I spent time with four: Mr Reed and Mr Stanford you know of, Mr Herring and Mr Winchcombe came with Charles. It was those three who tumbled Mr

Reed out onto the street for Mrs Farley, along with Tommy Bridgewater.'

'That's interesting. Tommy Bridgewater swears that he didn't know Reed, even though Reed called his name. Was Reed acquainted with any of the others?'

'I don't know. I don't think he knew anyone except me when he arrived. It would have been difficult to tell, anyway, as we were all wearing masks – apart from Tommy and Amelia.'

'Why not them?'

'They weren't invited. They should have stayed upstairs and out of the way, but Amelia came down to see what was happening and that's when Mr Reed caught sight of her and began to be unpleasant.'

'And everyone, men and women, wore masks, except those two?'

'That's right.'

'Why the masks? What's that about?'

'It's something Mrs Farley picked up in Paris. Masked balls were all the rage there a few years ago, but they're not so common here. It adds to the mystery and the elegance of the evening.' I winked at him. 'To say nothing of the excitement. The masks stay on, even when the clothes fall off.'

'Paris, again.'

A girl was leading a laughing man up the stairs. He watched them with a wistful expression until they disappeared.

'I think,' he looked back at me again, 'I think that you should speak to the gentlemen and find out whether they have been to Paris, and whether any of them had met Reed before.'

'Why me?'

'You want to help, don't you? I've got other matters to attend to. Mr Reed's death is not the only crime in London and we don't have enough men to hand.' He dropped some coins on the table and stood up. 'I'd better be going.'

'You're going home?'

'Not yet. I discovered the whereabouts of Mr Reed's lodgings. He was staying with a couple called Groves. Respectable people,' he added, unnecessarily. 'Mr Groves is a butcher.'

'You're going to see them now?' It was getting late and respectable people would be locking up for the night in an hour or so.

'Grimshaw told them I'd be around.'

I shuddered, remembering the scowling face and wide shoulders.

'Is Mr Grimshaw already there?'

'Not tonight. Mr Fielding has sent him and a couple of others to a warehouse off the Strand. Apparently, it's full of stolen property that needs to be returned to the rightful owners.' He finished his beer. 'But the men who are currently looking after it are not going to be happy about that. We're wondering if they have anything to tell us about Swann's gang.'

There would be a fight. No wonder Jack Grimshaw was going.

'I could come with you instead, then,' I said. 'I'd like to see where Mr Reed was lodging.'

He was taken aback. It was a bold request; I knew that and assumed he would refuse. He chewed the inside of his lip as he thought for a moment.

'Very well,' he said. 'You may come with me.' I stood before he could change his mind. He shoved his hat firmly on his head. 'Just stay close to me and keep your mouth shut. And remember: I ask the questions.'

Chapter Seventeen

We walked quickly up the street for several paces before he slowed down a little. William Davenport was a man who walked in order to arrive at places; he did not saunter or peer about at his surroundings. He was uninterested in food sellers and paid no heed to their melancholy cries offering us sustenance. He didn't appear to notice the cluster of thin grey children sleeping underneath a broken cart at the side of the path, or the half-naked woman in the window above them, lighting a small candle – the better to display her wares to the gentlemen who walked more slowly, looking for precisely those delights.

But he was alert; leading us confidently to our destination. We turned down several streets into an area near to Golden Square that was quiet and relatively free of squalor. He found the door of a decent-looking property. It was large, but neat and not at all showy.

'This is it.' He hammered hard on the wood.

A thin-faced woman in a plain cap opened the door to us. She was not old, but she looked like a woman with a life that was hard even if it was comfortable.

'What do you want at this time of night?' Anxious eyes flitted up and down the street, as if she were expecting robbers and murderers to be running up and down it. It seemed a quiet enough place to me.

'William Davenport, from the magistrate at Bow Street, mistress. I think you're expecting me? This is Miss Lizzie Hardwicke,' his voice faded, unable to explain me or my presence any further.

She looked at me, taking in everything she needed to form her own conclusions. 'We don't rent rooms by the hour, whoever you are.' She lifted her pointy chin at us, as though she had just said something very daring.

'We're not here for a room. As my colleague told you, I'd like to speak with Mr Groves about a murder.'

At that her face changed. She became flustered again, twittering like a little bird.

'Come in, please. Do forgive me. It's such dreadful, dreadful news and I am quite shaken by it. I'll call my husband.' She pulled us in and cried up the stairway. 'John! John! The constable's come about Mr Reed.'

We heard grumbles and mutters from the floor above and then a man slumped down the stairs to us with the nimbleness of a large pig.

'Well, let him into the back room, Susan.' He shooed us along the hallway to a dismal room. He offered us a seat around a wooden table while Susan fussed about lighting as many candles as she could find and bringing a jug of beer to the table in jittery hands before sitting down uncertainly.

'You rented a room to Mr George Reed, I understand.' Davenport declined the beer. 'Have you found a new tenant since he died?'

'Not as yet. I'm hopeful; it's a good room.'

We were in luck.

'I'd be glad to see Mr Reed's possessions, before you clear them, if you don't mind, sir.'

Mr Groves scratched at a hairy ear.

'I'm not sure I can agree to that. It don't seem right, you going through his things. He left them here, you know.'

Mr Groves wanted to pick over them himself. He would, like any man of sense, sell whatever he could.

Davenport looked thoughtful.

'Mr Reed was a visitor to London, sir. We haven't been able to find his relatives and I'm hoping to find something that will lead us to his home in Norwich.'

'Yes, he was from Norwich,' Susan cut in. 'Something in cloth, from what he said to me. My sister's in Norwich.'

'He was a cloth merchant; here on business,' Davenport nodded to her. 'But there may be people expecting him home and, apart from knowing the city he hailed from, we have no way of knowing who they might be. I'd be most grateful to see his room.'

I could see the sympathy beginning to rise in Susan's face. He was clever, Mr Davenport.

'You won't take nothing?' Mr Groves' fat face was still contorted with the thought we would carry away his loot.

'You can come up with us and make sure, if you like,' Davenport said, 'but I don't plan on removing anything of value – unless such items would belong more properly to his relations.'

I saw Susan shoot a wary glance at her husband. His mouth tightened a little but, clearly weighing up the situation, he nodded.

'All right. I'll take you up.' He heaved his frame out of the chair. 'Susan, we'll need those candles.'

Susan handed a light to Davenport and another to me, carrying one for her husband, before leading us up the stairs.

'We rent out the room for a bit of extra money,' she said as we climbed, her reedy little voice offering me an explanation. 'John's work at the butcher's is not always regular. And he's not so well these days.'

Overeating, probably.

John cleared his throat noisily behind us. Susan took the hint and we reached Mr Reed's room in silence.

The room was small and simply furnished, but it was not shabby. There was a low bed with a truckle underneath it, and an empty pot, a table and a straight-backed chair for writing, a cupboard for clothes, and a stand with a jug and bowl. A small mirror hung next to the cupboard, and the curtain at the window looked new, but apart from that there was no decoration or colour. There were no paintings on the walls. For a shrewd man of business, like Reed, this place had offered a good location for what I guessed was a minimal cost. I wondered aloud why he had chosen to rent a room like this, rather than stay at an inn.

'I think he liked it here,' Susan said, planting the candles on the table in the corner and patting the bed cover with a touch of pride. 'He said that he appreciated the quietness as he attended to his business.'

'Better than the noise of comings and goings he would have had at an inn, I suppose,' I said. She nodded. Well, he had sought some excitement outside these four walls, certainly.

I lifted my light as Davenport entered with John Groves.

'Here you are then,' said Mr Groves between gulping breaths. 'It's how he left it.'

'You've not touched anything?' Davenport looked about.

'Not a thing. It's all got to be cleared tomorrow morning. I think his chest is behind the door.'

'Was he planning to stay for a long time?'

Mr Groves shook his head.

'He was happy enough to keep on with the rent, but he said he was returning to Norwich shortly.' That was what he had said to me too. 'He wanted to keep the room here for when he came to London. He told me that his business was expanding and he needed to be here from time to time.'

'How long had he been your lodger?' I asked.

'Less than a week,' Susan cut in. 'He was such a good lodger for us too. A man of means, pleasant manners, very quiet and able to pay us promptly. The money was very useful to us.'

Her husband frowned at her and her shoulders sagged.

'I'd like to look at his possessions, please.' Davenport was keen to poke about – as was I.

Mr Groves shrugged and gestured towards the cupboard.

'There's not much. He was a modest gentleman.'

'He didn't seem that modest to me,' I muttered to Davenport.

'Well, as we know, he was wearing a fine waistcoat and his purse is missing,' he said, keeping his voice low, 'there can't be much left to find.'

'Except his papers.'

'Indeed.'

Davenport opened the cupboard and began rummaging through the shirts and coats. I took a candle and pulled the truckle cot from under the bed. Neither of us found anything of significance. The chest was full of more folded clothes and shoes, all of which were of good quality, but nothing else.

The table in the corner promised more. We found a writing set designed for travelling traders: a neat pen, a small inkhorn, and a pile of paper, unmarked and wrapped with a pale ribbon. An old newspaper hid a well-thumbed copy of *Fanny Hill* that fell open at his favourite pages. Small wonder he had been so greedy for young Amelia Blackwood. Apart from that there was nothing to tell us about him.

'No papers, Miss Hardwicke,' Davenport noted.

'Then he really must have been carrying them. He was most particular about the packet.'

'He was always scribbling something or other,' said John Groves, from the doorway. 'He would be keen to get to his desk whenever he was in.'

'He was up early writing in the morning,' Susan agreed.

'May I take these spare sheets of paper?' Davenport turned to Mr Groves. 'They're not worth much, but I can give you something for your trouble.'

Susan looked like she was about to say that it was no trouble at all, but her husband, mentally inventing the value of six or seven small sheets, said that Mr Davenport was a very obliging gentleman.

'We still have no idea about his home, or family,' I said, as Davenport fished a coin from his coat.

'I don't think there was a Mrs Reed,' said John Groves, hand closing over the money. 'He never mentioned a family, neither. But you never know.'

'He told me that his business was in the very centre of Norwich,' Susan said, her eyes squinting as she recalled a conversation that, at the time, had probably seemed unimportant; the sort of general chit-chat you make with a person you've only just met. 'Next to the Guildhall, I think he said. I imagine that if you were to go there you would find people that knew him. If he really was that worthy a gentleman as he told us.'

Well, that was the question, wasn't it?

Davenport looked thoughtful for a moment. He was weighing something in his head.

'I think,' he said, 'I think it would be useful to send a man to Norwich. Yes, I'll see if I can find someone to send over.'

It would take more than a day to ride there, nearer two, but the roads had just been relieved of one highwayman. Still, Fielding's men were stretched, as he had told me. I couldn't see the magistrate sparing a man for such an excursion.

'Come, Miss Hardwicke, I'll escort you home.'

'Thank you. I think that would be very kind.' With a man by my side I wouldn't be pestered. Very soon, the house would be opening its doors to the sort of gentlemen who wanted exactly the same as the pests, but who would pay more for it.

We said farewell to Mr Groves and his anxious wife and went back into the chill of the night. The small fires along the roadside gave precious little light, let alone heat. I pulled the cloak around my neck as we picked our way in silence along the squalid streets.

Chapter Eighteen

When we reached the house, I could see something was out of place on the doorstep. There was a crumpled body lying outside the front door. A small body in a pink gown, singing quietly to itself, out of tune. I groaned.

Sallie had not been sober enough to find her way back to Bess and Kitty's place, but she had been able to recall that I lived on Berwick Street. And for reasons known only to her gin-addled mind, she had decided to come and find me. I was in enough trouble with Ma already; if she discovered that this filthy, drunken scrap was anything to do with me, I would be looking for a new home.

'My sister!' Sallie stood up, arms open to embrace me. She swayed, tottered down the step and fell over in a heap.

Davenport looked from her to me. 'Your sister?' There was a touch of laughter in his voice. 'Whoring runs in the family, does it?'

I ignored him and tried to pick her up, shaking her shoulders as I did so.

'What are you doing here?'

'Came to find you, lovely wench. Need my sister. Need a bed for the night.'

I had to get her away from the front door before Sydney heard her. Before we had customers.

'You can't stay here. You'll not be welcome.'

'Why not? I'm just as good as you. Just not got the right clothes yet…' She was starting to shout – the way people do when they are drunk and unreasonable. Usually before they announce loudly to the world that they are your best friend.

She cocked her head over at Davenport. 'They all want the same thing, Lizzie. They all just want a fuck.' She leered at him. 'I'm cheaper than she is, sweetheart. You can fuck me for tuppence, if you like…' Then she fell on him as he tried to step away.

'No, thank you.'

I grabbed her arms and pinned them to her side.

'Right then.' I gritted my teeth, knowing I had no choice but to take her in, if I wanted to keep her quiet. 'If you're not going to go away, if you're going to stand here bothering decent gentlemen, then the only thing I can do is hide you in my room and put you to bed. You can sleep off whatever it is you've drunk.'

'My sister,' she said to Davenport, beaming a wide smile. 'Shesss very kind to me.'

'And stop calling me your sister, or I'll slap your cheeks so hard you'll wish you'd never met me.' I gave her another shake, to show I meant business.

'I need a piss first. Got to go. Sorry.'

'Oh, for the love of God. Walk ten paces away from the house, if you must do it in the street.'

She did.

I caught Davenport's arm. 'I need your help.'

He folded his arms and tried to frown, but he was, in truth, shaking with laughter.

'Well, I'm not taking her home with me, if that's what you want.'

'There's a thought. You can have her for tuppence – as she's already told you.' I giggled and gestured down the street. 'If you're not prepared to be so helpful as that, then there's an alley just a few doors down. It'll take us to the back of the house. I think I can get her in through the servants' rooms and up the back stairs without Sydney or Ma seeing. Would you come with us? It's dark.'

He nodded, solemn again, understanding my fear. He considered his sword but decided instead to pull a short knife from somewhere inside his coat.

I threw one of Sallie's arms over my shoulder and half-dragged, half-carried her, as he led the way into the darkness. The ground squelched softly, and the length of the narrow passage stank, but we reached the end safely and turned into the small courtyard that led to the back of the house.

The back door was unlocked. A single candle burned in the servants' room, and Old Sarah was dozing in a chair. Meg was nowhere to be seen. Whispering dark threats in Sallie's ear, I stole past Sarah and up the stairs to my room. Sallie had quietened down, but I was alert to the possibility of a commotion at any moment.

Davenport stood mute in the doorway still clutching his knife as I tipped Sallie onto my bed, pulled off her bonnet, and loosened her clothing.

'You can put that away,' I nodded at the blade. 'We're safe enough now.'

He tucked it into his coat.

'You'll need a bowl, I think,' he said, looking over at the sleepy girl. 'I wouldn't be surprised if she threw up before dawn.'

I hadn't thought of that.

'Are you in the habit of giving up your bed to drunks? I thought you said that this was a respectable house,' he said, as I put my washing bowl on the floor beneath her head.

'Don't breathe a word of it to Mrs Farley, or I'll be joining Sallie on the streets.'

'Sallie…' He stiffened. 'Is this the girl who was picking pockets? The one you spoke about in the White Horse?'

'Leave her alone, Mr Davenport.' Sallie was snoring quietly. 'She's just a girl. She's full of gin, and you've got Mr Reed's murderer to worry about.'

'I haven't forgotten. Turn her on to her side; otherwise, if she vomits, she'll choke.'

When I had arranged her to his satisfaction, I walked him down the front stairs, where we found Sydney and Mrs Farley welcoming a small party of boisterous young men. Davenport slipped out, unnoticed, as I made a great show of expressing my delight at their arrival.

Chapter Nineteen

I am experienced enough, by now, to know how to entertain men out of my bed, as well as in it, so Sallie was able to sleep undisturbed, while I stayed downstairs. It helped that Polly was with me all night – and that the silly boys drank a lot of wine. I crawled up to my room alone as dawn was approaching, a fat purse bulging with coins from happy customers who had enjoyed what they had declared to be the liveliest of evenings. Sallie had not vomited and was still asleep. I tried – with difficulty – to get comfortable in a chair until she woke.

Once awake and sober, she was as sweetly grateful as when I had fed her at the White Horse. Even so, I had to get her out of the house. While Ma might imagine Amelia working with us, offering gentle refinement and wide-eyed innocence, she would never dream of taking in Sallie. Sallie was attractive only to men who like their whores soaked in gin. She would not be welcome here. Once on the street, she would drink to numb herself in order to work – and she would work to buy the drink. And I had to put her back there.

It was late in the morning, and most of the household were sleeping off the night's work, so we left without being caught and walked together towards the location of Kitty and Bess's lodgings – which she now remembered.

She still couldn't recall where she had been on the night George Reed was murdered but promised to find me if anything came to her. I felt in my pocket and gave her a couple of crowns. She fell on my neck and thanked me extravagantly.

'You mustn't spend it on drink, though,' I had little doubt that she would do just that. 'Some rent for Bess, some pretty ribbons and food to put colour in your cheeks will be far better than gin.'

She clutched the coins. 'Oh, I will, I will. I promise.' She gave me a wicked grin. 'I'll have to land on your doorstep more often, sis.'

I pushed her away, not gently.

'I'll treat you to some more gingerbread, if you're lucky, from that chatty gingerbread man we met last night. But come and find me in the White Horse, not in Berwick Street next time, or I'll box your ears.'

She giggled, blew me a kiss and ran to find Kitty. I groaned, as I walked back home, knowing that I was saddled with her: my grubby drunken little friend who would wheedle coins from me in the rare moments she was sober – because she knew I felt sorry for her.

–

Several hours later I was back at the White Horse.

'It's full in here tonight,' I said, settling myself between Charles and John Herring and helping myself to a mouthful of someone's beer. 'I said there was nothing like a murder to encourage business.'

It was open again and heaving with people. Anne Bardwell had decided that one day was quite sufficient to mourn decently for Mr Reed. It was also enough time for news to have travelled widely.

Harry Bardwell, as short as he was stocky, was lost in the crowd, visible only by the small tray he carried aloft, to deliver the pots. He looked worn out when I finally caught sight of him. Anne was likewise red-faced with effort, perspiration on her brow. I motioned to her that I would like a drink and she rolled her eyes. I wouldn't be getting one for a while.

'I wonder whether Mr Bardwell has managed to clear the yard yet,' I asked, relying on someone to know the answer. 'Or whether Fielding's men have found anything in that stinking pile.'

'It still looked pretty sordid when I went out earlier,' said Joshua Winchcombe. He was turning a coin over and over in a state of agitation. Perhaps he was itching to get to a gaming table.

'Ah yes,' said Charles, draping an arm around my shoulder and drawling in that affected tone he knows I loathe. 'How is that dreadful Davenport getting on, do you know?'

'And what have you discovered so far, as Bow Street's latest recruit, Lizzie,' asked Mr Herring, pulling a silver snuff box from his pocket. 'Have you caught the fiend?'

I pushed Charles' arm from my shoulder and sat forward, as if ready to share information. They all leaned in to hear above the hum of tavern.

'As it happens, Mr Davenport wondered where you were, each of you, on the night of the murder. He wants to talk to you.'

'Don't be ridiculous. You can't think that any one of us had anything to do with that man's death,' said Charles, the drawl disappearing in favour of a sharper tone.

'And who's to say that you didn't strangle him for his gold?' said Herring in a mean voice. 'You wouldn't be the first harlot whose greed got the better of her. I bet that's what Davenport thinks.'

'Mr Davenport does not think I killed him, thank you, sir. And neither should you, if you wish to enjoy the hospitality of our house again.' I pursed my lips. 'Anyway, he asked me if you'd seen anything, not whether you'd killed Mr Reed. I told him what I knew. None of you saw anything because two of you were losing a fortune in a gaming house and one of you was tupping a cheap whore in an alley.' I glared at Charles. He glared back and then suddenly roared with laughter, downed his drink in one and kissed me, his mouth wet.

'Have any of you been to Paris?' I wiped my hand across my lips.

There was a flicker, a glance, that passed between them. Charles said, 'We've all been to Paris, Lizzie. It's how we three met. What of it?'

I had no idea how gentlemen of quality became acquainted. It intrigued me.

'You met there? When was that?'

Herring examined his pinch of snuff thoughtfully. 'It was before I married, certainly. And Louisa and I have been married for, ah, about eight months.'

Not happily, if he was falling into brothels already.

'Why were you there?'

'It's the tour, Lizzie,' said Winchcombe, hands painting the breadth of his travels in the air, 'you make the tour, and see the splendid cities of the continent.'

You do, if you are a gentleman of means. The rest of us are lucky to see the splendour of a clean room.

'I preferred Rome,' said Herring, sneezing into a lace-trimmed handkerchief. 'It was perfect.'

'No, Herring,' said Charles, drawling again, 'the sites of Paris were much the prettier.'

Winchcombe sniggered. 'Wasn't it in Paris that you discovered philosophy, Herring?'

'Oh, you'll love this, Lizzie,' Charles took up the hint. 'Herring became obsessed with the writings of some Frenchman, I forget his name, and used to attend meetings with very dull and earnest men to talk about life. Except,' he glanced at Herring who had tucked away the handkerchief and was beginning to turn red in the face, 'one afternoon he made a great fuss about inviting us to join his new friends. We went along, only to discover that Herring had the wrong day entirely.'

Herring shifted, in visible discomfort.

'He was so concerned with the working of man's mind that he quite forgot how to work his own.' Winchcombe finished off the tale with a line that the two of them had obviously used before.

'What happened?' I couldn't help but play.

'We took him to meet some new friends of ours. Some ladies. He learned a lot more about life from an evening with them than with those dreadful thinkers.' Charles slapped Herring on the back. Herring took it well and laughed heartily, but there was a hard look in his eye. He was a proud man and did not take kindly to being mocked.

Anne Bardwell finally arrived at the table with my beer, and more for the men. Charles leaned across the table and gathered the empty pots for her, helping to pile them on the tray.

'There's no need for you to bother, sir, I can manage,' she said, as if his assistance was unwelcome.

'Tell me, did you meet Mr Reed in Paris?' I asked, taking a gulp of beer when she had gone.

'Reed?' said Charles. 'Certainly not.'

Herring had his thin nose in his beer and Winchcombe scratched his cheek and blinked.

'What about you two?'

Herring withdrew his tankard and shrugged, still sore from the teasing. 'I don't recall meeting him until that night at your party,' he said in a tight voice.

Winchcombe shook his head with some vigour. 'No. Why do you ask?'

'It's just that someone on the street behind the yard said he was talking about Paris. I wondered if it was significant.'

'Why would Paris be significant?' Charles frowned at me.

'I think he was about to receive some money from a man from Paris.'

'Well, if he had a full purse, then even more reason to suppose he was killed for it,' said Charles. 'I still say it was Swann's men.'

I patted his arm. 'I think Mr Davenport is inclined to agree with you, but I'm not convinced.'

'And someone said Reed was talking about Paris?' Mr Winchcombe asked.

I was about to tell him about the gingerbread man when I saw Polly arrive with Sydney. She waved cheerfully to our group and skipped over. Mr Herring brightened as soon as he saw her. She put one arm around him, and another around me as she leaned down to our table and spoke into my ear.

'Ma says you're to go home, Lizzie. There's a gentleman asking for you, and only you will do, apparently.'

I had promised Mrs Farley that I would behave. Ignoring the usual dread of who or what awaited me, I nodded and said I would be on my way. Sydney, who had been sent to escort me home, loomed at the side of the table.

Polly was already beside me on the bench, next to Mr Herring, flirting and preening, although anyone could see from his face that he was hers for the night.

'My apologies, gentlemen, I am being called home. I hope that you have a pleasant night.' Charles kissed me again, with cleaner lips, and Joshua Winchcombe nodded to me from across the table as I stood to greet Sydney.

Two painted girls pushed their way through the crowd and, seeing me, came over, some relief and purpose in their faces. It was Bess and Kitty.

'Lizzie, we're so glad to find you,' said Bess. 'It's Sallie, she says she wants to talk to you. You'll have to come with us.'

'I'm not able to talk now,' I said, aware of Sydney's hand on my arm. 'I've got work to do.'

'Really, she sent us to find you. She says she's remembered something.' Kitty tugged on Sydney's sleeve, but he was not going to let me go with them. Mrs Farley wanted me home and we both knew better than to dawdle. Harry Bardwell pushed between us to gather empty pots on to his tray, meaning that Kitty had to shout.

'She says she knows something about Paris – if that means anything to you.'

It did. Sallie had heard my conversation with the gingerbread man, so I doubted that this was anything new. Even so, I couldn't deal with her now – not with Ma waiting.

'But we were just speaking of Paris, weren't we Herring?' said Winchcombe, in his booming voice, over-hearing, 'And how much you enjoyed your time there.' Herring's attention was fixed on nearer delights.

'What's this about Paris?' said Charles, 'Who's talking of Paris?'

Herring pulled his face away from Polly's neck and looked over at me.

'Just a girl we know, Sallie something. Wants to tell Lizzie about Paris.' Kitty's eyes swept over the men as she leaned over. 'You won't mind if Lizzie nips out for a while, will you? We can keep you company, if you like.'

'She's just repeating something I already know, I'm sure,' I said to Kitty. 'Tell her I'll find her tomorrow afternoon if she's sober.'

'But she said it was important. She keeps on about Paris and says it's a matter of life or death. You said you'd come.'

I felt Sydney squeeze my arm.

'I'll find her tomorrow, Kitty. If I don't get back to Berwick Street, it'll be my death I'll worry about.'

Kitty wasn't listening. She and Bess were squeezing themselves between Charles and Winchcombe, neither of whom were complaining.

Chapter Twenty

My head throbbed, and my body was sore. The room reeked of a night's toil. There is, as my father often lectured me, no peace unto the wicked. He would probably tell me again even now – if he were still speaking to me.

I lay quietly and listened. It was early, according to the bells. The house was almost silent – apart from some scratching behind the wainscot. This was my favourite time of day: before work, before the busy chatter of my companions rattled the tranquillity, before the sounds of London rang out incessantly.

I could hear a bird, I thought. There was a mouse or a rat pattering inside the wall; a bittersweet reminder of the countryside that I would never see again. The half-open shutter revealed a clear spring sky. I pulled the covers up under my chin and stared at the brightness, knowing that the same sky was reaching over the little room in my childhood home. I could not let myself remember; Berwick Street was my home now. And my father had no daughter.

I am clean forgotten, as a dead man out of mind. I am become like a broken vessel. The words drifted into my head. Psalm 31.

I turned over and went back to sleep.

Meg woke me later, clattering up the stairs to bring me water for washing.

'Good morning.' She heaved the jug on to the dressing table and hobbled about the room gathering up laundry. 'There's a man to see you.'

I turned my face to the pillow and tried to stifle the groan. 'It's too early, surely?'

'Not for the law.'

I looked up.

'It's that runner. Anyone would think he was sweet on you, the way he keeps calling.'

'Mr Davenport is not sweet on me.' I wondered why he was back so soon, though. I took my time dressing as decently as I could manage and made my way to the parlour.

He had been left alone; the house's inhabitants were either busy, asleep or out. Ma was nowhere to be seen. The servants didn't know what to do with him. He was poring over a pile of papers at the table, sipping from a cup of tea. A strange expression crossed his eyes as I pulled up a chair and eased my aching body carefully into it; a flicker of concern, perhaps.

'There's a cup here – would you like some tea? It's still hot.'

He was offering me tea in my own home, but it was done in kindness, rather than impertinence.

'Thank you.' I moved to get up, but he motioned me to be still and poured it for me. 'Thank you,' I said again.

He was quiet for a moment. So was I. I drank my tea and began to feel brighter. He continued to scan the papers in front of him, barely looking up. Presently, he said, 'Is everything all right, Miss Hardwicke?'

'Perfectly, Mr Davenport. It's just warm enough.'

The silence between us continued until my curiosity got the better of me and I tried to see what the papers were.

'Can you read?' he asked, as I craned my head.

I could certainly read. Not only my own tongue, but French, Latin and even a little Greek, if pressed. I had spent many hours of my life compelled to be indoors, translating texts and all the while longing to be out in the sunshine, but he didn't need to know that. I simply said, 'I can read. What are we reading?'

'These are the papers that you were so keen for us to find. Mr Reed's papers.'

I didn't manage to suppress my gasp.

'Where did you find them?'

His nose wrinkled. 'I sent one of our men to search the area immediately after Mr Reed was moved, he picked over the yard at the White Horse, but he found nothing. Then I sent Grimshaw over yesterday. He delayed in his task – I don't know why – but finally made it to the tavern at first light this morning. He found a packet of papers lying near to the back wall. I can't see how it was missed initially, but we have it now.'

I leaned forward to see if I could read anything of interest. If this was Reed's own hand, then it was not easy to discern. The pen was scratchy, and the letters formed badly. In some places, the ink had splattered. It surprised me that a man so particular in his business as Mr Reed was so lacking in care with his penmanship.

Davenport watched as I picked up the papers and stared at the words.

'What do you think, then?'

'He wrote in a hurry, did George Reed. Which is strange, given the care he gave to his appearance and his trade.'

'I agree. It seems to me that it is entirely reasonable to suppose, given the nature of the letters, that Reed rushed as he wrote. He hasn't taken any care with his pen because he is dashing off these notes with speed.'

I barely heard his comment because now, with one letter in my hand, I was reading what the words were saying. It was extraordinary and explosive stuff.

'...I am sure you wouldn't want him to know your secret... lies you tell... if it all became public... sordid truth... ten guineas and I can keep quiet for now...'

This was blackmail. Someone was being blackmailed. I grasped at letters. Who was Reed blackmailing?

Joshua Winchcombe. The gambler who, it became clear, was trying to hide his losses from his father.

'He was blackmailing Mr Winchcombe?' I looked up at him.

'Not only Winchcombe, it seems. There are a number of people here,' he said.

He began sifting the papers to find evidence.

'Um – here's Mr Herring too.'

'Mr Herring? Why? He seems a straight enough sort of person.' Well, he was foolish and haughty, but that's not unusual.

'Take a look.' He handed me a letter. Mr Herring was a man in peculiar difficulty. As I had already suspected, although recently married, he was not happily matched. His wife was engaged in intimate conversation with his own younger brother. This was a very difficult situation for poor Mr Herring. He could not expose his wife's infidelity without bringing shame on his own family. He was turning a blind eye for the sake of loyalty to his parents. Mr Reed was threatening to share this delicious morsel of gossip with the newspapers.

'Goodness me.' They had lied to me. They had known Mr Reed before the party.

'Indeed,' nodded Davenport. 'Suddenly we find people around who might have wanted Mr Reed out of the way.' He picked up another letter. 'Here's your charming Mr Stanford, too.'

'Charles?' I grabbed the paper and read through a page even more ink-splattered than the rest. A youthful affair with a young woman had ended badly and she, fearing she was ruined, had tried to kill herself. Her family had protected her reputation, but Reed, somehow, had discovered the attempt on her own life. He was black-mailing Charles who, whether from a sense of guilt or lingering devotion, was paying to keep the suicide attempt a secret. How did Reed know such information? Was it true?

Davenport patted the brown packet lying next to the letters. 'It seems you were correct.'

I frowned at the packet. Something wasn't right. I gathered the scattered leaves into a neat pile and put them back into the parcel. The folds were heavily made, as if the papers had been there for a while.

'Look.'

'What am I looking at?' he asked.

Gently, I pressed the top of the parcel and it gave way. He nodded slowly, seeing what I meant. There was a gap of half an inch.

'The packet isn't complete,' he said. 'There are a number of pages missing. I wonder what was in them?'

It was a tantalising thought.

'But more importantly,' I said, '*who* has the missing pages?'

He picked up the packet and strewed the letters again over the table, as if they might give us the answer.

There were pages filled with writing, and some with only a few words. There were blank pieces too. Davenport was trying to piece them together, to create whole letters from the incoherent mess in front of him. The brevity of some surprised me. Had Reed written more than once to his victims, pursued them for extra money?

I picked up one page, that was simply an amount to be paid and a date for payment. I held the paper up to the window, hoping vainly that seeing it in better light would tell me something about the writer – or about the recipient. I was rather surprised that the daylight did reveal a clue, of a sort.

Reed had written his letters with the pages on top of one another. I could make out the imprint of another letter, a previous note to someone else.

'Look at this,' I held it up for Davenport. 'There's something here; can you make out the words at all?'

He took the note from me and held it up for himself. He frowned and swore under his breath. 'His handwriting is not easy to read. This is impossible.'

He tossed the paper on the table and went back to his work. I picked it up for another attempt. He was right: it was too difficult to read. One word, though, I could make out. I could see a capital T and a looping Y.

'This says "Tommy".' I held it out to him again. Now he was interested.

'Where? Show me.' I pulled my chair closer to his and together we looked at the letter, held up to the light. Carefully, I pointed to the word I saw.

He squinted at it. 'I believe you're right. It does say Tommy. It's a great pity that we can't read any more, but this does, at least, tell us that he was blackmailing Tommy Bridgewater too – which means Bridgewater lied to me.'

It looked that way, although, without a letter, we didn't know why.

He scanned the table again and poked at another of the pages in front of him.

'Even so, your friends are not the only ones with cause to dislike Mr Reed.' He lifted the leaf and held it to my face. 'Do you see another name you know, Miss Hardwicke?'

I did. A small puff of air blew, unbidden, through my lips.

'Sydney?'

'There is quite a lot for your French bully to be bothered about, it seems.'

I took the paper from his hand. Sydney, in whose company we all felt so confident and comfortable, was, according to the papers, a man who preferred the company of gentlemen to ladies. I had already guessed this (how else could he live in a bawdy house without being tempted?); but seeing the words in front of me was still alarming. Sydney had, Mr Reed observed, visited a molly house – a place that catered for his sort of tastes.

How had Reed known this? Had he known Sydney before he had visited Berwick Street? It was all rather odd.

I looked at the paper. It was not a letter, but merely a series of notes. The date at the top of the page was the day that I had met him – the day before our party.

'This date here,' I pointed it to Davenport, 'it's the day I met Mr Reed. He can't have been blackmailing Sydney.'

'What do you mean?'

'This isn't a letter; it's simply some notes about Sydney. Reed only met Sydney twice before he died. That means he hadn't had chance to send him a letter or try to get money from him.' That was how it appeared to me.

'Hmm.' Davenport wasn't convinced. 'It might not have needed a lengthy correspondence. If he had noticed Sydney when he visited this house and discovered a little about him then who is to say that he didn't whisper a threat into the doorman's ear as he handed over his coat?'

It was a fair question.

'How would he be able to make so many notes on only one visit?' I didn't see this.

Mr Davenport shrugged.

'Looking at these papers, I would imagine that Reed was quite used to noticing other people's weaknesses. One look at Sydney would be enough – for a man who spent his time looking for flaws and imperfections in bolts of cloth. And once he found that one weakness then he would spend a reasonable amount of time asking around, building up his notes.' He tapped the paper. 'He could have discovered all of this in an afternoon and then dropped an insinuation on his way through the front door. As you've already observed, his writing reveals that he worked very quickly – scribbling as much information as he could in a short amount of time.'

'I like him less and less.'

'He does sound unpleasant, it's true,' Davenport agreed with a grimace. 'Here was a man who, to all intents, was a respectable cloth merchant. His wealth, in part, though, must have come through the unhappiness of others – and his exploitation of that unhappiness. In Sydney's case, he found something that, if discovered, would have not only carried embarrassing or pecuniary consequences, but potentially fatal ones as well.'

Most girls I knew were happy to tolerate the poor mollies, even if we didn't understand them. They weren't taking our business after all – but sodomy is a hanging offence and anyone who risks their neck for a lover is to be admired.

'Sydney wouldn't kill, that I know.'

'You don't know what a man will do to save his own skin. Even good men act rashly if their life depends on it – and they think they will get away with it.'

I shook my head. Not Sydney. He was vain, pompous and condescending, but not a murderer.

'I'll want to speak to him,' Davenport said. 'He wasn't at the front door when I arrived. I still need to speak with the other gentlemen too.'

There were voices in the hall. We had visitors. If Sydney wasn't around to deal with them, and Ma was out, then the servants would want some help.

'I'll need to leave you now, sir.' I put a hand on his arm and tried not to sound too weary.

He gave me a sympathetic look, packed the letters into his coat and stood up.

'I should go,' he said. 'Another house was ransacked last night. We've only just rounded up one gang of thieves, but there are whisperings that Swann's men really are in London, so we're looking for them as well as a murderer. I'll come back later to speak to Sydney.'

Chapter Twenty-One

It was late afternoon before I made it back to the parlour. Lucy had been shopping, so Polly, Emily and I had managed the guests between us. Men who arrive early in the day are usually desperate and quick about their business. There's not really much entertaining to be done with such creatures: they are simple in their tastes, swift in their activity and you can charge as much as you wish. The later crowd are more discerning and need flattery, wine and the sort of preening, coquettish behaviour for which we Soho ladies are famed. They are more difficult to please and try to haggle the prices. Lucy: precious, beautiful and utterly mercenary, came into her own with the evening crowd. She left the easy afternoon boys to us and would swish home at dusk, hike up her rates, and have them all in her thrall.

Davenport had returned. Someone had taken pity on him: I saw the remains of bread and cheese next to the pile of letters he was still reading.

'Have you caught the Swann gang already, then?' I asked, pinching a crust from his plate.

'No.'

'Are you having more luck with the papers?'

'There are one or two comments of interest, yes,' he said. 'You should know, I found that Mr Reed was about to start notes on you.'

'On me?' I sat down with a bump, coughing on the bread. 'He was going to blackmail me? About what?'

'I don't know that. I only found a sheet of paper with your name at the top, underlined, but with no comments.'

'Let me see it. Please.'

He took it from the top of the pile.

There it was, in his dreadfully scribbled hand: my name.

I stared at it for a moment and then at Davenport.

'I have no idea what the notes would say. I mean, I can hardly bring any further shame on my family, can I?' The words were out of my mouth before I could stop them.

He favoured me with a quizzical expression but decided not to press me about my family. Instead, he smiled a little and shook his head.

'No, probably not. Perhaps he realised that. Perhaps that's why there are no comments.'

Or he hadn't identified my weakness. I shivered.

'What?' He saw it.

'Nothing. Just a draught.'

Perfectly timed, the door opened, and Sydney came in, followed closely by Mrs Farley.

'I understand that you wish to speak with Sydney,' she bristled at the sight of Mr Fielding's man, once again, in her house.

Davenport stood up and bowed to her and to Sydney, who was standing very close to her, like a terrified dog. His tall frame, usually so impressive, was cowed and bent.

'Thank you, Mrs Farley, I won't take much of his time, or yours, but I am here again to ask questions about a man who was murdered the other night.'

'That dreadful Mr Reed, Sydney,' Ma explained to Sydney as if he were a child. He already knew that Reed had been killed.

Davenport motioned Sydney towards an empty chair. Mrs Farley hovered.

'You don't say anything you don't want to, Sydney.'

'Thank you, Mrs Farley.' Davenport was becoming impatient. 'I am sure that Sydney, as a grown man, is perfectly capable of answering all that is necessary.'

I reached over and squeezed Sydney's hand. His eyes were wide and fearful.

'I have some papers here that belonged to the dead man.' Davenport sifted through them, reaching the notes he was looking for. 'It appears that Mr Reed was in the habit of discovering information about people – information that they would rather keep hidden – and using it to blackmail them.'

'I knew he was a bad apple,' Ma sniffed.

'Sydney, do you know what blackmail is?' I thought it best to check. He is French, and although his English is splendid, I wanted to know that he had understood.

He shrugged. 'Of course. Blackmail is not only an English matter.'

'Good,' said Davenport. 'Well you'll understand why I am asking you about Mr Reed.'

Sydney looked puzzled and shook his head.

Davenport pulled out the notes Reed had made about Sydney. I could see Ma squinting over his shoulder, trying to read them.

'Mr Reed met you only briefly, Sydney, but he understood something of your nature immediately,' he looked down at the notes. 'Mr Reed made comments to himself about you and your... your unnatural desires for other men.'

'Mr Davenport! We'll have none of that in this house, please.' Ma was furious. Sydney was a favourite – and a very good employee. The thought of losing him on account of his habits was agitating.

Sydney, on the other hand, was nonchalant.

'I visit. I look. I do not touch, Mr Davenport; do you understand me?'

'That's what they all say.'

'With good reason, monsieur. But it is true, for me at least.'

'Regardless of what you do or do not touch, Sydney, Mr Reed guessed or knew that you visited certain notorious establishments. He wrote all of this down. My question to you is this: did Mr Reed send you a letter suggesting that you might pay him to keep silent about the molly houses?'

'No, monsieur, he did not. There was no letter.'

'Then did he, when he visited the house for the masked party, make a comment to you as he arrived? A quiet word in your ear as you took his coat?'

'Non.' Sydney's face fixed itself into a scowl. He was probably lying, but Davenport would not be able to contradict him.

'Very well.' Davenport gathered up the notes and put them back into his coat.

'Is that it?' Ma asked. 'You have no more questions for him?'

'No,' he said. 'I can search his room for a letter, of course, but Sydney has told me there is none. I might not believe him, but I have no proof that Reed made threats of blackmail as he came in through the door the other night. I have no need to ask any further questions.'

He stood to leave and then sat down again.

'Except... I wonder, Sydney, if you could tell me what happened on the night of the party – as you saw it.'

Sydney stared at him. 'Of course. I remember everything.'

As Sydney began to speak, I realised that he really did have an eye for detail. Our quiet giant of a doorman, whose disinterested contempt for whores and visitors alike we took for granted, was rather observant. He described the arrival of each guest immaculately, remarking on clothes, mannerisms and comments they made. As he described them, even their gait or voice, each one sprang to life in my mind.

While we had been upstairs, doing what we did, he had spent the evening reading by candlelight and noting the movements of the staff. We learned of excitements, such as Old Sarah scolding the kitchen girl for dropping a pan of milk; and he told us that the extra staff brought in to help with the food helped themselves to some of it as they carried away the trays.

Davenport, however impatient he must have been listening to all of this tittle-tattle, never took his eyes from Sydney's face. He knew that, eventually, the information he was waiting for would come. Now he knew that he had a keen observer of people as a witness he was prepared to wait.

Finally, Sydney gave us Mr Reed's eviction, with a view from the front door. He had been startled from his reading by my exchange with Mr Reed on the landing.

'Miss Blackwood started screaming. She screamed like a little girl, but the man Reed, he was shouting at her and pulling her arm. I think he wanted her for himself.'

'Go on,' Davenport shifted in his seat.

'I saw Mr Bridgewater appear suddenly on the landing.'

'Where had he been hiding, Sydney?' I asked.

'He had been watching much of the sport through the door, Miss Lizzie. When you marched along by yourself with a little candle, he hid behind the chest. I think he would have stayed there, if Miss Blackwood had not appeared and Mr Reed had not tried to cause her harm.'

So Tommy Bridgewater had been spying on our party, the dirty boy. Presumably he had enjoyed himself quietly all evening – until his darling Amelia became involved.

'He rushed out when he thought Mr Reed had wicked designs on his lady.' Sydney has a dramatic turn of phrase at times. Perhaps this is because he is French.

'And then the other men came out of the room. Some of them were wearing masks, most of them were not wearing many clothes. The ladies came behind and had not many clothes between them at all.

'Mrs Farley shouted, "Get that man out of my house",' he gave a fair impression of her tone, if not her accent, 'and four men bundled him down the stairs. I opened the door and gave him his coat and they threw him onto the street. I threw the wig. And his hat.'

He concluded with a flourish of the hand. It was as much as I could do not to applaud.

Davenport had not finished.

'Who put him outside? Which men? And what were they wearing?'

Sydney considered this carefully.

'It was Mr Bridgewater, Mr Stanford, and his friends, Mr Winchcombe and Mr Herring. There were four of them. Mr Bridgewater was fully clothed and not wearing a mask. Mr Winchcombe and Mr Stanford had their masks, but not shirts. Mr Herring had a shirt, but his mask had gone.' He paused. 'All of the gentlemen, except Mr Bridgewater, were unbuttoned.' He gestured to his breeches.

I was astonished that he could remember in such detail.

Davenport nodded, taking it all in.

'And what of the comments Mr Reed made about Tommy – what did you hear him say?'

Sydney closed his eyes, as if to remember better.

'There was a moment. At the door. Just as they were about to push him out. He managed to get free from them. I think that the gentlemen were unwilling to hurt him, even if they wished to humiliate him. He looked at all of them and then he started to laugh.'

'He laughed?' Davenport looked intrigued.

'I remember that too,' I said. 'He did laugh.'

Davenport raised a finger to me in warning, wanting Sydney to continue.

'I saw his eyes. He looked – how to describe it – content. And then he laughed and said that he knew who Tommy was. Then they put him out.'

'Exactly, Sydney. What did he say?' Davenport leaned forward across the table.

'He said, "I know who you are, Tommy boy."'

'Tommy boy?'

'Yes.'

I didn't recall him calling Tommy a boy, although he wasn't much more than a boy. Still, it sounded like mockery of a young man who wanted to protect his love, find a decent wage and settle down. Would that slight against his manly pride have been enough to make him kill Mr Reed? I looked at Davenport. He seemed to be weighing up the same question.

'Where is Mr Bridgewater at the moment, Mrs Farley? Is he still living here?'

She nodded. 'Yes, he is, but he isn't in the house today. He is still looking for work.'

Amelia's time was running out.

'I would be very grateful, Mrs Farley, if you could make sure that he doesn't leave this address. I would like to talk with him again very soon.'

She looked ashen.

'Very well, Mr Davenport, but if he did kill Mr Reed, then I hope that he hasn't got a taste for it.'

Sydney shuddered. We all hoped that.

Chapter Twenty-Two

'Miss Hardwicke, I would like the pleasure of your company for an hour or two.' Davenport stood up and offered me his hand. Mrs Farley raised an eyebrow. It was not unheard of for the law men to make use of the same women they cheerfully condemned, but this one had not shown any interest until now. This one required my mind, not my body – which he had guessed was in need of a rest. We were going out, it seemed.

–

There was a man lurking in the street below our front door, not at all neatly dressed, and with a battered old hat on top of a head of lank untied hair. He wasn't doing anything but standing with his hands in his pockets, looking up at the house. If Sydney had been at the door he would have shooed him away as bad for business, but Sydney was still sitting in the parlour with Ma, Old Sarah and even Meg fussing over him.

Davenport, who had halted briefly in the hallway to exchange pleasant words with Lucy, joined me as I waited by the railings. This was a decent street with elegant houses and a wide road, not overly bustling with people in the early evening. A man like that, who looked like a common knife-grinder without his whetstone, stood out. He was in the wrong place, as Sallie had been.

Sallie. I had forgotten about her, with the excitement of the letters. I had promised Kitty and Bess that I would meet her, even if I knew that she would only repeat the story the gingerbread seller had told me. Still, if Davenport and I were looking for three men in taverns and gaming houses, I might pass her on the way.

'Reading!' Davenport hailed the man with a raised hand.

'You know this man?' I hissed.

'Yes, of course. He works for me sometimes. John, come and meet Miss Hardwicke.' The man ambled towards me and grinned with toothless gums at Mr Davenport. He was not old, but his pock-marked face was that of a man who had seen a great deal. He hadn't had a bath for a long time — if ever.

'Miss Hardwicke, may I present Mr John Reading?'

I gave as much of a curtsey as I felt appropriate, trying not to breathe in.

'You work for Mr Davenport?'

'That's right Miss Hardwicke.' His voice was low and quiet. 'I watch for him sometimes. Keep an eye.'

I turned to Davenport.

'Keep an eye on what? Us?'

He shook his head.

'No. Reading has been searching for your friends in the nearby taverns. Any sign?'

'Mr Herring is in the White Horse, sir. I have not located Mr Stanford or Mr Winchcombe as yet.'

'Mr Winchcombe will be in a gaming hell somewhere,' I said, recalling the blackmail letters.

Mr Reading raised his eyebrows at Davenport, who chuckled. It was an unlikely sound.

'Miss Hardwicke is very nearly as sharp as you, Reading. She's a lot prettier too.'

'Y'know, if you're going to start operating whores, sir, the other men'll call you the pimp of Bow Street.'

Davenport was still laughing, but his eyes had become serious. 'Miss Hardwicke and I will go and meet Herring while you continue your searches for the others. If you find them, tell them I would like a word over a beer.'

Reading turned obediently and scuttled off down the street like a thin grey beetle.

'Where did you pick him up?' I asked as we, in turn, made our way towards the Bardwell's tavern.

Davenport watched his man disappear into the distance.

'Not far from here, as it happens. I thought he was fencing goods for a local thief in the hovel he calls his home, but it turned out that it was a neighbour. When I was asking questions, I saw that not only was he a reasonably honest man, but that he was observant. We caught the fence; we managed to take the thief as well, thanks to his careful descriptions.'

'Are you certain he didn't just lay the blame on someone else to save his own neck?'

He shook his head.

'No. He's been a reliable and useful informer ever since, so I don't think so. The small amount of coin that he gets from me keeps him just the right side of the law.'

'A beneficial arrangement to you both, then?'

'Mr Fielding's men need eyes and ears on the streets, Miss Hardwicke. There are precious few of us otherwise. We rely on people like Reading for information.'

'Well as long as he doesn't hang around Berwick Street too often, I won't argue. He fits the shadows of Seven Dials better than the gentler prospects of Soho.'

'He has plenty to keep him busy elsewhere, I can assure you. He was only waiting to meet me.'

We reached the door of the White Horse; it was already full and lively. Harry Bardwell greeted both of us like long-lost cousins. I could see that Anne was carrying trays full of plates to tables. The food smelled good – even through the tobacco fog.

In a quiet corner, Mr Herring the philosopher was exercising his silver tongue down a very pretty throat.

'Polly!'

She pushed him away and waved to me. 'Lizzie! Come and join us!'

I was strangely grateful to find her here; a friend in an uncertain time. Her mouth was over-kissed, and her cheeks were flushed with arousal. Business was mixing with pleasure again for lucky Polly. I hoped he was paying her well.

I shoved up next to her on the bench, while Davenport introduced himself and made the acquaintance of Mr Herring.

'It's busy in here again,' I said to Polly. 'And it's still early.'

'Anne Bardwell is pretending that the increased custom has nothing to do with the murder,' she said. I glanced across the room and saw Mrs Bardwell appreciating the full tables with a quiet smile.

'Well, I'm glad the Bardwells have done well out of Mr Reed's misfortune, at least,' I said, taking a mouthful of the wine she was ignoring.

'Have you gone any way to catching his killer, Mr Davenport?' she asked.

He wrinkled his nose.

'At the moment, my best guess is Miss Hardwicke here, and she's not much of a guess.'

'Lizzie? Why on earth would she want to kill Mr Reed?' Polly was incredulous. 'He wasn't the most charming of men but, really Mr Davenport, if we killed every man who was less than charming then we would halve the population of London overnight.'

He laughed at that. Pretty, flirty Polly was full of wit when she had drunk a glass or two. The tavern lad brought over drinks and a plate of bread and cheese for me and Davenport.

'There are others who might have had a reason to want him dead, it is true.' He turned to Mr Herring. 'I imagine that he wasn't a friend of yours Mr Herring, given that he had been blackmailing you for a while.'

'How dare you!' Herring was startled, and a flush of colour spread over his pale cheeks. 'I didn't know the man until the night he died.'

'I have written evidence to the contrary, sir.' Davenport lifted his beer to his lips. He smiled up at Mr Herring before taking a gulp. 'I am happy to show you your letters, if you would like, to remind you.' Herring put his head in his hands and groaned. 'But I see that you are beginning to recall the details.'

John Herring, married to a flighty wife who was, probably even now, in bed with his brother. Of course, the fact that John Herring was a frequenter of brothels and had been, moments ago, all over Polly like a rash would be of little consequence to most sensible people in England. Everyone understood that a man might have needs that took him away from his marriage bed; for a wife, finding love, fun and comfort elsewhere was a very different matter. But adultery with a relative was disastrous for everyone. No wonder Mr Herring wanted to hush it up.

Mr Herring spoke from under his fingers. 'I didn't kill him, Davenport. I really didn't. But I am very glad someone else did.' He peeped up at us, unsure of how such honesty would be greeted. Davenport carried on drinking his beer, unmoved.

'You are probably not the only one,' I said.

'When did he start writing to you?' Davenport put his tankard down, keener to find answers than make sympathetic noises.

Mr Herring closed his eyes and slowly rubbed his hands on his cheeks as if the memory needed soothing away.

'About a month ago,' his voice was quiet and unsteady. 'If you have read copies of those letters you'll be aware that things are not quite as they should be in my marriage.'

'Your wife is having an affair with your younger brother, I believe.' Davenport was not going to spare his feelings, then.

Polly, who had been gazing into the distance in a drunken haze, suddenly pricked up her ears and leaned into the conversation. Even the sweetest harlots love gossip.

Herring sat up a little straighter, puffing out his chest. We were left in no doubt that his wife had chosen the inferior brother, at least in his own mind.

'My brother is a very appealing sort,' he said. 'I used to admire him. He is not the cleverest of men, but he is pleasant to look at and enjoys riding about the countryside on fine horses. Louisa also prefers being out of doors far more than I do.' He looked wistful. 'I imagine they are far better suited to one another than she and I ever were.'

That was generous of him, I thought, even if it did sound like a practised line.

If Davenport was at all sympathetic, he wasn't showing it.

'You want to keep the scandal quiet because exposing your wife's unfaithfulness also brings shame to your family.'

He nodded.

'It may seem hard to believe, Davenport, sitting here with women like Polly and Lizzie, but I am a dutiful son and I do try to please my parents. That's why I married Louisa, I think, to please them and to extend the family line.' His pale eye lashes fluttered. 'Louisa is the daughter of an earl. She brought with her the sort of connections and society that my parents so desperately wanted.' He shrugged. 'I brought wealth.'

His parents wanted to move in better society and found a titled family strapped for cash. It was usually the other way around. Herring's family would gain no name or title by the marriage, but if his social-climbing parents longed to operate among titled people then this was their way in. Sadly, for John Herring, they chose to push the wrong brother in Lady Louisa's way.

'Do your parents know about the affair?' I asked.

'They know.'

'Have they tried to end it?'

He shook his head.

'They have spoken with Edward, but they don't want to cause a fuss. I think they hope it will end quietly.'

More likely they didn't care very much as long as they continued to enjoy their new-found social status. Any child born to Louisa would, at least, bear the Herring family likeness, so no one would ever know. For an extra-marital affair, it was surprisingly neat and tidy – until someone threatened to turn it into a very messy public scandal. Lady Louisa would be disgraced, of course, but so too would the Herring family, tainted by association, known to have turned a blind eye.

'Do you want her back?'

He looked at me as if I were stupid.

'Back? She hasn't left home.'

Well, that was all right then. Carrying on in the family home was acceptable. It was probably a very large family home.

'I don't mean that, Mr Herring. I mean, do you wish her to love you again? Above your brother?'

He considered the question as if for the first time.

'All I know is that my family would be in a very difficult position if the affair were made public. While it's quietly going on at home I am personally offended, but not publicly shamed.'

It had never been a love match and had not had time to become one. I had shared my bed with enough married men not to be surprised at this, but his indifference was odd.

'Mr Herring, were either of your parents aware of Mr Reed's threats to you?' Davenport cut in.

'No. I have means of my own to pay.' He seemed bored by the question.

'You don't have to pay him anymore, though.'

'I didn't kill him. I told you that.'

We were all quiet for a moment. Near to the door there was a scuffle taking place: a sure sign that someone had had too much beer — and that business was, once again, flourishing for the Bardwells. We watched as two men tumbled outside, laying into each other with fists as well as insults. Davenport was alert, ready to call for assistance should real injury occur, but prepared to let a drunken quarrel take its course. I saw his hand drop down to his sword. Associates of the scrapping pair fell out on to the street with them and pulled them apart, dragging each to safety and, it should be hoped, sobriety.

'How did you first meet Mr Reed?' Davenport pulled his eyes away from the door and fixed on Mr Herring again.

Herring glanced at me before answering. He couldn't lie this time.

'I was in town with my family some months ago. Just before Christmas. We were at a party, my brother and I. Reed was there. We were introduced. I saw him at dinner, but did not sit near him.'

'And did either you or your brother tell him about your unusual arrangements?' Davenport raised his eyebrows.

'Of course not. No one is foolish enough to share such matters with a complete stranger.' Herring gave a contemptuous sniff. 'He must have overheard a conversation I had with my brother.'

'You were discussing your wife?'

'Indeed. We were in a small room, away from the main party. I had some things that I needed to say to him and, as far as I knew, we were talking privately.'

The Herring brothers had sat discussing the wife they shared. Polly and I exchanged a knowing look; I wondered if their conversation had been as vivid as the ones we had about the men we knew and shared.

'And shortly after this, the letters began to arrive?' Davenport pressed on.

'Yes. About a week later. It was clear from the phrases he used that he had been listening to us; eavesdropping on our tête à tête.'

'I see.'

I wondered what he had felt when he saw Reed at the party. Davenport was thinking the same.

'You came across him in person at the Berwick Street party. Did you exchange any words with him there?'

He hesitated. Perhaps he was trying to remember the evening – or else make sure that his story was straight in his mind.

'We were all wearing masks, you will recall. I'm not certain that he knew who I was, although I recognised him; more from his conduct than his face.'

'His conduct?'

'Greedy. Eating and drinking a lot. Being too loud.'

Interesting, though, that he seemed able to remember Reed's manner from only the one encounter. He was lying again.

'And then there was that business with the young girl on the stairs.'

'Amelia Blackwood.' I supplied the name for him.

'Yes, that was it. Amelia.' He shrugged at Davenport. 'Well, I expect you've already heard that we threw him out?'

Davenport nodded. 'Who did the throwing?'

'I think we all did; Stanford, Winchcombe and me. And that young man – Tommy somebody I think he was. I hadn't seen him earlier, but he was doing most of the shouting.'

We didn't need Herring's half-remembered account when we had Sydney's precise recollection. I cut across Davenport's questions, still puzzling over the lies.

'Can you say again, Mr Herring, whether you had spoken to Mr Reed earlier in the evening or not,' I said. Davenport swung round at me, scowling at the interruption. Then his face softened and, slowly, he turned back to Herring.

'Miss Hardwicke is right. You didn't answer my question. Did you speak to him at all before he was thrown out?'

Herring's mouth twitched a little.

'I did answer you, sir. I said that I recognised him, but we did not speak.'

Davenport was quiet, letting the answer go unchallenged. This time I held my tongue. Davenport finished his beer and then stood up.

'Well I think it's time I rooted out Mr Winchcombe and Mr Stanford and left you to a pleasant evening.' He looked down at me.

'Are you coming, or are you expecting to meet someone here tonight?' His eyes suggested that he wanted my opinion. I glanced about the room. I didn't want him to think I was too easy, after all. The prospects for work were promising, but distinctly less exciting than searching for answers with a runner. Besides, despite myself, I was beginning to enjoy his company. I took his hand.

'I'll help you find Mr Winchcombe. I probably know the disreputable establishments better than you do.' I looked at Polly winding her arm around Herring, 'I'm not sure I'm needed here.' He nodded and tugged me up from the seat. I blew a kiss to Polly and swished my skirts through the crowds as I left the tavern.

Chapter Twenty-Three

I looked out for Sallie as we searched the streets and taverns, peering into every dank alleyway we passed. We were making our way in the direction of Seven Dials, the air thickening with the smell of human existence as we went. The further we went into the squalor, the more I expected to find her, until I really needed to concentrate instead on navigating the squelching mess underfoot. The soil men worked half-heartedly in this part of town. Food stalls offered hot snacks and painted women exuded cheap perfume, but neither could mask the stench of waste that had been emptied, here and there, into the open road. A man across the way raised a hand to us. He was almost hidden in the shadows, but the brazier a yard away meant that we both saw it.

'Come on,' Davenport caught my elbow and steered me swiftly towards the dark doorway. It was John Reading. His hat was pulled down and he wore a scarf that covered his mouth.

'I've found Mr Winchcombe.' He gestured with a thumb at the door behind him. It looked a desperate place. It was certainly no place for a gentleman.

'What sort of state is he in?'

Reading pulled down the scarf and rubbed his misshapen nose.

'Pretty deep cut, sir, and losing badly.'

'Is Stanford with him?'

'No sir.'

Davenport scratched the side of his chin.

'We're not going to get much sense from him now.' He nodded at the door. 'Reading, keep an eye on him and watch where he ends up. I'd like to speak to him in daylight – preferably sober. Make that clear to him. And keep looking for Stanford, would you? I'm sorry, Miss Hardwicke, we seem to have had a wasted journey. I'll escort you back to the White Horse, it's near my way home.'

'You live near the White Horse?' I hadn't really thought about where a man from Bow Street would reside.

'Gerrard Street. Close enough to Covent Garden to do the bidding of Mr Fielding, but far enough away to breathe purer air.'

Strange that a place called the Garden should be thought so clogged and rancid, but in our quieter squares and streets around Soho there was a lot less of a stench. Fewer bodies jostling for space as well. We picked our way back down the dark roads to the White Horse, avoiding the foul stuff under foot as best we could. Soho's streets were cleaner, but even they were never free of filth – and in the dismal light could be just as hazardous for pretty shoes. I was glad I'd worn my sturdier boots.

The lights of the White Horse shone brightly through its windows. It was still heaving with custom and I could hear the music from out on the street. Davenport tipped his hat and made to move on and I was about to push on the door when, through the glass, I saw Charles. It was only a glimpse, but I knew him from his shape; the tilt of his head, the way he carried himself.

'Oh, Charles is here, after all' I said. Davenport spun round.

'Here? When we've been all the way over to Seven Dials to look for him?' He muttered a blunt curse and pushed open the door. 'I suppose I'd better speak with him now. It's late, but there's no knowing where I'll find him tomorrow.'

I wanted to know the story of Charles and the woman mentioned in George Reed's letter. The woman he had loved.

He was, as I might have expected, sitting with a red-cheeked blonde, laughing and drinking. He saw me, trotting behind Davenport, and raised his eyebrows as we neared his table.

'Is this the best man you can find tonight, Lizzie? Dearest, you are down on your luck.' His tone was merry enough, but his eyes suggested disapproval.

'You're a fine one to talk,' I said, nodding at the cheap trollop who was snuggling into his coat. 'Off you go, little girl. Go and find yourself another gentleman to clap. This one's mine.'

She opened her mouth to protest – she looked the whining sort – but Charles gave a short laugh, kissed her full on the lips while looking at me, then pushed her roughly away. She got up and stood pouting for a moment until he pressed a coin into her hand and waved her off as though she were a small child or a puppy. I took her place next to Charles and pinched his arm.

'Is this what happens if I leave you alone for a moment?' He shrugged and lifted his tankard to his lips.

I thumped him on the shoulder, deliberately causing him to splutter into his ale. I nodded over at Davenport, who had taken the seat opposite and was watching us, frowning as our drinks were brought to the table.

'Mr Davenport's not interested in me at all. He's come to talk to you about George Reed's letters. One of the other runners found them in the yard.'

'I heard,' he said in his drawling tone, scowling at me as he wiped beer from his cravat. He turned to Davenport. 'I bumped into Herring as he was leaving. He told me you gave him a tough time about his marital problem. I presume you're going to quiz me about Emily now.'

'If you would be so kind, sir. The letters explain a little, but I would hear your side of the story.'

'I'm not certain I wish to tell it.'

He sat staring at Davenport, saying nothing. Then he sighed and ran the back of his hand across his forehead.

'You'll appreciate, it's a story that does not show me in my best light. It happened when I was young, and I was... well, I should have known better.'

'I appreciate your reluctance, sir, but you can be assured of my discretion.'

Charles shrugged. 'It's not complicated. Her family is decent but has no wealth or standing. She believed that we would be wed, when I, of course, had no intention of marriage.'

It was an old and familiar story. He wasn't the first man to hint at marriage to get a girl into bed. At least he seemed to recognise that he had done her a great wrong.

'Her parents didn't encourage you to marry her?' I asked.

He rubbed an eyebrow. 'They might have done, but Emily tried to drown herself. I told them that she was mad, and that talk of marriage had been her own fabrication. They believed me, rather than her.'

'You told them that she'd thrown herself at you?'

He nodded, gazing at me for a moment before hanging his head. 'I'm not proud of what I did. In fact, I'm ashamed of myself, truly.'

The poor girl. The flimsy dreams of marriage to a wealthy and attractive man had vanished once he had tumbled her, and her subsequent distress had only served to confirm her as a flirt. And a mad flirt at that.

'How did Reed find out about it?' Davenport's question cut across my thoughts.

'Well, I didn't tell him,' Charles' eyes flashed with annoyance.

'You told me once that you grew up in Norfolk, with your uncle,' I said. 'Did he know about Emily? Might he have said something? George Reed was a merchant from Norwich.'

He gave me a scornful look and pulled away from me.

'Don't be ridiculous,' he said in a tight voice. 'My uncle had his faults but associating with merchants was not one of them.'

He let out a long breath. 'But now I think about it, Emily had an aunt who was rather indiscreet. I had to leave the county for a while because of her insinuations. Some of the lines in Reed's letters had the ring of her voice in them, I'm sure.' He sighed again. 'Stories told by gossips are lapped up by dull people with no intrigues of their own.'

'You lived with your uncle, sir?' Davenport said. 'I hadn't realised that you inherited from your uncle rather than your father.' His voice was smooth. He took a gulp from his beer and waited.

'My parents both died when I was an infant. My uncle took me in and made me his heir.'

'That was a kind thing for him to do, even if it was a family duty,' I said.

Near to us, several young men were noisily discussing moving on to a gaming house. Charles knew them well enough to raise a hand. He wished to go with them, I guessed.

'I lived like a prisoner there,' he said. 'He barely gave me an allowance and disapproved of all the usual vices a gentleman takes for granted. I imagine that was why I chased after Emily and behaved so badly.'

It sounded like an excuse for his behaviour; probably one that he had told himself for a while.

'You decided to make up for it when you came into your inheritance?'

He laughed heartily and smacked my thigh.

'I most certainly did, you gorgeous wench, I certainly did.'

He kissed me hard, his tongue tasting of beer. Then he stood up, clearly indicating that his interview with Davenport was over. We had learned a little, but his wildly rakish behaviour now made sense. He had been contained for most of his life by a dutiful but earnest relative, away from excitement. Now he was spending money as though he had an endless supply, living a fast life and enjoying every moment of new-found liberty. I felt a pang of envy.

Davenport nodded solemnly as Charles grasped one of his friends by the arm and fell, still laughing, towards the door. No doubt Mr Davenport would have extended his sympathy to the uncle rather than to the nephew. I would have offered mine to Emily.

The tavern was emptying of young men. I was not in the mood to entertain any of the old goats who were hanging on in the hope of desperate whores. I was not so desperate. I could only hope that the gentlemen I would inevitably find back at Berwick Street were younger and richer than the poor culls in my view.

'I think I should make my way home, sir,' I said, standing. I didn't even wish to finish my drink.

'I'll walk you there.'

I hesitated for a moment but judged that I would reach home unbothered and a good deal faster if I walked with my arm through his. I would not make a habit of it.

Chapter Twenty-Four

Berwick Street was quite safe enough, even at this late hour, but Davenport insisted on walking me as far as the front door. He had been silent ever since we left the White Horse and I was glad not to talk. The shops and the elegant houses of the street were, mostly, shut up for the night. Ours wasn't. Our house was never shut. I could see windows still blazing shamelessly with candlelight – a sure sign for any passer-by that the folk of this house were not quietly tucked up in their beds but cavorting about on top of them. For any gentleman looking for pleasure, the windows offered a welcoming sight.

For me, they were a reminder that a night's work still stretched ahead, however weary I was. I would be bright and sparkling; competing with the lights and commanding far more attention.

'Are you coming in, sir?' I asked because he was a man on the doorstep of a brothel, and I was expected to ask. Ma would expect me to ask.

There was a short, rather awkward silence.

'No. But thank you for the invitation.' He smiled, took my hand and, quite gently, lifted it to his lips. It was such a tender gesture that I was amazed. No man was ever usually so courteous, unless he wanted to take me to bed.

He bowed stiffly and then walked back the way we had come. He didn't look back.

I stood, watching him until he was gone, then climbed the four steps from the railing to the front door and pushed it open, smile at the ready, expecting to be rebuked by Sydney for my late return.

Instead I found Ma pacing up and down. She spun around as I came in.

'Where have you been?' Her face was anxious, rather than angry.

'Hunting for men.' True enough, although not in the sense that she would understand.

She dashed out of the door and peered into the street, this way and that. This was unusually undignified for Ma. But there was something odd going on. The house was very quiet.

'Where's Sydney?'

She pulled herself back in from the doorway, closed the door and leaned heavily against it.

'He's disappeared.'

'What do you mean, disappeared?'

'Gone. Left us, walked out, I don't know, Lizzie.'

She rubbed her hands over her cheeks, closing her eyes. Sydney had a life beyond Berwick Street – that we all knew – and he wasn't permanently fixed to the stool in the hallway, but this was different.

'Hasn't he just gone to wherever he goes when he leaves the house?'

She looked at me wearily.

'He left a note, telling me that he needed to be some-where else. He never leaves a note when he visits other establishments. He has never written to me before. I've had Meg call at every molly house I can think of.'

Poor Meg. She would not be pleased to be hobbling about the streets looking for Sydney.

'Has Meg returned?'

'An hour ago. No sign of him. He's gone for good, I think.'

This was bad. A bawdy house without a decent doorman was prey to all sorts of unsavoury visitors. Sydney, despite his affected bearing towards us, was a large deterrent, useful with his fists, wiry and strong.

It was Sydney, I recalled, who had finally thrown George Reed out of the house at the party.

Other concerns crept around my head and entertained themselves. This sudden departure had something to do with the interview with Mr Davenport. Sydney was, then, being blackmailed by George Reed, even if there was no letter. Had he left because he believed that his sexual depravity would be exposed if he stayed in the house? Or was there a darker reason? Was Mr Davenport right to be suspicious?

Sydney's flight suggested that possibility, even if I found it hard to believe.

I wasn't the only one to make the connection.

'Of course, he's been frightened by that runner you brought to the house.' Ma folded her arms and glared at me in accusation. 'I've lost the best doorman I've ever had because Mr Davenport made insinuations.'

I said nothing. There was little point arguing with her. She was distressed at Sydney's disappearance and casting around for someone to blame. I was standing next to her and it was I who had brought not only Mr Davenport, but also Mr Reed to the house.

'May I see his note?'

She rummaged inside voluminous skirts and plucked the note from her pocket.

'Here.'

She thrust it at my hands and turned away towards the parlour.

'You see if I'm wrong. He's gone for good. And where am I to get a new doorman as fine as Sydney? I'm damned if I'm going back to Paris for another one.'

I raised my eyebrows; Ma was quick enough to disapprove of the rest of us when we cursed. She was really rattled. The paper had been folded twice, very neatly. The handwriting was unfamiliar but clear, almost childlike – the hand of a man writing carefully in a foreign language.

'*Mme Farley, I am very sorry to disappoint you, but I need to be somewhere else. I thank you for your understanding. Sydney.*'

It wasn't as clear to me as it was to her that this was a permanent decision. He might need to be somewhere else for any number of reasons. But something nagged at me. If he had never written a note to her before then this departure must be, in his mind, more significant.

There was little I could do this evening. I wandered into the parlour where Ma was pouring herself a glass of gin. I had never seen her like this.

'Are there any gentlemen in tonight?'

She slumped into a seat, glass in hand.

'I think Emily is engaged, but the others are out. I am discouraging visitors. I'll lock up later.' That was unheard of. 'I can't manage the house and the entertainment without a doorman. I need Sydney.'

She threw the gin down her throat and motioned to me to pour another. The bottle smelled strong, even from across the table. Goodness knows what was mixed into it.

'Do you want me to wait for the others? Leave you to have some peace here?' I didn't want to spend all night by the door, but the guilt of having brought Mr Davenport into the house was eating at me. And if Ma was going to drink herself into a stupor she didn't need to be doing it in view of the street.

'You're a good girl, Lizzie. I've always said so.'

The gin was obviously starting to take effect already.

In the hallway I sat for a moment on Sydney's stool, reading over the note and trying to think. Could Sydney have strangled George Reed? Was that why he had run away? I found it hard to believe. More likely he had been frightened by the fact that his little secret had been discovered by a man from the magistrate's office. In which case, surely he wouldn't choose to hide in a molly house? It would be the first place we would go looking for him, he would know that. So where had he gone? Was he still in London or had he left for the country? Returned to France? No, I couldn't see Sydney being anywhere other than London. He had told me that he was pleased to have left Paris. And he would be so out of place in the countryside: his dark skin, which made him seem so elegant and unusual in town, would invite too much attention of the wrong sort elsewhere. He had to be in London.

I poked around the hallway quietly for a few minutes, looking for anything that might offer a hint.

There was no sound from the parlour; perhaps Ma was asleep. As softly as I could I tried the handle of Sydney's room. It was a small cubbyhole by the front door, conveniently placed for a man who was supposed to be our guard. It was locked. I had never been into Sydney's private space and I imagined that the only other person to have a key would be Ma.

I stole down the hall to the parlour and peeped through the door. She was snoring, mouth open, feet resting on a stool. The keys might be on the table or in her pocket, if I could just find them and take them without waking her...

The front door flew open with a bang. I jumped out of my skin.

'God's blood, Lucy!' I hissed.

'Lizzie, what's the matter? You look scared half to death. Where's Sydney? And what are you doing, creeping about down here?'

'Shh. Ma's been on the gin. Keep your voice down.'

Lucy hobbled to the stairs, sat down and kicked off her shoes.

'Lord, but my feet ache! Mr Gideon's chair wasn't free, so I had to walk in those wretched shoes. Miles I've walked. Remind me not to wear them again.' She rubbed her heels. 'What did you say? Ma's been on the gin? What's happened?'

Lucy knew, as I did, that Ma only got the gin down after a very bad day. Gin was the ruin of prostitutes and it was a mark of Berwick Street's superiority that we never drank it. We had fine wine on our table from Portugal or France. Of course, we did drink gin – beyond Mrs Farley's reach and knowledge – but we all knew girls who had gone to the bad on it.

'Sydney's missing.'

'Oh, he'll be fine. We know where he goes.' She waved a dismissive hand, more concerned about her aching feet.

'No Lucy, he's written a note,' I held up the little sheet of paper. 'He's never left one before.'

She shrugged, unconcerned, barely glancing at it.

'Well I suppose we'll need a new bully. We can't operate a place like this with no one but you to open the door.'

She was a heartless little piece sometimes. Grumpy too, and it wasn't just the shoes, I was certain.

'Mr Gideon's still not invited you to stay, then?'

'Shut up. You don't know what you're talking about.'

She stamped, barefoot, up the stairs. No, her dreams of a rich man to keep her in silks and jewels had not yet come true. I hoped that they would one day – not only for her sake. She would be a nightmare to live with until one of her lovers made an offer to keep her as his mistress.

Her loud clomping brought Ma, bleary-eyed, out from the parlour. She grunted something incomprehensible at me and followed her noisy tenant up to bed. The keys went with her.

I put Lucy's shoes neatly on the bottom stair, wrapped her abandoned shawl around my shoulders and padded back to the stool to watch for the others. If I was prevented from searching Sydney's room, then I was tempted to fetch the gin bottle for company but decided to keep a clear head and think matters through. I was no closer to finding out who had killed George Reed than I had been when I saw his body at the White Horse. Now that he had the letters, Davenport had stopped thinking of me as a murderer – thank God – but I hadn't helped him much at all.

It was near dawn before Polly finally rolled home. I drew a bolt across the door and, for once, our home closed for the night.

Chapter Twenty-Five

Sydney had not returned by the morning. Ma had stationed Meg at the door, which was a bad idea for many reasons. Sarah had been asked to take on Meg's chores – but she was refusing to do them, on the grounds that she needed to cook. Lucy was forced to pick up her own laundry and carry it downstairs – along with the rest of us – but while the rest of us got on with it, Lucy was not happy. She was still complaining about blisters on her heels, as if such injury would excuse her the menial household tasks. Meg, meanwhile, had positioned herself on Sydney's stool and now, in this exalted position, with the weight off her bent legs, had begun to take on some of his airs. She was unable to help with the housework because someone needed to welcome guests with dignity and elegance, she said.

I carried water up the stairs and met Polly, bucket in hand, coming down from lighting fires. Neither of us spoke but rolled our eyes at one another. As soon as I had completed my tasks, and as soon as it was possible, I escaped. Someone needed to go and look for Sydney, I said to Ma. And Meg, after all, was far more crucial to the hospitality and good order of our house than I was.

Meg, from the lofty height of the stool, said nothing, but cast a look of extreme disapproval at my choice of gown as I went out. Well, if I have to dress myself, I'm going to look shabby.

I decided to walk west, rather than east, suspecting that Meg had gone towards Covent Garden last night. It was nearly noon, and the air had a moistness about it; threatening rain. Ahead of me, not far from Golden Square, there was a small commotion – an unlikely sound at this time of day, I thought, but even more unlikely given the source of the fuss. It was Susan Groves, George Reed's landlady.

She was flapping her hands at two boys, squealing as if they were trying to murder her. They looked to be no older than ten and all that had happened, as far as I could make out, was that they had bumped her arm and upset her basket. More startled than malicious, they had returned her cries with high-pitched wails of their own and all three were in real and unnecessary danger of attracting a crowd.

'Mrs Groves!' I greeted her fulsomely with waves and smiles as I scurried towards her. 'How lovely to see you again.'

She looked confused; she didn't recognise me.

'Lizzie Hardwicke – I came to your house with the magistrate's man, Mr Davenport.'

We hadn't had much time to talk as Davenport and I poked about her guest room, but I must have made a good impression, for now she gripped my hand like an old friend.

'Oh Miss Hardwicke, how good to see you. Look what these dreadful boys have done,' she said with sniffs, her patched red shawl falling off her shoulders. 'The food's all over the ground now.'

The lads, wise enough to realise that my arrival offered the chance to escape any further scolding, took flight immediately. I bent down to the cloth parcels that had, indeed, landed on the street.

'There's no harm done, dear Mrs Groves, don't be distressed. Look here, the bread has been perfectly protected because you've wrapped it so carefully.' I handed up the two items – bread and, I imagined a portion of cake – and she examined them fretfully.

'Oh no, oh dear, the cloth is so dirty.' She fussed about with it.

'But it's only the cloth,' I said, 'I'm sure the bread is just fine.' I began to suspect the reason for her agitation had little to do with the dropped bread. 'Where are you going at this hour?'

Her face fell. 'I'm taking this basket of food to John's place – to the butcher's – I forgot to give it to him before he left. He sent a message home.'

I took the bread parcel from her shaking hands before she dropped it again and, rubbed some of the dust away with the corner of my cloak. I gave her a half-smile. 'Perhaps if we put the bread at the bottom of the basket, no one will notice the dirt on the cloth. I think it's mostly clean now.' I crouched down and tucked the bread under the rest of the food, along with the cake, and spread the paper packets of meats and cheese over the top. 'He'll never know.' I smiled up at her. Her face, beneath its squashed brown bonnet, was a mixture of astonishment and embarrassment.

'Thank you very much, Miss Hardwicke. You're really very kind to stop and help.' She fought a sob that was growing in her throat. 'You must think I'm very foolish to make so much fuss about a bundle of bread.'

I shook my head. 'Not at all. Would you like me to walk with you to the butcher's — to prevent any further accidents?'

She hesitated for a moment. It was understandable: respectable women don't walk with the likes of me. Then a soft glint of rebellion appeared in her eyes. 'I'd like that.'

We walked arm in arm, silently at first, as neither of us wished to pry into the life of the other. Then she said, 'Are you… on your way home?'

'I'm looking for a friend who has gone missing.'

'A friend?'

'Our doorkeeper. His name's Sydney. He disappears sometimes, but this seems more than just a casual flit. I'm worried that he's gone for good.'

'Why would he want to leave your house? Is he in trouble?'

She was sharp, for all she was timid.

'Possibly. I don't know. I hope not.'

'But you're concerned for him?'

'If he is in trouble, I want to help him,' I said.

'Does this have anything to do with poor Mr Reed's death? Has his murderer been found? Is it anything to do with that highwayman?' Her shoulders tightened, as if she were fearful of imminent attack. 'They say he has men roaming London.'

'I don't think Mr Davenport is any closer to finding out who killed him. He discovered some letters, though. They were in the yard at the White Horse. Blackmail letters sent by Mr Reed.'

Her eyes widened.

'No!'

'It's true. He wasn't as respectable as we thought.' Well, I'd never supposed him to be respectable, but then, I'd seen a lot more of him than Mrs Groves.

We turned down a narrower street, Mrs Groves still turning this information over in her mind and saying, 'Well, I never' to herself and shaking her head, when she stiffened a little.

'We're here. This is the butcher's.'

It was a large place. The shop front was already hung with hams; a young lad was lifting strings of trotters high up onto hooks with a long crook-ended pole. The hooks were above the hefty rounds of pork; he was concentrating so hard on his task that he didn't acknowledge our arrival. Even so, Susan Groves dropped my arm.

'I won't come in, if you don't mind,' I said, sensing her apprehension. 'I'm not keen on butchery – all that blood makes me feel ill.'

She gave me a grateful smile. 'I won't be long,' she said, 'if you don't mind waiting.'

I nodded and watched her step into the butcher's, head lowered. It was the sort of place that was doing well – feeding the well-to-do who lived in this pleasant neighbourhood. Not grand enough to command the attention of the finest houses, the frontage – with its carefully displayed wares – nevertheless suggested that the customers would be discerning and moneyed. The actual butchery was around the back of the shop. I could smell it – and see traces of blood and bits that had splattered along the gutter – and knew that it would be full of carcasses on the ground and joints of curing meat swinging from the ceiling. A better establishment would site it further away, so that housekeepers, cooks, or even lowly maids from the finer houses in St James would not have to meet with the distressing reality of entrails. This butcher, although still rudimentary, sold decent meat. Mr Groves was earning a comfortable living. The fact that he kept his wife short of money – I'd seen the patched-up clothing and battered bonnet – was something to wonder at. A man who bullies or beats his wife won't care about letting her go about the street without any air of fashion – and that, too, is an unkindness.

She emerged smiling.

'I didn't see John,' she said, breathing quickly and trying to hide the relief of having avoided him. 'Gave the basket to one of the lads.'

I took her arm and tugged her away. It was starting to rain and, even though her cheap hat might be improved by the dampness, I didn't want my own beribboned creation to get wet unnecessarily.

It was one of those sharp spring showers; usually over quickly, but heavy enough to drench anyone unlucky to be caught in it. Shop keepers began to drag their wares inside, or pull large awnings down to protect their goods as the shower became heavier. Servants with baskets scurried a little faster to finish their errands and, as the heavens poured forth, some took shelter in doorways.

I tugged Susan Groves into a shop without thinking; the nearest one. It was not my usual sort of establishment, being a gentlemen's outfitter. I realised my mistake only after we had run inside, but, rather than appear foolish, I loudly suggested to Susan that we examine the buckles displayed in neat rows in the window. We might as well pretend that we had intended to shop here. The buckles would, I said, look very fine on her husband's shoes. Gamely, she played along, picking up items and staring thoughtfully at them in the grey light of the window. The old tailor eyed us suspiciously, as if he thought we were likely to slip a buckle or two into our pockets. His younger assistant was gazing at us – well, at me – as though he'd never seen a woman before. I winked at him and his face coloured as he began to rearrange the bolts of cloth. One of them fell on the floor.

'So,' I said, noting that the rain had eased to a light drizzle, and nudging her arm, 'do you think he would like a new pair of buckles after all, or might he prefer a new pocket handkerchief?'

She stifled a small giggle. Turning to the shopkeeper she dropped a neat little curtsey and thanked him for the opportunity to look at his wares, assuring him that she would return presently with her husband to make a purchase. She did this with such gentility and seriousness that I saw his face soften and smile at the expectation of a future sale. Mr Groves, I was confident, would not be wearing new buckles from this shop or any other.

'Thank you,' she said to me as we found ourselves on the street once more. 'That was a delightful shop and I really did enjoy myself – more than I thought was possible.' I bade her farewell, knowing that I needed to be back in Berwick Street, doing my best to avoid the puddles of rain that had collected in the street's ditches. Susan Groves trotted off with a lively gait, oblivious even of the children jumping into the same puddles, splattering muddy water everywhere. If a few minutes looking at shoe buckles had made her so merry, then this was truly a woman who did not have much to keep her entertained at home.

'Lizzie!'

The shout came from across the street. Lost in my thoughts, I hadn't seen the two girls leaning against a doorway, arm in arm. I waved to them, wished them good day, and then remembered that I had yet to speak with our mutual friend.

'Where's Sallie?'

Kitty shrugged. 'She's gone off.'

'Gone off? Gone off where?'

'We don't know,' Bess said, kicking at a stone, unconcerned. 'We think she went over to Covent Garden.'

I crossed the street to speak with them.

'Or maybe she's down the Strand?' Kitty said.

The Strand: last refuge of the desperate. I was not Sallie's sister, despite her jokes, nor even a close friend, but I did feel oddly responsible for her. 'When did you last see her?' I frowned at Kitty, but she was watching a young man who stood preening himself in front of a shop window.

She turned back to me with a sigh. 'She went out yesterday in the early afternoon and she hasn't come back yet. She's probably drunk somewhere.'

'Or maybe she's found herself a new pitch. Somewhere more suitable to her own sort,' said Bess.

The cheap sort. The I'll-do-whatever-you-want-for-a-meal-sir sort.

'I thought she had something important to tell me – a matter of life and death, wasn't it?'

'Can't have been that urgent after all, then,' said Bess, pulling a face.

'Probably not.'

Neither of them was worried. I left them to their business and continued on my way home, telling myself that they were right and that Sallie wasn't my problem. She would turn up eventually. Even so, as I passed the knife-grinding boy outside the White Horse, I decided to ask if he'd seen her. He was always there in the daylight hours. He had taken over the family business when his father had died a few months ago and was working hard, but knife-grinding is a dull occupation and I guessed he spent his time watching the comings and goings. I asked him whether he remembered Sallie, the girl I had brought to the tavern.

He nodded. I had guessed right.

'Thin scrap. She had a pink dress and bonnet the other day. Looked worse for drink.'

'That's her. Did you see her yesterday?'

He shook his head. 'Saw the other two she's been walking with, but not her.'

Out of impulse, I pressed a shilling into his hand.

'When you finish for the day, will you go and have a look for her? Can you go as far as the Strand? See if anyone's seen her. She's gone missing and I need to find her.'

He looked at the coin in his hand, and then nodded again.

'All right.'

'Come and find me if you hear anything or see anything. Or leave a message.'

'I will.' He went back to his grinding.

I hoped he was a boy of his word, otherwise I had just lost another shilling on Sallie.

I hadn't found Sydney, either, for all my intentions.

Meg, still wearing a superior expression, waved me upstairs when I returned home – noting, as I dutifully ascended, that there was mud on the hem of my gown and suggesting that I might change it for the evening. She was very nearly as astute as Sydney; I might have known.

Chapter Twenty-Six

I could not hear birds when I woke the next morning. It was their absence that made me think of home again.

When I was a child, I would wake with the birds and make every effort to be outside in the open air. My mother died when I was very small, but I had a governess who was almost a mother to me; happy to indulge me, seeing every blade of grass and every insect as an opportunity for learning. She taught me to look, to observe and to understand what I saw by research and by contemplation. The sky was above me, the fields spread before me and the whole world was mine to study and enjoy. Then, one day, she found a husband, and was gone, and my father took charge of my education.

My two older brothers taught me to ride, dragging me out on wild adventures that muddied my gowns and boots, and blew the wind through my hair. And then, becoming young men, they too had left, while I remained at home.

My father was the rector of a rich and pleasant living; there were many opportunities for enjoying social inter-course with local families. But my father, concerned at the streak of wilfulness that he discerned in me, counselled me to cultivate a quiet and godly demeanour. Wilfulness led to disobedience, wantonness, and ruin. He lectured me often on this. I had tried my best to curb the desire for adventure but had embroidered cushions and read improving sermons with increasing agitation.

I was beginning to feel the urge and swell of lust, but I hadn't known, in those days, quite what it was. I was frustrated; constrained by home. My father should have encouraged me towards a sensible marriage. Instead he sent me, when I had just turned eighteen, to stay with my aunt. Aunt Anne, who did not enjoy good health, was in need of a companion. All was well – if excessively dull – until my uncle arrived home from London.

My father spoke of his older brother Francis as a libertine, a devil, but adored him nevertheless. Francis was equally full of devotion to my father. Despite this, and being the devil, my uncle decided that his niece was just to his taste and set out to relieve me of my burdensome innocence, knowing, with uncanny insight, just how much I wanted to discard it. I was fascinated by him, and foolishly imagined that I knew what I was doing – not recognising that I was dealing with such an experienced player of the game. Once I had given myself willingly to him, then, like the devil, he preyed on my growing shame and regret, threatening to tell my father every time he came to my bed, reminding me of how far I had transgressed, how I thrown myself at him like a cheap slut from the streets.

He taught me my trade; taught me every trick I know. I had been forced to learn.

At least now the devils I deal with must pay me for their pleasure.

I closed my eyes. I lay still in my bed and tried again to listen for the birds. I couldn't hear them, and a sensation of panic crept over me. Here, in London, I was as trapped as I had been at home. In this vast city swarming with people, expanding, so it seemed, on a daily basis, I was contained; suffocated. I had no prospect beyond what I could earn – and only a short time in which to earn enough to last beyond my youth. I was ill-equipped to be a servant; I didn't want to be an oyster seller and I had no craft to speak of, save a little music and some small ability in drawing.

And I excelled in my trade.

I sighed, rolled out of bed and opened the shutters. The sky was grey, and a fine drizzle had wet the street. No wonder there were no birds. The weather matched my mood and I was tempted to climb back into bed and disappear under the covers until I was required. Instead I knelt in front of the bed, pulled up the corner of the rug and carefully lifted one of the floorboards. Under it, pushed almost an arm's length to the side, was my box. Wooden, square and inlaid with silver, this was my most precious possession. The box itself I had brought with me, snatched up hastily with my clothes and belongings while my father had paced the floor of the hallway. The box was my past; its contents were my future.

My independence.

I sat on the floor, a shawl wrapped over my shoulders, and opened it slowly. Inside were the coins and notes that I had kept hidden from Ma and the others. There were small trinkets, offerings from grateful and indulgent men that I had failed to declare; jewellery I had taken from my home that would, one day, need to be pawned.

I counted it all again, and was, as always, happy that I had it, but frustrated at its meagreness. Here was my paradox: to leave this grotesque way of life I had to embrace it wholeheartedly. To make more money I had to earn more money. That was the reasoning I had employed since arriving in London. But I had nowhere near enough in the box yet.

I touched the scars on my left hand; the sight of my disfigured skin made me tremble even now. I pushed a memory back down into the darkness, returning the box to its secret location and covering the floor with the rug just as Meg knocked on the door and offered me water.

'You've got visitors.'

I sighed. Of course I had.

'It's two little strumpets,' she said. 'Sydney wouldn't have let them in the house, and neither would Ma, but he's not here and she's out. Old Sarah's put them in the kitchen and told them not to touch anything.'

She could only mean Kitty and Bess. They were not so low that I would call them common strumpets, but they wouldn't be the sort of girls Ma would want in her house, and Meg knew it. I would have to get rid of them as fast as I could.

As soon as I saw them I knew something bad had happened. They were in no fit state to pinch the food or the silverware. The two of them sat, damp from rain, white-faced and silent at the table. I knew before they told me.

'It's Sallie,' Kitty said with a little sob in her voice. 'She's dead.'

Oh God.

'She drank something bad, didn't she?' She had wandered off and died in a doorway, and I had let her go. I sat down; a lump rising in my throat. I had been so caught up in other excitements that I had not properly looked for her.

Bess' hard little eyes were tear-stained.

'It wasn't the drink, Lizzie. She's been pulled out of the river. We've just found out. That's where we're going now. We thought you'd want to know.'

'What was she doing by the river?'

'We don't know why she was there. They pulled her out at Hungerford Stairs.'

Poor girl. She really had been trying her luck down on the Strand.

'It was that knife-grinder from Compton Street that told us. He said you'd given him a coin to go and find her – and that we were to tell you immediately.' Bess blew her nose on the corner of her cloak.

'I'll come with you,' I said. 'Did the lad tell you anything more?'

'He's with us,' said Kitty. 'He's outside in the street. Wouldn't come in.'

I doubted that Old Sarah would have let in a knife-grinder, even if he had been keen. I picked up my cloak and hat and gathered up the two girls – with some hunks of bread and cheese for the journey – and we stepped out of the house. The mist was, finally, beginning to lift. We found the young lad sitting at the bottom of the steps, which certainly would not have pleased Mrs Farley either, had she seen it. I pressed another coin into his hand, thanking him for the information, even though it was bad news.

'She went to meet a man, miss,' he said as he turned the coin over in his hand. 'I had it from the oyster girl on the corner of Wardour Street. She was boasting all that day about a handsome gentleman who wanted to take her for a night-time walk along the riverside.'

'Did anyone see the handsome gentleman?' I asked, knowing it was unlikely.

'No. The girl wasn't even sure if he really existed.' He confirmed what I expected, and looked a little sad as he wandered away, as if he really had hoped to bring better news.

'Come on,' I linked my arms with Kitty and Bess and called on my own courage to make my voice as bright as I could. 'We should go and take a look.'

Chapter Twenty-Seven

We were mostly silent as we walked down to the river, to where the knife-grinder had directed us. There was something dreadful about the prospect of seeing her. She had latched herself to me like a leech and called me her sister, bleeding me of coins to spend on cheap clothes and nasty gin. But there had been something sweet about her; a vulnerability, perhaps, hidden under the cheeky smile. I realised, with a stab of guilt, that I had never asked her how she had ended up on the street.

We were sisters, of a kind. I had landed well, when I fell from grace. I had stepped from the coach at Charing Cross in the autumn and straight into the path of one Polly Young, who had scooped me up and brought me to Berwick Street. I had been lucky. A minute later and I would have found myself in London, with only a small trunk and my wits to keep me from the life that Sallie had led. A minute later, and it might have been me they had pulled from the Thames.

The river was as busy and stinking as ever, an expanse of noise, as much as water. On the water's edge, avoided by every waterman, porter and trader who passed it, was a body, covered by a dirty length of cloth that might once have been white.

We could tell it was Sallie even before we reached her. Someone had tried to deal with her decently; possibly the person who had found her and pulled her out. Kitty gripped my arm tightly as we came near.

'You have seen a dead person before?' I asked.

'Of course,' Kitty said, trying to sound brave.

'Come on,' I patted her hand, also pretending to be confident. 'It might not be her after all.'

As we reached the body a man yelled to us from the alehouse by the bank. Tankard waving in his hand, he marched over.

'Oi! Leave it alone!'

Wind-chapped cheeks and sun browned hands told me that he spent most of his life on the river – probably fishing bodies out of it. I guessed it was he who had found her.

'We mean no disrespect, sir, but we think this is our friend. We heard that she had drowned here.'

He looked us over, as if mentally assessing whether we might be friends to a drowned whore. Clearly, we looked as though we were. He wandered off, still clutching his pot, leaving us to it. I crouched down and touched the grubby cloth at the head, hesitating to draw it back, and witness death. I looked up at Bess and Kitty clinging to one another, and then again at the body, slowly folding back the fabric. I swallowed hard as bile rose in my throat.

Her bonnet was hanging limply from a ribbon around her neck and thick weeds had wrapped themselves over her brow. Her face was bloated and grey. The pale pink gown was tattered and soiled. She didn't look a rose bud anymore; just a trampled bloom discoloured with blood and covered with brown slime. Bess wailed loudly. Kitty whimpered like a dog.

'Rest in peace, little sister,' I whispered, touching the cold forehead.

A shadow crossed her white face. The boatman had returned with a man I recognised. I stood up.

The boatman had sent for a constable, probably some time ago. But dead girls pulled from the river were not a priority in Bow Street, so he had arrived only now. Davenport was surprised to see me.

'What are you doing here?'

'It's Sallie.'

'You'll need to be more careful, Miss Hardwicke, this is the second friend of yours to meet their death in a matter of days.' Was that a warning, or was he attempting a joke?

The girls curtseyed half-heartedly, at once distrustful and curious.

Davenport nodded to them and then crouched by Sallie's head.

'What's happened to you, then?' he asked her, as if she might speak.

'Just a drunken bunter who fell in the water. They drown more often than people imagine, you know.' The boatman said, standing impassively – his tattered shirt flapping in the breeze.

Davenport tugged the cloth and exposed Sallie's whole body. I could still smell the gin, along with rot. Maybe she had simply fallen in, as the man said.

Davenport began examining her carefully. I watched as he opened her lips and felt around her jaw, with the attention of someone who had done this sort of thing before. He tipped her gently on to her stomach and pushed her shoulders.

'Well, she didn't drown.'

I knelt beside him.

'She was dead before she went into the river, you think?'

He didn't look up. He was examining her hair, wiping slime away. 'There's no water in her, for a start, and look here at this...'

I looked at where he was pointing, although I really didn't want to. There was a lot of blood in the matted strands.

'She's been hit hard.' He was feeling around the wound. 'The skull's broken here.'

'Is that what killed her?'

He rolled her gently over again on to her back, pulled the bonnet away from her neck and checked around it, not answering. There were no marks on her neck, as far as I could see.

He picked up her left hand, which was clenched into a fist, and then moved down her body lifting her skirts. Bess sobbed again but he carried on, ignoring her. The brown stockings were full of holes, but then, they always had been. There were no bruises on her legs. She had not been ill-used, which was a small comfort.

Davenport sat back on his heels, wiped his hands with the discarded cloth and groaned quietly.

'What a life, eh?'

'Will you find who did this to her, sir?' Kitty's eyes were wide and tearful.

He stood up with a heavy sigh.

'I doubt it.' He looked down at Sallie.

'She knew something, I think.' I said. 'She had something to tell me about Mr Reed and about Paris. Surely, that means her death has something to do with his?'

He thought about it for a moment.

'It's possible that she may have seen or heard something, but more likely she *thought* she had. She probably just wanted to get money from you – you know that.'

'Someone killed her, hit her on the head; can't you do anything?'

'I'll do my best. I can ask around as I go, someone may have seen something, or know something but, really, there's not much I can do.' Fielding's men were busy hunting for Swann's gang. Sallie was unimportant. No one would be asking questions. No one would miss her. No one would care.

He reached inside his coat and pulled out some coins.

'I'm unlikely to find out who killed her, but,' he dropped the coins into my hand, 'perhaps this will help to bury her decently. And maybe you can buy these girls a drink with what's left.' He looked almost as upset as Bess. He put a hand out to her. 'If you have to live as you do, try to stay nearer Soho. It's hell down here.'

He turned to go. 'I'm sorry,' he said. I think he meant it.

I stroked Sallie's clenched hand. A dark blue thread hung between her fingers; it was attached to something in her fist. Her hand was already in the grip of death and prising open her fingers was not easy, but I tugged gently on the line and a button fell from her cold grasp. A button from a gentleman's coat. It was gold and it shone well enough to suggest that it was new. There was a small bird embossed on the front of it; I'd not seen a button like it before.

Kitty squeaked and called him back. 'There's a button, here, look! Do you think this will help you find whoever killed her?' Her face was almost radiant with hope.

He took it from me and examined it. Then he returned it to my hand.

'It's just a button.'

'I think it's quite distinctive,' I said. 'There's some sort of a bird on it.'

'Could you look, sir?' Kitty pressed him now, excitedly believing that, somehow, this small clue pointed us to a murderer.

'I haven't got the time to check the closet of every gentleman in London. I wish that I had. Perhaps Miss Hardwicke can take it to any of the tailors she knows and make enquiries.' It was his quiet way of letting her down gently.

'I can do my best, Kitty,' I said. There must be several hundred of places to buy buttons in London. His response was disappointing, but understandable.

Davenport tipped his hat to us and walked away. I watched him kick at the wheel of a cart as he went. The girls fussed about straightening Sallie's bonnet and pulled the greying cloth back over her. The boatman was still standing nearby, watching us, tankard in hand.

'Are you able to find us an undertaker, do you think? I can pay.'

He rubbed his stubbled chin. 'I can find you one near St Martin's, if you want. I'll take fourpence.'

I thought fourpence was daylight robbery, and that he was making money from our grief, but decided not to argue. He knew the area better than I did and would find someone faster than I would. He pocketed the coins and then favoured us with what he probably hoped was a compassionate expression.

'I'll get going now, then. Don't want to leave you ladies down here for too long, do I? An' I got stuff to do, besides.'

His 'stuff' involved sitting in the alehouse rather than ferrying passengers, most likely. There was nothing to do except drown our sorrows in the same alehouse while we waited for him to return. We sat by ourselves, huddled together in silence around our drinks as if it were winter. Sallie had wanted to speak to me about something. I was troubled by the thought that, had I been more interested, she would still be alive.

'What was it that she wanted to tell me, did she ever tell either of you?'

Bess, about to take a mouthful of the not-very-pleasant beer, paused and looked thoughtful.

'She said it was something about Paris.'

This again. I sighed. 'You told me that the other night.' I had hoped for more, a small clue that would help me locate Reed's killer – and possibly her own.

'I haven't been to Paris,' said Kitty, to no one in particular. 'But I've never been to the sea in this country, even.'

'What?'

'I said I've never been to the sea.'

I shook my head. She couldn't be that drunk on one pot of weak beer. 'What's that got to do with Paris?'

Kitty gave me a superior look. 'Sallie said that Paris had a beach. That means it must be by the sea.'

I laughed. It was the first time I had laughed for hours.

'Sallie was an idiot even when she was sober. Paris isn't on the coast.' But even as I laughed, something nagged at me. 'Did she tell you something about Paris, Kitty? Something about Mr Reed and Paris?'

'That's what I'm telling you,' Kitty rolled her eyes. 'She said that she heard Mr Reed on the night he died. He was having an argument with someone. She didn't think anything of it until you told her you'd buy her gingerbread whenever you saw her.'

That was not what I had said.

'She heard my conversation with the gingerbread man. Go on.'

'Well, she told me that Mr Reed said he had missed the beach in Paris.' Kitty raised her head, proud of herself for recalling a vital piece of information. Bess scowled. She hadn't heard this. Sallie must have only shared it with Kitty.

'Missed the beach?' I propped my elbows on the table and rubbed my temples. I was trying not to become exasperated. 'Missed the beach? What did she mean by that?'

Kitty looked confused. She scratched at her hair.

'I don't know. How am I supposed to know? That was what she told me. Mr Reed said that he had missed the beach in Paris.'

It was drunken nonsense. Whether it was Sallie's own drunken nonsense, or Kitty's in the retelling, I wasn't sure. I was quite certain that George Reed, having been in Paris, would know that it had a river, but no sea and no beach.

I felt in my pocket for the gold button, running my thumb over the little bird. It was my only link to Sallie and her killer. Silently, I swore on it, that I would find out the truth, knowing that the button was a better witness to it than either of these two girls, or even Sallie herself.

Chapter Twenty-Eight

The undertakers were efficient when they arrived and even managed to appear dignified. This was, in part, because I was dressed, if not like a lady, then certainly like a woman of means, and they were hoping for a few coins by way of gratitude. I obliged them; it's how things work around here, but even though they might just have been happy to take my money, they gave a good impression of earnestness and honesty. I watched them go off in their dismal cart. Kitty and Bess went with them, leaving me to walk back towards Soho alone. There would be no grand funeral for Sallie. Mr Davenport's money would give her a little dignity, but she would be lost among the masses of the wretched in death as in life and no one would weep for her.

As I passed St Martin's, I wondered whether God the Father, whose blessed son loved prostitutes, would welcome her to a better home. Or perhaps, as my own father would have said, he would send her to everlasting damnation.

Thinking about my father was never a good idea. I decided to do something useful: find the owner of the gold button.

-

The world of gentlemen's clothing is less of a mystery to me than it used to be. I have become, in the last few months, well-acquainted with breeches, shirts, neck ties, waistcoats — brocade or wool — coats and hats. Discarded over my floor in a hurry by eager young men, or carefully folded by the less-energetic ones able to afford to take their time, I have seen them: the best new fashions that money can buy — and the over-darned stockings that are coming towards the end of their natural life.

I am aware of how a garment feels as it is removed from the body it encloses, warm and soft. I know the sound of breeches buttons fumbled open, the hasty shrugging off of a coat, the noise a shoe makes when, tugged from a foot, it falls to the ground. Bolts of cloth, lying untouched, unworn in a tailor's emporium, present a wholly different world for me though.

Men, like women, come by their clothes in different ways. I do know that. Not everyone buys everything new. I don't always. Great business is to be had in London by the selling on of second-hand garments. You can't always tell a person's income from the cut of the clothes they wear: a decent coat taken from a dead gentleman and hawked about by an undertaker might be picked up for a fair price by a baker or a bookseller, as much as another gentleman who had fallen on hard times. What would tell you that this was a second-hand purchase might be the quality of the cloth, or the fashion of the cut — but you would have to look closely. Dresses worn by duchesses, in silk or satin, would be copied — sometimes very well — by discerning garment makers in cotton or wool. The lower orders liked to wear the same as their betters: every slut in London could feel like a lady, if she had rummaged through the second-hand markets of Monmouth Street. Or at least, she could look like the courtesan who had been forced to sell her clothes when she was down on her luck at the gaming tables.

There were clothing shops across London. I could comb every inch, every alleyway and wide street from Cheapside to Piccadilly and still have plenty more places to try. This was the nub of the problem. I had a button with a dark blue thread. It could have been stitched onto any coat made in London in the last ten years. I was looking for a needle in a haystack.

The only place to start was where I was. The Strand, famed for its cheap women, was also well-known for tailors. Men of quality walked along this way looking for both.

It was early afternoon. Women of pleasure were only now beginning to emerge into the streets, and their numbers had not yet reached the level where they plucked at men's sleeves to attract attention. The tailors were doing the brisker business for now. I found one shop: a middling establishment with bolts of cloth displayed to good effect. Brocades, watered silks and velvets in rich reds, purples and greens were hung in the bay window to show how they might fall when made into coats, pooling together in the window's ledge. I pushed the door open and smelled warm fabric and the fresh tang of gentlemen's perfume.

Three shop assistants were demonstrating their brocaded waistcoats to two elegant but disinterested gentlemen. The assistants were working hard to make a sale; inviting the customers to note the cut and the quality of the cloth as they admired their physiques in the mirror. The gentlemen were less enamoured of the waistcoats than their own reflections. Then they all turned to look at me.

'Can we help?'

I ignored the tone, and the way the senior assistant's mouth pursed as he addressed my interruption. He was a thin-faced man, past his prime and bitter about it. The two younger, prettier, assistants stared at me. I was not a Strand girl, not a twopenny-whore, but they wouldn't want me in the shop for long. I put on my haughtiest manner.

'I hope that you can.' The two fine gentlemen tore their gaze from the mirror, took in my dress, my carriage, my brazen step into their world and knew immediately what sort of woman I was. I could almost hear them haggling over which of them would go first. I ignored that too.

'I have a button. It came to me... ah, from a friend, and we are trying to trace its owner.' I presented the button to the assistant for inspection as if I were carrying a family heirloom. He glanced briefly and then waved his hand dismissively.

'It's just a button,' he said, echoing Mr Davenport's opinion. 'Have you any idea how many buttons we see every day?'

I kept my hand out. 'But this one is interesting, don't you think? It has a small bird on it.'

He shrugged. 'Buttons have designs on them. It's not unusual.'

'Please,' I said. 'I'd really like to know who it belongs to — so that I can return it. Some gentleman might be missing it. Walking around with a shabby coat.'

203

One of the younger assistants gave an involuntary shudder, as if the thought of a half-finished coat caused him physical pain. The older man looked down his skinny nose.

'Perhaps you should ask your *friend* which coat she pulled it from,' he said. 'I can't help you. Leave my shop, slut.' He turned his back, picked up a tape measure and hung it around his neck. The pretty shrimps took the hint and began to fuss over the waistcoats as if I had already left.

'Thank you for your assistance,' I said, in the sort of acidic voice I had heard Ma Farley use with tradesmen. 'I'll be sure to recommend your establishment to everyone I know.' One of the gentlemen grabbed my arm as I passed and offered his own helpful suggestion of how he and I might spend the afternoon together. I shrugged him away; there were a thousand other shops to look at. Besides, there would be enough men like him waiting for me at Berwick Street.

It was the same story everywhere that I tried. With varying degrees of disdain, shop assistants shook their heads and told me that a button, with or without a bird on it, was unimportant or untraceable. I trudged home past plenty of mercers and tailors, I tried buckle-sellers and shops selling belts and swords and pocket watches. I gave an hour to the rag markets in the better corners of Seven Dials – where one thieving wretch tried to grab the button from me and several others offered to buy it for a pittance – and the trail of second-hand emporia on Monmouth Street. Everywhere I was met with a wall of disinterest. I was told that embossed buttons were not special, that they had never seen one with this sort of bird on it, they didn't know where it came from and I should quiz my friend if

I really wanted to know. It was a pity that she was dead, I thought, as I reached Berwick Street in the darkness, otherwise I would have shaken the information from her to save my aching feet.

Chapter Twenty-Nine

The sky was appropriately dismal for Sallie's funeral.

I put on my most sober outfit and left off the rouge, slipping out before Ma could see me so undressed. To anyone who passed me, I was a presentable, even modest, young woman going about my business in the grey morning. At least it wasn't raining, but the wind was cold enough to make me scowl. If there were any other whores out on the streets of Soho, they were either desperate for coin or going to a funeral.

I tugged my cloak more firmly around my shoulders and sank my chin into its folds, in an effort to keep out the sharp chill as I hurried to St Anne's. A woman, basket over her arm, gave a brisk wave with a gloved hand. It was Susan Groves.

She was smiling, her face free from anxiety. I supposed that her husband was safely at work – with enough food to satisfy him this time.

'You'll never guess,' she began speaking before I had time to greet her, 'John's buying me a new bonnet.'

She told me this with as much joy in her eyes as one might behold from an expectant grandmother, or someone who had suddenly come into a surprise inheritance.

'How delightful,' I responded to her genuine happiness, rather than to the actual news about the hat. 'Is it a very fine hat?'

Her face fell a little. 'I have yet to choose it,' she said. 'But he has promised me a new one,' she added defiantly. So, there was no hat in existence yet.

'Well, my congratulations on the soon-to-be new bonnet, then,' I said with mock solemnity. 'I look forward to making its acquaintance soon. You must press him for it without delay.' I grinned, hoping that she would take my teasing in good heart.

She gave a timid smile and plucked at her cloak. It wasn't as thick as mine and her bony shoulders suggested that she needed a new cloak more than a bonnet. I doubted that Mr Groves would offer her both. Even so, his extravagance puzzled me.

'Has your husband come into money?' It was an impertinent question and polite ladies do not ask such things. But I am not considered polite anymore, so felt free enough to ask it. Her expression became more conspiratorial.

'Well,' she leaned closer, 'I thought we would be short, having lost such a good lodger as Mr Reed, but John has told me that he's discovered a way of making money, and that we will be flush with it soon enough.' I had a prickly feeling down the back of my neck. Perhaps Mr Groves had taken up where George Reed had come to an abrupt end. There could be a great deal of cash in blackmail – especially if Mr Groves had searched Reed's room before Mr Davenport and I had reached it and found a few scribbled notes. Taken some of them and thrown the rest over the wall of the White Horse...

'Has he shared the source of his good fortune?'

She shook her head. 'No, but I think that his partner is looking to sell up. The butcher, I mean.' She must have seen me looking doubtful.

'He'll buy his partner's share of the business, you think?' I was worrying over nothing. This was a man on the edge of a deal, and nothing more.

'He's not said exactly. But that's what I've guessed. My husband will control the business and the profit.'

I didn't know how far to trust Susan Groves' guesses. She seemed far too innocent in the ways of the world – unlike her husband.

'But where are you off too, looking so sombre?' She interrupted my musings with a chirrup.

'A funeral.'

Her bright smile evaporated with an agony of having said the wrong thing. She clutched at my arm.

'Miss Hardwicke, I am so sorry. Do forgive me. Was this a close relative?'

I was touched that she believed my family would still be speaking to me. I could hardly call them close.

'An acquaintance,' I said. 'A young woman from the streets who met a very sad end. She was pulled from the river yesterday.'

Her face crumpled in sympathy. Mrs Groves was solidly respectable, but she was not without compassion. She put a hand on my arm.

'I am sorry, if she was a friend of yours.' She rummaged in her basket and took out a stem of rosemary. 'Here, have this. For remembrance.'

'Thank you.'

She gave me a careful look.

'Yours is a hard life – especially for one born a gentle-woman.'

She was shrewd enough to have noticed that. Perhaps she was right about her husband's business plans, after all.

'Thank you, Mrs Groves. It's not the life I chose, but no woman gets a free choice, does she?'

She gave a look of uneasy acknowledgement before leaving me at the gate of the church yard and wandering away down Princes Street, shoulders hunched against the wind.

I saw Kitty and Bess next to a yew tree, clutching one another and giggling. Neither of them had any idea how to behave, but I suspected anxiety rather than devilment. At the far corner of the church yard I spotted the rector in a round wig and a voluminous white surplice that kept whipping up in the breeze. On the ground, between him and the undertaker's men, lay a rough-looking coffin. Sallie.

I scooped up the chattering girls and we made our way to the grave. The rector took his fat hand off his wig only to take the coins I pressed into it; the funeral might be paid for by the parish, but I wanted it done decently. Even so, he flipped open his prayer book and began to recite the words of the burial service at speed, as keen to finish as the rest of us. Keen to get back to a warm tavern, from the look of him. I wasn't going to argue when there was a cold wind chafing my ears. The girls fell silent, as if in awe. He slurred a couple of the words, but he managed not to make a mess of the psalm.

On his signal, the two other men stumbled forward, picked up the coffin, and eased it, as gently as they could, into the pit. I tried not to look into the ground, but it wasn't easy to avoid signs of other occupants in this plot, who had been hastily dusted over with quick lime and soil. The men would have shovelled more soil into the pit immediately, but the rector, in a lame attempt to afford Sallie some sort of dignity, and mindful of my coins, held up a finger and finished the prayers, before clutching his wig again.

He reached the conclusion, nodded to me, ignored the girls and walked back towards his church. At that, the grey-faced men began to tip the soil from their wheelbarrow. I took a deep sniff of the rosemary that was still in my hand, before casting it into the grave with the lime. Bess and Kitty threw their posies.

Then there was little else to do but take them to the White Horse, to remember Sallie in the traditional way.

A familiar figure stood leaning against the churchyard gate, watching us. He looked as though he had been standing there for the whole service, impervious to the cold and unruffled by the wind, hat in his hand. I hailed him.

'You've found her killer, then, Mr Davenport?'

'No. Just paying my respects.'

He eased himself away from the gate and fell in with us as we made our way towards the warmth and comfort of the tavern. He didn't say anything more and we walked in silence as the girls chattered away a few paces in front of us – the sad event of minutes ago now forgotten as the prospect of drinking and earning money beckoned.

We reached the door of the White Horse. Bess and Kitty were disappointed: it was far too quiet. This was not surprising, given it was before noon, but they were hoping for some fun after having been forced to be religious for a whole ten minutes.

'Come on,' I said, pushing them to a table. 'I'll buy you a bowl of hot punch to share, and something to eat. We should raise a glass to Sallie, at least. She'd do the same for us – especially if someone else was paying.'

'And the bowl was very big,' Bess giggled.

Chapter Thirty

Davenport decided to leave us alone with our punch, guessing, probably accurately, that we would spend all afternoon getting steadily and noisily drunk enough to face whatever waited for us in the evening. He skulked over to Harry Bardwell and engaged him in conversation, presumably about the night of Reed's death.

I am not fond of punch – it makes my head spin too quickly – so sipped at a large glass of brandy while the girls knocked back what I'd bought them. It wasn't long before they began to annoy me with their antics. Davenport looked over when Kitty squealed with laughter and I caught his eye, silently pleading with him to be relieved of my nurse-maid duties to these infants. He hid the smirk as well as he could and turned back to Harry. He continued to talk to the landlord for a minute or two before stepping from his stool and wandering over, beer in hand.

'May I have a quiet word?'

Relief flooded over me as Kitty, even then, let out a screech and sent a slice of bread skidding off the table.

'Oh yes, please.' I stood up before he could change his mind. We moved to a table over the other side of the room. The girls barely noticed. They were trying to attract the attention of a couple of young, serious-looking clerks who had wandered into the White Horse for light refreshment. The poor fellows had probably wandered west, imagining that the taverns of Soho were quiet; the haunt of gentlemen. Such innocent wretches were easy prey for Kitty and Bess — now filled up with drink and game for anything. I turned my back, knowing that Anne Bardwell would soon throw the jolly pair out if they started harassing decent customers. A bit of a joke was one thing, creating havoc was another. Anne glared at me. I shrugged back at her: I had only bought the drink. How they behaved having drunk it all so quickly was their own concern.

'Were you as wild as that, when you were their age?' Davenport asked, nodding over to their table.

'What makes you think I've left those ways behind?' I asked with a wink.

His mouth twitched into a smile. 'You're far too refined.'

'Well, you'd have to pay to find out just how wild I can be,' I smiled back at him, taking a delicate sip of my drink, happy enough to flirt. 'You might be surprised.'

He sat back, clasped his hands behind his head and regarded me for a moment, without speaking. His was not the sort of gaze I was used to. Men watch me all the time. They look me up and down, working out how much I'm worth, what I might look like without my stays, or how I'd feel lying beneath them. This one scrutinised me as if he were weighing my soul. I shifted in my seat.

'Why are you looking at me?'

'I imagine that you're used to being looked at.'

'Not like that, I'm not.' He was one of those strange ones, perhaps. The ones we tried to avoid. Every girl had a story of a peculiar customer.

'I'm just wondering what you're doing here, that's all.' He continued to watch me. 'I mean, you're not like most of the girls I see. You're clearly not someone who's grown up on the streets like those two, you're not a servant making a few shillings on the side, you don't strike me as country lass tricked into sin – you're far too smart for that. You have the manners of a well-bred gentlewoman, but although I imagine you're older than you look, you're not old enough to be a widow fallen on hard times. You've already confessed you're estranged from your family, but you've told me nothing more. So, you see,' he relaxed his arms and rested his elbows on the table, 'you are an enigma to me, Miss Hardwicke. I would rather like an explanation – to put my mind at rest, if you understand me.'

He wasn't a customer. He wasn't even odd. He was simply intelligent and curious – as a magistrate's man should be, I suppose. He wanted to know who he was dealing with. I was surprised that he had thought so carefully about me, though.

'Are you beginning to suspect me of killing George Reed after all?'

'Maybe.' He was quiet again. Then he said with a grunt that sounded like frustration, 'You don't belong here. You just don't fit. I can't make you fit. So, I wonder who you are, where you come from, Lizzie Hardwicke – if that's even your name.'

Oh, he was a smart one. I had gone to a lot of trouble to lose my name and lose my past along with it. No one had questioned it before; I was Lizzie Hardwicke at Mrs Farley's establishment. But then, no one had needed to question it. Now I was staring at a man who might still think me a murderer, and anything could be construed as guilt if he had a magistrate on his back, demanding results. It was better to tell the truth than have him suspect me just because I didn't 'fit'.

And perhaps I wanted to tell him.

'Well, I didn't kill George Reed, any more than I killed Sallie.' My mouth had become dry. 'But I wasn't born to this life. You're right about that.'

The tavern was just noisy enough to cover my confession. It was too early for the real fun to be happening and, although more people had wandered in for food and conversation, and a decent drink, it wasn't heaving with customers. Harry and Anne were occupied: Harry was telling a tale to some older men at a corner table. It was evidently going to be a long tale, because he had sat down with a beer and filled himself a pipe. Anne, rolling her eyes at him, was on her way to evict Bess and Kitty. The timid clerks had wisely moved tables and left the girls engaging in a spitting contest – the men having foolishly bought them more punch before escaping. It was only a matter of time before things became messy. Anne was very happy to serve drunkards – as long as they kept their drink inside them. She, experienced landlady that she was, knew the signs and was making a move.

Davenport leaned across the table. 'You're gently born. You can't hide it.'

'It's what Mrs Farley calls my "edge". I have an edge over the others, apparently. What I lack in beauty or experience, I make up for in knowing how to talk, how to behave politely. It brings a better sort of gentleman to her house, she says.'

'Hardwicke isn't your real name?' He asked it as a question, but we both knew it was a statement of fact.

'No. It was my mother's name. But I am Elizabeth.' That was all he was getting. He appeared to understand this.

'How did you end up in Berwick Street?'

'Polly found me when I arrived on the coach last September.'

He frowned. 'Before that, I mean.'

I took a careful sip of drink and felt the liquor warm my mouth. It was difficult to know how to start; how far I could pretend not to care.

'My father threw me out.' I shrugged, as if it didn't matter. He waited for me to continue. No one ever gave me chance to talk. No one was ever interested in who I really was. But this man was.

The brandy had made my throat thicken. I cleared it. 'My father threw me out because one day he arrived home earlier than expected and found me in bed with the squire's son.' My voice was confident enough, but the memory of that day made me tremble, even now.

He grimaced. 'He found you? He saw you? That must have been unfortunate for all concerned.'

It had been. I closed my eyes, remembering the look on my father's face as he had stood in the doorway. I would never forget it.

'He didn't allow you to marry the man?' Davenport was saying. 'Keep it quiet and make a decent thing of it?'

It would have been the obvious solution. I had, indeed, been fond of Edmund and marriage to him would have contented both our families. My father may even have recovered, in time, from the shock of what he had witnessed. Edmund had been, I thought, a fine and vigorous young man, of good breeding and decent fortune. I had fixed on him as the way of escaping my uncle; carefully and quietly using my new-found skills to draw him into bed – and, I hoped, into marriage. He had been happy enough to take a tumble with me, but I had not reckoned on his utter cowardice when confronted by my father.

'Ah, well now, Mr Davenport, you need to know two things. Firstly, my father was, and still is, a clergyman, the sort who is extremely committed not only to morality but also to his lofty social position. To be fair, he was in a state of distress, as well as anger at the time.'

'Even so –'

'And secondly,' I said, ignoring him, 'my sweet lover chose to lay the blame entirely at my feet. He told my father that I had seduced him, that he was certainly not the first man to have been in my bed, and that, in fact, I was nothing more than a common strumpet.' My voice began to wobble a little. I cleared my throat again. 'My father, you'll recall, had already seen enough with his own eyes to reach much the same conclusion. He decided that if I were a common strumpet then I couldn't also be his daughter, and there was no place for me in his house. There was no place for me in his family.'

There was a long pause. He sat watching me, saying nothing, while around us people chattered and laughed.

'Was it true, the man's insinuation?' he asked.

The answer was more complicated than he knew.

'It was true.'

There was a look of disappointment in his face. I was, then, as I had first appeared to him. I was just like Kitty and Bess, but with better clothes. I felt my face grow hot with shame. I did not want him to think badly of me.

'It was my uncle.' The words escaped in a rush, louder than I wanted. The serving girl who, at this point in the day was only serving beer and not herself to the customers, stared at me for a moment before carrying on with her work, gathering up empty glasses and tankards on to a tray.

'Your uncle?'

'The man... the one before Edmund... It was my uncle who...'

I saw him begin to comprehend.

'Your own uncle?'

'My father's older brother. He took a fancy to me last year, and...' I didn't want to say any more.

'Ah.'

He was constructing his own interpretation of my past. It would be almost accurate.

'You said that Hardwicke *was* your mother's name. She's dead, I take it?'

'She died when I was an infant. I have two older brothers.'

'You couldn't speak to them about your uncle? Or tell your father?'

'No, of course not. My father would have been appalled if he had ever found out. That's what my uncle told me, and I think he was right.' I stared at my drink. 'I couldn't speak of it to anyone.'

We were both silent. I drained my brandy.

'Still, I've been lucky so far, haven't I?' I swept a hand around the room, smiling brightly to dispel the possibility of fear or self-pity. 'I mean, who would want to miss all of this?'

'If lucky means a well-bred lady ending up in a brothel.'

'I could have ended up in places much worse than Mrs Farley's. I may be paying a heavy price for my transgressions, Mr Davenport, but I am not out on the streets.' I sat up straight and shook the cuffs of my gown, reminding him – and myself – of my relative prosperity and freedom. 'I'm warm and clean and I don't have to beg for food or lift my skirts just to eat. I've enough of a reputation that I can earn money while I still have my looks, but I'm not so stupid as to think I'll be in luxury for ever. I'm saving for my retirement.'

A tiny smile flickered over his mouth.

I banged my fist on the table. 'Don't laugh at me.'

'I swear I'm not laughing at you. I'm only smiling because you're the first working woman I've ever met who has a retirement fund.'

I shrugged. 'Some girls hope to become mistresses of benevolent gentlemen. They spend all their money on hats or gorgeous gowns in their attempts to snare one. Since the day I left my father's house I've never trusted any man to care for me. I don't trust anyone. I keep a little back from Mrs Farley; accept gifts from men and hide them away. She doesn't need to know about my secret store – I've earned it and it's there for my future.'

'So, where does your future lie? What are you going to do with your savings, when you retire?' He was smirking again.

I ignored the smirk.

'Maybe I'll take over from Mrs Farley one day. Or perhaps I'll open a shop and sell ribbons to young ladies.'

'No firm plans then?'

'All I know is that I didn't intend this life, but I will make the best of it, and one day I will leave it. Too many girls catch the pox, or something worse, and die alone in the dark. I would like something else.'

'Would you marry?'

Such a ridiculous question made me laugh aloud. He began to laugh with me until the two of us were almost losing breath. And then it wasn't funny anymore. The cold truth was that no one decent would marry me, even if I wished it. I had lost all respectability the day I caught my uncle's eye and, full of girlish lusts, flirted with the devil. If you fall into sin, you pay the price. That much I had learned from my father.

There was a commotion at the door. Jack Grimshaw was trying to get into the tavern with another man. He had the man's arm twisted up his back – something that this gentleman was not taking to kindly. He was protesting quite loudly.

It was Mr Winchcombe.

Chapter Thirty-One

Jack Grimshaw half threw Mr Winchcombe across the room. He landed at our feet, stumbled to his knees and then groped his way to a seat.

He slumped across the table holding his head and groaning a little.

When he finally raised his eyes, I could see that they were bloodshot. He had not been to bed for a long time.

Grimshaw stood behind him, arms folded and face like an angry dog. There was a cut to his cheek, small but deep, and bruising was forming around it. It looked as though he had been punched by someone wearing a jewelled ring.

Mr Winchcombe's magnificent amethyst glittered on his right hand. I could almost see the blood on it.

'Ah, Mr Winchcombe, how good to see you,' said Davenport, finishing his beer as though he had all the time in the world; no longer interested in my past, but Fielding's man once more. 'My name is William Davenport, and I am acting on behalf of the magistrate to find out who strangled Mr George Reed in the yard of this tavern six days ago. I see that you've already met Mr Grimshaw.'

Winchcombe was silent.

'It's taken us a while to meet,' said Davenport. His manner was curt, he was still annoyed that we had taken an unnecessary journey to find Mr Winchcombe the other night. 'You knew that we wanted to speak with you, ask a few questions about the night of the murder. Miss Hardwicke told you, I think, as did a man called Reading. Yet you seem to have been avoiding us.'

Winchcombe shrugged.

'I've been occupied in my own affairs.'

Grimshaw sloped off, presumably in search of refreshment.

'I need a drink.' Winchcombe's voice was rough. A drink was the last thing he needed, but he raised a hand and the girl came scurrying over to take his order.

'I gather you're not having much luck with the dice at the moment.' Davenport said.

A jug of wine was slopped down in front of the unfortunate Mr Winchcombe and he grasped at it, pouring a glass and drinking almost all of it in one go. He wiped his hand across his mouth and stifled a belch. His skin, I noticed now that I was close to him, was greasy and marked with small spots, as if he hadn't washed it in weeks. His lips were dry and he needed a shave. Very little of the spring sun had caught his handsome face.

'That's putting it mildly. Everywhere I go they seem to have queer dice. Although I'm no luckier with cards.'

'Why the need to play, when Mr Herring says you have a reasonable allowance?' I asked.

He looked at me with a frown.

'That's not your business,' he said.

'It might be my business, sir, to know just why you are so keen to secure a winning streak at present,' Davenport cut in. 'I understand that the places you have been visiting recently are notorious for their high stakes.'

'Don't I know it.' He fiddled with a loose thread on his cuff. I wondered if he had been sleeping in his coat, the sleeves looked so crushed. There were wine stains on his breeches. He was a mess.

'Excuse me for a moment.' Davenport rose abruptly from the table and made his way across to Jack Grimshaw. I could see that Grimshaw was engaged in a rather animated conversation with another man – almost as large and ugly as himself. Another runner, perhaps, or someone who acted as an informer, like John Reading. The two of them spoke to Davenport and I saw the third man pointing over at our table. Winchcombe was oblivious, drinking.

'Are you dreadfully in debt, Mr Winchcombe, or is it the thrill of it that keeps you returning?' I leaned over the table to him, touching him softly on the hand.

He shrugged. 'A little of both, I imagine. When you win, it's such a thrill – especially when you have a large win. And when you lose, well you just keep going to get it all back.'

I, who had only recently possessed my own money, could not understand the desire to lose it so lightly. My small box of coins would, slowly, and over time, be my complete independence. It was only the thought of what I would do with it that kept me from despair. Despair drove women to desperation and all sorts of poisonous powders designed to lighten their mood – and the powders cost them their fortunes. Girls who had once been the toast of the town, who had rolled themselves in silks, had died penniless and alone because despair had driven them to packets of powder or gambling dens. We'd all heard the stories.

'I had no idea it was so diverting.'

'Not so much diverting, Miss Hardwicke, as compulsive. A little like being intoxicated, or in love, I imagine.'

'You are out of control, then?'

He was about to answer when Davenport returned to the table. His face was grave. Grimshaw was lurking a few yards away, dabbing at his wound with a handkerchief.

'Can you tell me what you know of John Swann, Mr Winchcombe?'

My mouth fell open a little. I saw Grimshaw smirk.

'John Swann? Nothing. I suppose you mean the robber they just caught?'

'I think you know very well who I mean, sir.'

'Yes, of course I know of the highwayman.' He looked down his nose at Davenport. 'I could hardly fail to know, given the ludicrous songs that assail one's ears in every London tavern.'

Davenport pressed his fingertips together in a steeple and looked directly at Mr Winchcombe.

'And what of your own dealings with his gang, sir?'

Mr Winchcombe began to say something, then stopped and shook his head. In his eyes there was fear as well as defiance.

'I have nothing to tell you about John Swann – or any of his associates.'

Davenport sat back and watched with bright eyes as his quarry shifted uncomfortably. I was entranced. What had Mr Winchcombe got to do with John Swann?

'I don't think you are telling me the truth, sir.'

For all Mr Winchcombe's breeding and wealth, he was now sweating like a common cull caught with his hand in someone else's pocket.

Grimshaw moved to stand at Winchcombe's arm, blocking his path to the door. As if his presence wasn't threatening enough, Grimshaw shoved his hands into his pockets, better to display the pistols he had tucked into his breeches.

'You met a man, someone who gave you money,' said Davenport.

Winchcombe eyed the pistols but shook his head.

'And then he wanted something in return,' Davenport continued. 'You were overheard, negotiating the details. Gamblers in those places are never very discreet. Do you want me to tell you what they said?'

Winchcombe slammed his fist on the table, causing his wine to spill. Despite myself, I gasped.

'I swear, Davenport, I had no idea who he was!' His voice was hoarse, afraid.

The runner watched him, without saying a word, well-practised in letting a man talk himself into his own noose. Winchcombe could yell and bluster for as long as he wanted; he would wait.

Mr Winchcombe wiped the back of his hand across his mouth again, even though it was dry. It didn't take him long to blurt what Davenport, surely, already knew.

'He offered to lend me money. I was losing hard, and he told me that he could help me out.'

'Who?'

'Damn it, I don't know. Some man.'

'Go on.'

'He gave me a small purse filled with coins, which I managed to use up pretty quickly. I swear, sir, I had no idea who he was.'

Davenport stared at him, incredulous.

'And it never crossed your mind to wonder why a complete stranger would give you, a losing gambler, a pile of money?'

That did seem an obvious point. Whoever in this world gives their money without wanting something in return? Certainly no one in my business. Winchcombe was a fool and even I could see where this story was leading.

Winchcombe, though, was perplexed by the question.

'People offer me things all the time,' he said. 'I suppose I thought it a little odd, but I was desperate, and I'd been drinking.' Every man's excuse for everything.

'What happened?'

'I decided to call it a night, having lost the money, and went to find the stranger, to apologise and see how I might be able to repay him. He pulled a knife on me and began to make heavy threats.' He licked his cracking lips. 'I'll admit I was damned terrified. There were a couple of men with him. They came out of the shadows. Fearful creatures they looked all together. They told me they needed a place to keep some of their belongings. I could pay them back by storing it in my rooms.'

I couldn't believe so fine a gentleman could be so stupid.

'You've been *fencing* for them?' I said.

He looked at me, surprised.

'You know what that is, Miss Hardwicke?

'I've spent long enough hanging around taverns to know what goes on among thieves. Didn't you know?'

He shrugged. It was a pathetic sight. A broken man, mired in his debts, caught in a world of crime by his foolishness. He appealed to Davenport.

'I had no idea. No idea at all that they were from Swann's gang. I knew that they were no good, but I thought that they would return quickly and take their things.'

'Not their things,' said Davenport calmly. 'Other people's things. Stolen property.'

Winchcombe closed his eyes as if in pain.

'I didn't know. I swear I didn't realise.'

Davenport leaned forward and grabbed Winchcombe's cravat sharply, pulling him forwards until their faces almost touched. Winchcombe's eyes popped open and met Davenport's hard expression.

'You see, sir, I have no idea whether you are telling me the truth — that you are, indeed, extremely stupid and gullible — or whether you're a very clever liar and the fence for Swann's gang that some of us have been wanting to find for a while.'

Winchcombe didn't speak. He just gaped like a fish. Davenport released him, and he fell back. Grimshaw edged closer still, standing right behind him in case he decided to bolt.

Davenport sat in thought for a moment. Then he turned to me.

'You recall what was in Mr Reed's notes about this man?'

I did recall.

'That he was gambling his father's money and his father was losing patience. Reed was asking for money to keep quiet about the losses.'

Mr Winchcombe looked extremely exercised.

'What a nasty piece of work that man was. He knew of my father's principles and exploited them to get money from me.'

'You met him in Paris?' I had to ask. Davenport stared at him. He was probably about to ask the same question.

Winchcombe nodded miserably.

'Herring and I met him when we were over there. It was such a gossipy place. Too many people were ready to tell him about my predicament, even as I was doing rather well. My luck changed when I returned to London, alas.'

'But he knew enough to make life difficult for you?' I asked.

'My father believes that I am making my way in the world and living a good and honest life. If he knew the sorts of places I visit – and what my life is like...'

'You would be disinherited, I imagine.'

'More than that. His disappointment would be more than he could bear.'

He looked so utterly crushed by the very thought of it that I formed the impression of a man who really did love his father and hoped to please him one day. I reached out to touch his hand.

'You've never pawned your ring, I see.'

'It's his ring, his gift to me, Lizzie. I cannot lose it. Not even for a win.'

He had a shred of dignity left. It was a small hope.

'But why did you continue to visit the gaming hells – why did you go to those fearsome places beyond St Martin's – if you knew Mr Reed was dead? Surely, with your tormentor gone you had the opportunity to pull yourself together?'

He shrugged at me.

'I was still desperately trying for a win. And that's when I met the men you tell me are Swann's men.' He looked up at Davenport. 'They tricked me, sir. They tricked me royally and now my life is in such shit that I am lost.'

Davenport was not interested in his self-pity. He straightened his back and nodded to Grimshaw.

'Mr Winchcombe, your debts will land you in the Fleet, I have no doubt, but the magistrate needs to hear more from you concerning the stolen property you have in your rooms, and the death of Mr George Reed. You'll come with us, please.'

There was no alternative. Jack Grimshaw pulled him to his feet. Davenport stood too, grim-faced.

'Miss Hardwicke, I don't think I'll be needing your assistance from this point.'

He had caught his man. Davenport thought that Mr Winchcombe was a murderer as well as being in league with John Swann's men. I wasn't so sure, but there was little I could do.

Mr Winchcombe looked terrified, as if the realisation of his situation was only now sinking in.

'Lizzie,' he begged, 'find John Herring for me. Or Stanford. Tell them. Get them to find help. I haven't done anything wrong, you must believe me.'

I nodded. I think I did believe him, even if the case against him, whether for fencing or for murder, looked perfectly reasonable. I've known men hang on flimsier evidence, especially if there were other men willing to testify against him to save their own necks. He had mixed with highwaymen, wittingly or not, and the penalty for such a stupid risk might be his life.

Besides, if he had killed George Reed, or was involved in his murder, then perhaps he had killed Sallie too.

Chapter Thirty-Two

I didn't have much time to worry about Mr Winchcombe when I returned home; I was engaged for most of the afternoon. The miserable weather had brought in the men, seeking warmth and solace. A few more coins made their way into my secret store, even as I brought the lion's share down to Ma in the parlour.

She sat, as she always did, at the table, with her ledger and pen, noting down our earnings with care one moment – and greedily shovelling what she referred to as our 'rent' into her strong box the next.

Emily and Polly joined us, and we sat drinking tea, while there was a lull in the custom. We chatted, and Ma quietly counted and added up the daytime takings.

'Where's Lucy?' I asked. 'She's never around when we're busy.'

Polly rolled her eyes and hitched her shawl back onto her shoulder.

'You know Lucy. She'll have found a lovely old gentleman and gone off in a carriage to a large house with discreet servants—'

'—A widower—' said Emily with a faint sneer.

'—an extremely rich one—' I added. They were always rich.

Polly started laughing. This was a familiar conversation.

231

'She'll have spent less than five minutes on her back and the rest of the afternoon stroking his fine porcelain.'

'Is that what we're calling it now?' I started to giggle. Even Emily was beginning to crack a smile.

Ma Farley looked up and narrowed her eyes. For an old bawd, she could be ridiculously disapproving of lewd conversation, even when we were by ourselves. I nudged Polly and she tried to contain her mirth but ended up snorting into her tea cup.

'Sorry Ma,' I said. 'It's been a long afternoon.'

She patted the box.

'I know,' her eyes glittered. 'But not quite long enough. I hope you'll all be busy this evening, just like our Lucy.'

How Lucy managed it, though, we never quite understood. She was simply the best at hooking rich men and she never had to strain herself with overwork. To say I was envious, after the afternoon I'd had, was an understatement.

We heard the front door open. Emily, Polly and I eyed each other, as if gauging which of us was the least exhausted and most in need of money as we readied ourselves for the men who would be seeking our pleasures. Meg was still answering the door, so Ma hurried out to greet the guests and the three of us sat in silence, straining to hear voices.

The visitors were women, not men.

Lucy had returned. Amelia was with her.

'I found her out on the street… no, down by St Anne's…' Lucy was still speaking to Ma as they came in. Amelia's clothes had that crinkled look about them as if she had been out in the rain earlier and only recently begun to dry. Her face was pale.

I gave her my seat, nearest to the fire, and poured her some tea. Ignoring Ma's look, I spooned several lumps of sugar into the cup and pushed it towards her. She was unused to walking the streets. I wondered how she had dealt with the attention that would have, undoubtedly, come her way if she had been on her own. She didn't have the smart remarks that every street-wise harlot knows. She wasn't sharp or scheming, like Bess and Kitty. She was more vulnerable, even, than Sallie. I shivered, remembering Sallie's battered and bloody body by the river, and imagining Amelia in her place.

Emily's mouth started to twitch. She was becoming impatient with Amelia. A girl this pretty could be raking in the gold, just as soon as she stopped dithering and got on with earning. What Emily couldn't see was that it was different for Amelia. The rest of us had started our careers already ruined by careless or heartless men. We had nothing to lose and plenty to gain by charging for what others had taken for free. Amelia was destitute, young and beautiful; she was also, as far as we could tell, unspoiled and untouched. In a world that prized virginity – even as it wallowed in whoredom – her decision mattered.

'She hasn't gone and offered it up on the streets has she?' Ma was near-enough shaking Lucy by the arm, as if it were somehow her fault.

'No – at least, I don't think so,' Lucy looked almost as white as Amelia. 'She was just wandering about in the rain. I took her to a coffee house and got her warm.'

Ma Farley let out a curse in exasperation. This was not a good sign.

'I'm not having it!' she snapped at Lucy. Lucy's eyes widened. She wasn't used to being spoken to like that by Ma. It happened often to me.

Ma agitated the heavy gold rings she wore during working hours.

'Are you all right, Ma?' Polly could see, as I could, that something was amiss. She had been off with us ever since we came down to the parlour.

Ma sat down and looked directly at Amelia, who was staring dismally into her tea.

'Amelia, I think the time has arrived for you to make a decision. I cannot keep you in this house unless you are working. You are stretching my patience and my hospitality.' She laid her hands on the table and spread out her fingers, as if trying to calm herself. 'I'll have your answer by tomorrow morning. There's a very wealthy gentleman waiting on my word. He would like to spend an evening with you.'

Amelia's head lowered further towards the cup. We held a collective breath for a long time until Ma suddenly stood, nodded to us, and hurried out of the room.

There was little that we could say. We all knew that if Amelia was going to stay in Berwick Street she was going to have to pay rent. And rent only came by one means. She didn't have much choice.

I only hoped that the gentleman Ma had lined up for her was as kind as he was wealthy.

Amelia managed to contain the sob that was so obviously rising in her throat.

'What were you doing out on the streets?' I asked, trying to break the awkward silence. 'Lucy said you were down by St Anne's?'

Lucy nodded. 'That's where I found you, wasn't it?' She patted her shoulder in an unusual display of kindness. 'With a damp cloak and a battered hat.'

'It's been so miserable this morning,' Polly said. Talking about the weather like a benign grandmother helps any situation, as we know.

Amelia lifted her head slowly and sniffed back the tears.

'I decided to go and see my father.' The voice was quiet and querulous, so I guessed that it hadn't been a happy meeting.

'Why ever did you go and see him?' I said. 'I thought he had thrown you out?' My own father would set the dogs on me if I went home.

A fat tear slid from her left eye and splashed in the tea cup. She didn't seem to notice.

'I thought that I could persuade him to take me back, forgive Tommy and let us marry.'

She was brave, I'll give her that. Stupid as well, though.

'He didn't receive you?'

She shook her head and another tear dropped down her nose.

'He wouldn't allow me inside the house.'

'And Tommy still hasn't found work?' Lucy asked.

The tears told their own story.

'He's disappeared.'

'Disappeared?' I pricked up my ears. 'Have you any idea where he's gone?'

She shook her head.

'He was looking for work. He went out yesterday afternoon and I haven't seen him since.' Her shoulders sagged, whether at the loss of Tommy, or the realisation of what awaited her, I couldn't tell.

Emily passed her a handkerchief.

'Cheer up,' she said as she pressed it into Amelia's hand. 'I can teach you a few tricks if you like; help you earn a few guineas.'

I pinched the top of Emily's ear.

'Ow! What's that for?'

Polly scowled at her.

'You're so heartless sometimes, Emily,' Polly said. 'This isn't any easier for Amelia than it was for us.'

'You've become such an old hand at whoring that you've forgotten what it's like,' I added. She could be such a mean crow.

Emily bristled. She wasn't old by most people's standards, but she was no longer considered fresh, and she knew it.

'I'm only making a kind offer...'

'No.' I said. 'You're not making a kind offer at all. At least, not one Amelia wants to accept.'

Emily shrugged, but backed out of the room, leaving the rest of us to deal with Amelia. Polly rubbed her heaving shoulders and Lucy got up to find some more tea. I stood and watched the street from the window, wondering why an innocent man like Tommy had made a run for it – for surely that was the truth of it. He would not have abandoned Amelia otherwise, knowing Ma's plans for her.

Amelia had lost her protector, and even Polly's tender words would not help. She was a lamb about to be thrown to a ravenous wolf. As I had been once.

I had an idea. Before anyone could notice and ask questions, I snatched my hat and cloak and set off into the darkening streets. I hadn't been able to do anything for Sallie, but I might be able to save Amelia — or at least give her a better chance of avoiding a life like my own.

Chapter Thirty-Three

The streets were still damp. It wasn't so cold now, and the wind had dropped, but the air had a faint chill to it and I was glad of my cloak.

I knew what I had to do to help Amelia, much as it would injure me personally. I knew just the place to hide her; a place where she would be fussed over and cared for like the child she still was. The cost would be Ma's wrath, if she discovered my treachery, and my own hard-won retirement fund to pay for the rent. I told myself that I wasn't doing this just because I felt guilty about Sallie.

The pace of my walk, and the thick cloak wrapped about me meant that no one bothered me. Head down, I rattled along the streets in the direction of Golden Square, until I came to a halt outside the house belonging to Mr and Mrs Groves and banged on the door.

Her porker of a husband was out — he might have been late at work, but I suspected that he was eating and drinking their money away. It turned my own stomach to think that my secret retirement stash would soon be funding the expansion of his belly.

I explained Amelia's circumstances as delicately as I could, and Mrs Groves was sympathetic. I had guessed that they would be pleased to have a new lodger; they were still in need of rent after Mr Reed's demise. Of course, she would consult with her husband, but, in principle, she would take Amelia in and let her stay for a reasonable deposit and rent – paid by me until Tommy found a job. I assumed that, as long as the money rolled in, Mr Groves would be content with a pretty lodger like Amelia.

We shook hands and shared a small glass of port wine and some apple cake, and by the time I left the house, my spirits had lifted a little. I liked Mrs Groves. Without her husband to cow her she was a bright and capable woman. She had never had children of her own and had longed for a daughter, she told me. I felt a pang of envy as I foresaw the kindness that she would lavish on such a darling as Amelia. But I couldn't lapse too far into self-pity; not now I was a whore with extra rent to pay and the prospect of a diminished retirement fund.

As I turned the corner, I found myself standing outside the tailor's shop, where I had sheltered with Susan Groves only two days ago. There were a few candles burning inside. This was not a flashy store, brazenly lighting up to entice wandering customers in from the evening air, but the owner was astute enough to remain open late and compete with his rivals. The shop was empty of buckle-hunting gentlemen, and the tailor and his assistant were scooping buttons into a box.

I put my hand into my skirt and felt Sallie's button. It was worth a try.

The two men looked up when I pushed open the door. If they recognised me from the other day, they didn't show it. I put Sallie's button on the counter.

'I'd like to know about this button.' I didn't elaborate. They stared at it.

'You want to know about a button?' The tailor's face was a mixture of incredulity and disdain. It was a look with which I was becoming wearily familiar whenever I showed anyone the button. Whenever I walked into a shop.

'It has a small bird on it. I wondered if you could tell me about it,' I pointed out its finest feature for the seven hundredth time. The tailor shook his head.

'It's a canary button,' said the younger man.

'A canary button? What's that?' It was the first glimmer of interest I'd had.

'The bird,' he said. 'It's a canary. Means it was probably made in Norwich, or maybe for someone with connections there, who wanted the bird on his buttons.'

Norwich. George Reed's city.

'What's the canary got to do with Norwich?' I was genuinely interested – beyond the link with Reed.

'That'll be the weavers,' the younger man became animated. 'My mother's family is from there.' The tailor was not impressed and cut in.

'The weavers in Norwich: yes, lots of them keep song birds. They say it helps them work.' He frowned at the assistant. 'Go and fold the neck cloths, Jack. This matter need not detain you from your tasks.' The young man's face dropped a little; he had just begun to enjoy telling his story. He sloped off into the back room to get on with his folding.

The tailor turned the button over in his hand, feeling the weight of it. He looked at it in an odd way, as if he recognised more than just the canary, now that he held it.

'You've seen this before? Do you know who it belongs to?' It was more than I could hope. His eyes narrowed at me.

'Why? Where did you come across it?'

'A friend of mine found it.' It was not quite a lie. 'Can you tell me anything more?

He hesitated. 'We made a coat, some months ago. I'm sure, now that I see this button properly, I'm sure it had these buttons.'

I could hardly breathe for excitement.

'Could you tell me, sir, please? Who did you make it for?'

He looked uncertain. He didn't like to talk about his customers, I could tell. I exercise the same professional restraint. Then, in a very helpful, if unprofessional way, he went around the back of his counter and pulled out a ledger. He flicked through it, turning over pages until he found what he was looking for.

'Mr Beech.'

'Excuse me?'

'A Mr Beech collected the coat. I'm afraid that's all I can tell you.' He shut the book firmly. It was all that he was going to share.

The younger assistant popped a head around the door. 'Mr Andrews, I've been thinking about the canary button. I think I recall the coat.'

'Thank you, Jack,' the tailor said sharply. 'I've given this person everything she needs.'

The boy lowered his eyes and pulled himself back to the work he was supposed to be doing. I wasn't sure I did have everything I needed, but there was a prickling sensation on my neck. Mr Beech. I knew the name but couldn't quite remember why.

'I'm grateful to you, Mr Andrews,' I said, putting a hand over the button and drawing it back into my pocket. 'It isn't much help, but it may be something. My friend will be glad to know.'

We nodded to one another and I left the shop thinking to myself that I had missed something.

The beach.

I stopped walking. Sallie's ridiculous message now became entirely clear. 'Missed the beach' and 'Mister Beech' sounded almost the same.

That was what Kitty said Sallie had told them: George Reed had 'missed the beach' in Paris. She had been adamant about it, but she had also been full of gin, had only half-heard. George Reed, in an argument that had no connection with either sand or sea, had spoken of a 'Mister Beech' in Paris.

Or else he had spoken *to* Mr Beech. There was a man walking the streets who we did not know; another of his blackmail victims, perhaps. Was this a man from Norwich, or Paris, who Reed had wronged in some other way? And was his coat missing a canary button?

Chapter Thirty-Four

The house on Berwick Street was quiet when I returned. I thought I might manage to sneak upstairs unnoticed, but the bottom step squeaked – as it always did – and Mrs Farley poked her head around the parlour door. She had been at the gin again. Sydney's absence was causing her a great deal of anxiety.

I felt guilty as soon as I saw her. Tomorrow, her precious virgin would be spirited out of her clutches and away to a secret location. Little did she know – and she never could know – but the Judas of the act would be me. I was glad that she had been attacking the gin; she wouldn't notice my discomfort.

'Lizzie! Where have you been?'

'Nowhere special, Ma. Probably a waste of my time, I'm afraid.'

She shook her head, assuming I had spent my evening with poor customers.

'Ach. You waste your time too often on bad pennies, Lizzie. You should look to Lucy for advice...'

'Maybe,' I cut in before the customary lecture began. She had forgotten the coins I had dropped in her strong box only hours before and settled, instead, into the familiar whine. 'Have you opened the gin, Ma? I could do with something before I retire upstairs.'

I stayed away from gin, as a rule, but something was bothering me about her behaviour. I needed to talk, and Ma seemed in an expansive mood.

She lurched back into the parlour and I followed, determined to have only one small glass. Ma poured me a large glass and helped herself to another with an unsteady hand. I wondered how many she'd had.

'You all right, Ma?' I asked casually as I sipped my drink. The bitter taste stung my tongue. 'You seem a bit out of sorts.'

She rubbed her fingers into her temples; strands of grey hair worked themselves loose from where they had been pinned.

'Oh, I don't know. It's having that runner about. I'm still worried that we'll be closed down. And I'm fretting about Sydney, about getting a new doorman, about where Sydney has gone and why he might have left us.'

'How long before you abandon hope of him returning and find a new man?'

She sighed heavily, knocking back the evil liquid. 'I'll have to look soon. I can't have the door left unguarded at night. Most of our neighbours are locking up earlier, not that locks will keep out Swann's men, from what's said of them. You know how dangerous it could be for us without a man at the door.'

A house full of women, visited by men high on drink and lust. It was always potentially very dangerous. I was surprised she hadn't found a replacement already. Instead, along with Meg, she had become our doorkeeper, knocked out on gin and weak on her feet, rather than the lady of the house, exuding welcome and the promise of pleasure. The strain was getting to her. We sorely missed Sydney's solid male presence.

Still, the descent into drink was unusual. A hard-headed business woman like Ma should have been out scouring London for a doorman, not sliding into ruin before our eyes.

'Are you sure it's just Sydney, Ma? Nothing else bothering you? You seem so out of sorts.'

Her hands went back to her eyes. She was pressing hard at the sockets now, as if trying to shut out some darker problem. I waited. Eventually she removed her fingers; her eyes were red and sore.

She shook her head. The voice, when it came, was barely a whisper.

'That man, George Reed.'

I looked as encouraging as I could and poured her more gin.

'Mr Reed?'

'He was a very evil man.'

Oh, dear God. She had killed him. I had no idea how or why but something in my bowels told me she had killed him, and this was a gin-addled confession. I held my breath, not sure how to handle whatever came next. I necked a gulp of gin and felt it burn my throat.

'He's dead, Ma.' My voice rasped.

'He's evil, I tell you. Even beyond the grave he's taunting me.'

What was she talking about?

'Taunting you? How?'

'The bastard had some information about my past, Lizzie. It was a long time ago. Years ago. When I was young and living in Paris. There were some...

indiscretions. Some things I would rather no one knew about, I mean.'

I wondered what sort of indiscretions might embarrass a bawd. Enough to make her language coarsen, at least. This, like the gin, was a sign of her distress.

'He started to send me letters.'

'Ah.'

'Blackmail. Like he did with Sydney, although with me he had real stories and not speculation. Stories that might hurt me – and others.' She rubbed her face again, pinching her cheeks. This had really troubled her. No wonder she had been so upset to find him at the party that night. No wonder she had been so angry with me.

'He's dead, Ma,' I repeated. 'He can't hurt you now.'

She looked at me with bloodshot eyes.

'You don't understand, Lizzie. I thought it was all over when he was killed.' She groaned. 'I vowed I would shake the hand of the man who strangled him. He deserved nothing less as far as I could see. But then it all started again.'

'What do you mean?'

'A couple of days ago. I had a note pushed through the door. Sydney brought it up to me – before he disappeared. It was from George Reed.'

'It can't have been. He's dead, very dead. I saw him myself.'

'I tell you, it was the same handwriting. Same comments. Same request for money. And another one since then.'

It made sense now: she hadn't found a new doorman because she was looking out for whoever was delivering the letters. There was no loyalty to Sydney. She was watching the street all day, every day. It wasn't just the gin that caused her red eyes.

'Have you paid him money?'

She nodded.

'Where did you take it? How did you pay?'

She started to pick at a fingernail, worrying a piece of skin around the edge.

'I had to take it in a plain packet to a bath house near Covent Garden. The man at the reception received it and I had to tell him it was for a Mr Beech.'

The gin hit the back of my throat and I coughed wildly until I had thumped my chest for a moment.

I guessed that the man at the desk would be taking a cut for his trouble. It would be worth making a trip to the baths and engaging in flirtatious conversation with him to find out more about Mr Beech. Something about her comments bothered me, even as my mind was racing with this new line of thought.

'Do you know this Mr Beech, Ma? Is it someone you knew in Paris?'

She shook her head, surprised. 'No. I've no idea who he is.'

'You're expecting more of these requests, aren't you?'

She sighed heavily and ran a hand through her hair. It looked like a bird's nest once she'd finished. This was not the Mrs Farley I knew.

'This person, Mr Reed, or Beech, or whoever he is, has intimated that he knows enough about me to ruin this business. I could be finished, Lizzie, if I don't pay up. And you girls will be looking for a new home too. I have to get more money together before the next letter arrives.'

Amelia. This was why she had decided to sell her off. She had sold Amelia's virginity to the highest bidder, because she needed the cash. And I, treacherous jade that I am, was now planning to steal Amelia away to a safe place. Ma would be out of pocket and without the means to pay her blackmailer. If she discovered my plot, she would be so far beyond furious that I would never work again. If she left me alive, that is.

I thought about my retirement fund, hidden away in my room.

'I'll do what I can to help you, Ma. If another letter appears.'

I am too soft for my own good. Or guilt-ridden.

She patted my hand.

'You're a good girl, Lizzie. Just keep smiling that smile of yours at the rich gentlemen and we'll be just fine.'

I laid my hand over hers. She was a tough old bird, but something about the letters had rattled her. Someone – and someone other than George Reed – knew something about her past that she would rather keep hidden. Had it been enough to make her kill Mr Reed?

Chapter Thirty-Five

I had managed to bring Sallie into the house without anyone noticing; now I was going to get Amelia out of it. It had to be done carefully, but at least I wasn't dealing with a drunk this time. Amelia could cry noisily enough, but she would appreciate the need for quiet, and she wouldn't be shouting to the world that she was my sister. It was still dark when I dressed, listening hard to the creaks of the house and straining to hear whether anyone was awake. Mrs Farley liked to rise early to go to the market – a somewhat eccentric trait that she had brought back from Paris – but she had been downing gin and I gambled on her staying in bed with a headache. Sarah, I hoped, would also be in bed. Meg, flushed with her new importance, was unlikely to rise early because Sydney never did. None of the girls would be up before dawn; Lucy wouldn't emerge before noon.

As quietly as possible I stole up to Amelia's room and tapped gently on the door.

Amelia had not been to bed. She was dressed and sat gazing forlornly out of the window. Her face was thin and pale. She wasn't eating much, by the look of it, although whether it was Tommy's absence or the reality of the life stretching before her that caused the lack of appetite, I didn't know.

Whichever it was, the man paying Ma for her supposed virginity would surely not be impressed by such a bag of bones, but even with her cheek bones starting to protrude and dark circles around her eyes, she was still extremely pretty.

'Gather your belongings, Amelia, we're going to leave,' I kept my voice quiet but firm.

The wide eyes grew even bigger.

'Leaving?'

'Yes. But we need to go immediately. Do you have a bag? Many clothes to carry?'

She continued to stare at me, not understanding.

I began hunting around the room for clothes and trinkets, throwing them into a large shawl on the bed while I hissed at her. 'Do you want some disgusting old man pressing his attentions on you this evening, or will you hurry up and help me?'

At that she sprang away from the window and put on her shoes.

'I don't need any more, Lizzie. If we're leaving, then I can leave now.'

I tugged the ends of the shawl together into a bundle and we slid as quietly as we could down the stairs. There was no one in the hall, but the door was locked and bolted; impossible to open without Ma's keys. There was nothing for it, but to steal through the kitchen to the back. Meg and Sarah slept in a small room, to the side of the kitchen. The door was pulled to, but not closed, so I touched a finger to my lips in warning to Amelia. She nodded understanding and we padded as softly as we could to the door. The key was still in the lock but turned without a sound as I held my breath. The hinge, which needed rubbing with grease, gave a low squeak, and I stood, frozen, waiting for the servants' door to be flung open.

No one stirred. It is good to know that the back door of our house is so diligently guarded.

I found myself wishing that Davenport was with us again, as we came to the head of the passage. This time, though, it was nearing dawn and although it was dark, I could make out a patch of grey ahead of us in the blackness. Nevertheless, Amelia made a small sound of distress as I motioned to her that we needed to go through it.

'It's all right,' I whispered. 'I'm sure we're quite safe. I've done this before.'

Once before, and with a man carrying a knife, but she didn't need to know the detail. I took a deep breath, grabbed her hand, and led her, as fearlessly as I could manage towards the dim light ahead. I was very relieved, and almost giddy with my own achievement when we stepped into the street, familiar houses ahead of us.

I hurried her along. The street was nearly empty of people, which meant that we might be easily noticed by anyone looking out of the window. I glanced back once or twice, but we quickly turned a corner along Knaves Acre and were out of view. Only then did I slow the pace a little.

'Where are we going?' She noticed that I had relaxed.

'I'm taking you to Mrs Groves. She's a good woman who wants a lodger. It's not another bawdy house,' I said quickly, seeing the look on her face. 'Mr and Mrs Groves had that Mr Reed as their lodger – until he was killed. I've met them. She's quiet, a bit of a mouse, but intelligent. He's a fat pig, but he won't trouble you.'

She nodded, her head drooping a little.

'How am I to pay them?' she said.

I shrugged.

'Don't worry too much. I've come to an arrangement with Mrs Groves. I'll make sure you're not put out on the streets.'

She was astonished.

'You're paying the rent? Why would you do that for me?'

I trudged along the street, still with her bundle over my shoulder. It was hard to explain. Not without telling her about my own life. Not without telling her about Sallie, and she didn't need to know about Sallie. Instead, I said, simply,

'The life we lead in Berwick Street — it's not for everyone. It's not for you.'

We walked for a while without speaking until we came nearer to Golden Square and to the Groves' house.

She looked up at the windows with apprehension.

'Come on,' I said. 'You'll be safe here. Far enough away from Berwick Street to escape Mrs Farley, at least.'

'Will Tommy be able to visit me here?'

I squeezed her hand. If he ever shows up again, she meant.

'Maybe not for now. Best be as respectable as you can.'

She turned and looked me in the eyes, her own blue saucers beginning to fill with tears.

'Lizzie, I don't know how I'll ever repay you. This is such a kindness.'

'Oh, don't be silly,' I said. 'It's no trouble. Just pray that Tommy finds work soon and returns to make you an honest wife.'

'I will,' she said with passion. 'And when I am married, I will make it my business to pay you back every penny we owe. No, don't shake your head, Lizzie. I mean it.'

'Very well. I'll agree to that.' I grinned and put out a hand. She shook it. It would be wonderful if my money returned, but I wasn't pinning my hopes on seeing it again.

Susan Groves opened the door. She was up early and ready to meet us, as we had arranged. Her dress was neat, unfussy.

'You must be Amelia,' she said, her dainty face greeting us from under a plain white cap. 'I've heard all about you from Miss Hardwicke. You are very welcome here. Please, come in.'

I watched Amelia's shoulders loosen as she stepped across the threshold and into the tender embrace of Susan Groves. I followed her with the bundle and, after making sure that we were not observed by anyone in the street, found myself once again in the Groves' parlour.

Mr Groves was there, lounging in a chair with his feet on a stool. He wasn't long out of his bed, but unlike his wife, he had made little attempt to make himself tidy, although I imagined he would be leaving for work soon. He had no wig and was in need of a shave. He was puffing on a pipe; the sweet scent of tobacco almost masking his own unwashed odour. Susan Groves swept Amelia quickly upstairs to her room, after the briefest of introductions, leaving me to attempt polite conversation.

'Where's your runner friend, then?' Mr Groves said with a grunt. 'Any news of who killed my lodger?'

'No.' I wasn't going to tell him about Mr Winchcombe.

'Ha!' He was almost gleeful. 'These runners, they think they're so clever. Waste of money, I always say.'

This was obviously one of his pet subjects for conversation. I imagined he had bent the ears of many in the local taverns with his views.

'Have you formed any opinion as to who killed your lodger, Mr Groves?'

He scowled at me.

'What's it to do with me?'

'Well, where the runners may have failed to notice something, you, surely, would see it and note it as important. I imagine that very little gets past you.'

He raised himself up on the arms of the chair, fingers like sausages. He responded to the flattery, as I knew he would. I am good at flattering men.

'Well now, as it happens, I might have had a thought.' He paused, presumably for dramatic effect. He would have shared this thought several times over the beer, too. 'I think he was killed by one of his servants. Must have followed him here to London.'

I tried not to laugh at his pompous air.

'That's certainly an avenue of thinking that Mr Davenport has not explored.'

'No, well he won't, will he? Doesn't have the information like I do.' He smiled a lazy smile, sank back into his seat, and tapped his greasy nose.

'What information?'

'From Mr Reed himself, of course. The first day he was here, Susan was fussing with the maid, trying to get her to read her letters. Susan thinks that it will be good for the girl if she can read; then she can be sent out to buy food without forgetting things.'

I was struggling to see what this had to do with Reed.

'He said to me that no good came of teaching servants to read. Servants who had too much learning got above themselves, so much as to think they ought to take the master's place.'

'That sounds like the sort of thing any sensible man with traditional beliefs would say,' I said. Men like that always held that women and servants should remain illiterate. I disagreed with such sentiment, being a literate woman.

'Ah, but then he told me that some servants became so full of themselves, just because they had some letters, that they killed their masters.'

He grinned, triumphant at this splendid piece of information. He no longer possessed all his teeth.

I shook my head in amazement.

'Well, Mr Groves. That is news indeed. I will be sure to pass it on to Mr Davenport when I next cross his path.'

He grunted again. 'You and that runner think you're so clever. I'm the one with the information; the sort of stuff that could make me money, if I chose it.'

It sounded as though he had access to Reed's blackmail letters, or at least had sight of them.

'What stuff?'

His toothless smile returned, but he shook his head. If he knew anything about the letters, he wasn't going to share it.

Susan came skipping in.

'Amelia is settled,' she said. 'I'll make sure that she is cared for.'

'She needs feeding. I think she's been starving herself.'

She nodded. 'I'll do my best.'

'You make sure the rent is paid as well, Susan,' her husband bellowed from the chair. 'This is not charity.'

I reached into my pocket and pulled out a small bag of money and put it into Susan's hands.

'That should do for a while,' I said. 'You know where to find me if you need more.'

I knew I could rely on Susan's discretion. Mr Groves, although less likely to be discreet, would not haul his fat carcass towards Berwick Street and his tavern of choice would, undoubtedly, be the one he could stagger to across the road, rather than any I visited. Still, I was anxious that Mrs Farley knew nothing about this. As I thought about Ma, I realised that I needed to return home.

I shook hands with Mrs Groves and bade a polite goodbye to the slumped figure of her husband before making my way back to Berwick Street as fast as I could.

Chapter Thirty-Six

I managed, by some miracle, to retrace my steps without incident. The back door was still open; Meg and Sarah were up and about, but neither of them was in the kitchen. No one saw me climb the stairs, I was certain of it. Even so, my heart was pounding as I shut the door of my room and listened for voices.

I removed my outer clothes, to make sure that I looked as though I had been in my room and then, to be even more cunning, untied my hair and got into bed.

I heard a shuffling, thumping sound on the landing, and then a sharp rap at my door.

'Just a minute, Meg,' I called, trying to keep the tremble from my voice. I arranged myself carefully. 'Come in.'

Meg looked at me, I thought, with an odd expression. Or maybe I was just feeling guilty.

'Mr Stanford is here with Mr Herring. Apparently, it's urgent.'

It was early in the day for them.

'Tell them I'll be down presently. They can wait in the best room.' I had a sudden thought. 'And tell Mrs Farley when you see her that my head is sore after last night.'

Her eyebrows rose.

'Gin,' I lied. 'Remind me not to touch it ever again.'

She grinned. 'It wasn't that stuff she keeps in the lower cupboard, was it? Looks lethal to me.'

I rubbed my head. 'It is if you're not used to it.'

She scuttled away down the stairs and I imagined her chuckling to Ma about my inability to deal with gin. Such weakness would amuse them, but at least they wouldn't suspect me when Amelia's flight was discovered. I scrambled out of bed, dressed my hair and made my way downstairs, where I found John Herring sprawled in a seat and Charles Stanford pacing about, waving his hat in his hand, agitated.

'Lizzie, you'll never guess what's happened.'

'What? What is it?'

'Winchcombe's been carted off to the magistrate. Turns out our friend was working for the Swann gang.'

I slapped a hand to my brow and groaned. 'Charles, I am so sorry — I did know, and I was supposed to tell you. Poor Mr Winchcombe wants you to help him.'

'All this time,' said Herring in a weak voice from the chair, 'we never knew.' He shook his head with exaggerated sadness. 'The associate of a highwayman, no less.'

'What are you going to do?' I asked.

'Do?' said Herring, raising himself up a little to look at me. 'Are we supposed to do something? I've not had a felon for a friend before.'

'Well, shouldn't you go to him, perhaps? See if there's anything to be done to help him.'

Herring's face suggested that he would rather not; that commenting on a friend's misfortune was one thing, but that assisting any friend in trouble was a terrible chore and best avoided. I turned to Charles. 'I think that's what he would want.'

Charles weighed up the situation with more sympathy. 'Come on, Herring, don't you want to see inside the gaol? Might be your only opportunity, unless you start keeping company with robbers like dear old Josh.'

Herring stirred himself at that, his interest piqued, at least, if not his compassion.

'I wouldn't mind joining you, if you can bear my company,' I said. 'The last time I saw Mr Winchcombe, he looked like he hadn't eaten or slept in a while. I'll bring some food and wine if you'll wait.' And I needed to speak to Davenport, to tell him about Mr Beech.

Charles' arms were around my waist in an instant.

'Such a caring creature you are. I hope that's the only comfort you'll be offering our friend.' He began to cover my neck in fierce kisses, to remind me that he, not being locked in a cell, was ready for my comfort at any moment. I pushed him away and wriggled free, laughing.

'You think an unwashed man in a piss-stinking cell would be attractive? I don't think he has gold enough to tempt me, thank you, sir.'

I left the two of them to call a carriage, while I loaded a basket with bread and cheese from the kitchen and found my hat and cloak. Within very few minutes we were clattering over the cobbles to Bow Street.

—

The magistrate's house stood among the taverns and brothels at the far end of Covent Garden. It was an impressive building. It looked much like any other of the fine houses in the area, save for the courthouse next to the front door, the iron grille at the window of a locked cell, and the thick-set constable standing outside it. When

Henry Fielding had become the magistrate, he had made the astonishing suggestion that people might report crimes to him and his associates at Bow Street, and, even more astonishingly, they had. In a matter of years, his small band of men, a rag-tag band of constables, thief-takers, clerks and others, had suppressed several ruthless gangs of robbers and murderers. Henry had died, exhausted by his efforts to rid the streets of London of the horrors of crime, and his brother John had taken his place as magistrate. He was not as well-known as his literary brother, but he was much less of an old rake. Instead, Mr John Fielding had set about cleaning the streets with a more meticulous strategy: he was not only interested in the bravado of gangs and the highwaymen, but in the low-level activity of petty criminals and street girls. He was blind — the result of an accident in his youth — but his sense of hearing was legendary. It was said that he could identify thousands of people just from hearing their voices, and that once he had heard you speak in his court, he would never forget you. I sincerely hoped he would never have the opportunity to hear my voice in such a setting.

My companions had no such reason to fear the magistrate. Charles swung himself out of the carriage with all the nonchalance of a man who was visiting his tailor, or about to enjoy an evening at the theatre. Mr Herring was similarly unperturbed. I, on the other hand, was doing my best to hide my anxiety by tugging at my sleeves and straightening my bonnet.

It did not take long for us to establish that Mr Winchcombe was still in the cells. My companions had spent the journey from Berwick Street deciding that they would try to secure his release — by speaking of his family name and his good character. In the courthouse office we found Grimshaw and three other men gathered around a table, covered in documents and rolls of paper. The men appeared unmoved by the petitions, although this may have had something to do with the presumptuous air in which both Charles and Herring addressed them. Mr Winchcombe, we were assured, was going nowhere, regardless of his respected name.

I stood in the doorway with the basket over my arm, watching with growing irritation. Davenport was nowhere to be seen.

'He hasn't given us enough yet,' I heard one of the men say. He was a tall man; leaning over the table he looked like a tree bent by the wind.

Another, much shorter, and almost as thick-necked as Grimshaw said, 'The magistrate wants to know if he also killed George Reed.'

'He didn't kill Mr Reed,' I said – louder than I intended.

They all turned to look at me, just a woman in the corner of the room. The tall man straightened up, impressive in height and in the width of his shoulders.

'Who are you?'

'This is Miss Lizzie Hardwicke,' Grimshaw said, before I could open my mouth. 'Soho harlot.'

His words were supposed to silence me. I ignored him and spoke to the tall man.

'It's all about the letters, you see, not John Swann. Where's Mr Davenport? He would understand.'

'He's not here,' said the man. 'Some business with his wife's family.'

I was taken aback. I hadn't thought of Davenport as a man with family. There was a wife, then, and perhaps children. Strange that he hadn't said. But then, there was no reason for him to mention a wife to the likes of me.

'What letters?' The third man at the table, older than the others, had been examining the papers with his spectacles held to his nose, ignoring the argument about Mr Winchcombe. Now he seemed interested.

'Mr Reed was writing blackmail letters, sir. There were a number of recipients – including Mr Winchcombe and these two gentlemen here – but also some letters are missing.'

Herring swung around at that.

'Missing?'

'The packet Mr Grimshaw found in the yard of the White Horse was not complete.'

Grimshaw reached for a tankard of beer on the table. 'She's right. That's what Will said.' He took a drink, watching me.

'Go on,' the man at the table gestured to me that I should continue.

'Mrs Farley – the woman who is my landlady – she received letters from him too. But she has received further letters since his murder, suggesting that someone might have been interested to make use of the information in the letters. Interested enough to kill for it.'

'I suppose you're now going to tell us who this person is,' said Grimshaw, smirking.

I frowned. 'I did think it was a butcher called John Groves. He lives just off Golden Square. Reed was lodging with him and he said something very odd to me. But really, I think there is someone else, someone we don't know. There's a man called Beech involved.'

'Beech?' Charles said. 'Who is this Beech?'

'I don't know.' All I had was a button.

'Any ideas, Herring?' Charles pressed his friend. 'Have you heard of a Mr Beech at all?'

'No,' said Herring. 'Perhaps someone else who had a letter from that terrible man?'

'No, he's the person collecting the money, whether for himself or someone else, I don't know,' I said.

'I don't know about this Beech,' Herring spoke over me, 'I thought we were interested in Bridgewater. Isn't that what you told me, Stanford?'

Charles shrugged.

Grimshaw took another mouthful of beer and pondered this.

'Tommy Bridgewater? The young man with the skinny little moll at Ma Farley's place? He's got a temper, that one.'

'It was his name Reed called out when we all threw him onto the street,' said Charles. 'Tommy boy, he called him.'

'That's right,' said Herring. 'What's happened to Tommy boy?' He looked over at me, expecting me to know. They all looked at me.

'He's disappeared,' I said.

The older man at the table straightened up.

'Interesting.'

It was certainly confusing. Mr Winchcombe might be involved with Swann's gang, but the letters to Mrs Farley suggested that someone had killed Reed for information, not just money. Blackmail was a lucrative business

– especially if someone had done all the research for you. But I had nothing more to say to these men. None of them would want to hear about Sallie, or the button, or how she had told Bess and Kitty about a beach in Paris. I needed Davenport, but he was engaged on family business.

'Perhaps you should be looking for Tommy Bridge-water, rather than trying to turn our friend into a murderer,' Charles said. 'In the meantime, we will see Mr Winchcombe – make sure that his accommodation is suitable for a gentleman.'

'I have food for him.' I said, gesturing to my basket.

Grimshaw stepped towards me, took the basket from my arm and lifted the cloth.

'I'll make sure he gets it.' He put the basket down on the table. I strode over and put a hand on it.

'I would rather take it myself.' I wanted Mr Winch-combe to enjoy the contents, not Grimshaw.

Charles and Herring left the room, with the tall man leading them. Grimshaw laid a hand over mine.

'No. I said, I'll make sure he gets it,' he repeated in a mean voice, eyes on mine. He leaned on my hand, crushing my bones, just so that I understood.

'Very well.'

He chuckled, pressed harder on my fingers, and stepped nearer. His eyes wandered down to my breasts, with a look I knew all too well. I could smell the beer when he leaned closer and breathed at my ear.

'Perhaps I'll pay you a visit sometime, Miss Lizzie Hardwicke; see if you're as clever on your back as you are on your feet. I like redheads.'

I swallowed back all my usual insults; he was hurting my hand. But, dear God, the thought of having this man in my bed made me want to be violently sick. He released me, and I stood back quickly, unwilling to look him in the eye. I pulled the edges of my cloak tighter about my neck, covering myself as best I could.

'Good day, sir.'

He gave me a nasty smile. I nodded to the other two men and fled the room.

—

Charles had gone from the hall of the courthouse. He and Herring were, no doubt, poking about in the gaol, fussing over Mr Winchcombe and complaining about his treatment to the turnkey and the tall man.

There was a boy by the door, charged with showing people in and out. He couldn't have been more than nine or ten, solemn-faced and smartly dressed. I imagined he saw and understood a lot of what went on, even though he was just a child.

'Where is Mr Davenport today?' I asked him. 'He's a friend of mine and I expected to see him here.'

He narrowed his eyes, deciding whether to favour me with information.

'He's gone away for a day or two, miss. Mrs Priddy says he's out near Twickenham.'

Family business took him away from London, then.

'He is with his wife?'

The boy looked puzzled. 'No, course not. His wife's dead, and his baby. Mrs Priddy said it was a year to the day his wife died; that's why he's gone to see her mother.'

His wife and child dead. I thought I had seen sadness in his eyes; now I knew its cause. The poor man was still grieving and had gone to share that grief with her family.

'He's gone to his mother-in-law? He has a sense of duty.'

The boy looked thoughtful as he stepped from the doorway. 'Mrs Priddy says it's guilt what takes him. He was a medical man, she says, but he couldn't save his wife and boy.'

I assumed Mrs Priddy was a housekeeper or cook. There had to be a woman somewhere, supplying all these men with food and drink.

'And what else does Mrs Priddy say?'

He was suddenly anxious. He knew that he had told me too much. 'I probably shouldn't tell you any more, miss.'

'You won't get into trouble on my account,' I said. 'Mr Davenport has become a new friend to me and I'd like to know if I can help him.' We were out on the street now. Men limping with bandaged legs were not going to persuade me that their pastries were the best, nor would girls with pimpled skin sell me sweetmeats, but the boy might like one. I plucked a penny from my skirt.

'How did a physician end up working at Bow Street, do you suppose?'

He eyed the penny and I watched him wrestle with his conscience and his hunger. Hunger won out.

'Mrs Priddy says he was just about managing without his wife and son. He was finding comfort in his work, knowing that even if he hadn't been able to make them well, he could save others. Then, she says, it was his father's death that turned his heart.'

This was an odd phrase for a child to use. I imagined Mrs Priddy chewing over the situation with the servants in the kitchen, unaware that her exact words were being locked into a nine-year-old memory. The boy would make a good witness.

'What happened to his father?' I let the penny catch the light.

'He was attacked in the street, they say. Knocked over and whacked on the head for sixpence. His heart gave out. After that, Mr Davenport came to us at Bow Street. Mrs Priddy thinks he's looking for the men who did his father in and that Mr Fielding likes having such a clever gentleman in his company.'

'And what do you think?'

He wrinkled his face, giving my question some consideration. I imagined his opinion was rarely sought.

'He always says good morning to me, miss. I like that.'

I gave him the penny. 'I think you're right to like it. But I won't tell anyone what you said. Thank you for leaving your post and escorting me.'

He shoved the penny into his coat, gave a swift bow and then ran away across the street.

I stood for a moment, watching the swell of people at the market. I remembered the way that Davenport had dealt with Sallie's body at the side of the river; calmly and methodically, like a doctor examining a patient. He had been frustrated too, because he was unable to help. Now I understood why.

Chapter Thirty-Seven

I took a carriage home. I wasn't looking forward to returning. Once Ma discovered her little bird had flown and her opportunity to pay the latest blackmail letter had gone, she would either hit the gin or hit out at the rest of us. Probably both.

With a sigh, I pushed open the door.

Mrs Farley was boxing someone's ears. That someone, shrieking murder, was Sydney.

I sprang to defend him, pulling her away as best I could. She was a strong woman and her hands continued to rain blows on his head even as I dragged her off him. He leapt into his room like a frightened stag and bolted the door, screaming.

Ma was also still screeching and ran to the door, pounding it with her hands, as if, unable to clatter Sydney, she would make do with the wood.

'Ma!' I tugged her arms. 'Ma! For pity's sake, calm down!'

I was yelling now as well. Faces appeared over the bannister rail as Emily and Polly peeped down to see what the commotion was about.

'He's not going to come out, Ma. Leave him for a while. Come away.' I pulled her sleeve again and she gave up, collapsing into great sobs. I could smell the sour odour of gin on her breath. Sydney, behind his door, was crying quietly and soothing himself.

'Why? Why has he come back to us, Lizzie?'

Ma had fallen into a chair, her head in her hands.

'You didn't ask him that before you started beating him?'

Her red eyes glared up at me.

'Foolish girl! Of course I asked him! He said that he came back because this is his home. What does he mean by that? His letter said that he was leaving us.'

'And then you started beating him?'

'Well, he made me so angry. Such a silly thing to say. And then he was screaming at me that this was his home and asking why I was shouting.'

'You still have his letter in your pocket?'

Her hand rustled through her skirts and drew out the crumpled note.

I patted her on the shoulder and wandered into the hallway.

'Meg,' I called out. 'Can you come and make Mrs Farley some tea? And find her something good to eat? I think she needs a bit of care.'

Meg came to the hall, wide-eyed with anxiety. Polly and Emily were still on the stairs.

'She won't bite you. She just needs something to calm her down. Nothing that comes from a bottle.'

'What about you?' Polly asked from behind the safety of the rail.

I nodded toward the locked door.

'I'm going to talk to Sydney. Without boxing his ears.'

'Good luck.'

'I'm not sure who I'd rather deal with, Sydney or Ma.' I grinned at her as she went into the parlour. I waited for a moment and listened for the sounds of Meg and Polly beginning to offer comfort and then stole to Sydney's room and tapped on the door.

'It's me, Lizzie. I promise not to hurt you if you let me in.'

There was silence. The sobbing had stopped.

'Sydney, I'm not going to hit you.'

Still there was no response.

'Mrs Farley is in the parlour and has calmed down. Just let me in, please. I need to talk to you.'

The key was turned, and the door opened a fraction. Sydney's fearful eye met mine.

'It is safe?'

'Let me in, please. We need to talk.'

He opened the door and, before he could change his mind, I pushed past him.

Despite my time at Mrs Farley's, I had never had cause to enter his room before. It was small, but extremely tidy and even elegant in its decoration; the room of a fine gentleman, rather than the doorman at a brothel. The room was on the front of the house, near enough to the main door that he could be there as soon as anyone knocked, but it was a private space. His space.

There was a small table in the corner, upon which sat a few books, some paper, and a pen. The paper was covered with dots and splodges of ink; this was at odds with the good order of everything else in the room.

Sydney retreated to the end of his bed and put his head in his hands.

'Why? Why does she attack me, Miss Lizzie? I do not understand her. What have I done to deserve such treatment?'

I gave him the crumpled paper from my hand.

'Maybe it has something to do with the note you left her. Where did you go? Where have you been these past days?'

He looked up, sniffed and unfolded the paper. He read it and then looked up at me with puzzlement in his eyes.

'What is wrong with my note?'

I grabbed it from him and read it aloud. 'Madame Farley, I am very sorry to disappoint you, but I need to be somewhere else. I thank you for your understanding. Sydney.'

He shook his head.

'I thought that she would appreciate a letter.'

'She believed that you had left for good.'

'Why would she think that? I have not said so in my writing, have I? I have been away before.'

'"I need to be somewhere else", you said. "I am sorry to disappoint you". Why would you say that if you were not leaving us? When you've never written a note to her before?'

He was silent for a moment.

'Miss Lizzie, you must understand, I have never written to anyone before. Did I get it wrong?' His eyes were full of shame.

Suddenly I saw it. The childish handwriting, the ink-splattered paper, the small stack of novels on his table, the shameful face. Sydney, the elegant Frenchman who kept us all on our toes, was learning to read and write. His letter to Mrs Farley was him showing off a new-found skill.

I started to laugh.

'Miss Lizzie, what is so funny?'

'Oh Sydney, you've no idea the trouble this letter has put us to.'

'Am I in trouble?' The worry was etched on his face.

'No, no, not at all. It only needs a little explanation to Mrs Farley and all will be right with the world again.'

I touched his arm.

'Did you tell anyone that you were learning to write?'

He shook his head.

'No, I did not. It seemed that writing was a talent that I should have mastered as a child. I hid my inadequacy from everyone.'

'Who has been teaching you?'

His eyes lowered.

'Mr Slim. Mr Slim has been teaching me.'

I sucked my teeth. 'I won't ask how you've been paying him.' Thomas Slim was well-known around our part of London for his attraction to dark-skinned young men.

'He has been very generous with his time.'

'I imagine you've been generous with yours, Sydney. Is this where you've been? At Mr Slim's house?'

He shrugged. 'Mostly, I have been there, yes.' He was not going to tell me anything more.

Ma greeted the news with grumbling.

'I don't need a doorman with his nose in a book. I need one who will be handy with his fists.'

'He'll always be our Sydney,' I said, 'his size is enough to deter intruders, but perhaps his conversation will be more learned.'

'He's already pompous,' said Meg, cross that Sydney was back in the stool she had recently occupied. 'He's

272

forever lording over the rest of us. Reading and writing will just make him even more superior.'

'Then maybe it's time you learned your letters, Meg,' I said, 'so you can read the same books and argue back at him.'

She snorted.

'I've no time for books, miss, and I can argue with Sydney whenever I want. I don't need books to do it.'

There was no disputing that.

'Well, at least it means that he's back with us, and you don't have to find a new doorman, Ma. Next time he leaves us, he'll write a note to you without causing such grief.'

'Perhaps, next time, he might ask permission first,' she frowned. 'Or, at the least, tell me when he is going to return.'

She was pleased that he was back, but she wasn't one to show her gratitude – to Sydney or to me.

Chapter Thirty-Eight

Meg took the tray from the table and left us.

Ma had calmed down considerably, but she was still picking the edge of her sleeve. I guessed why she was anxious, but the guilty feeling in my gut meant I didn't dare comment.

She reached across the table and clutched at my arm. 'Have you had any thoughts about those dreadful letters?'

'No, Ma, I'm sorry. I've been trying to help poor Mr Winchcombe.'

'Mr Winchcombe? What's he got to do with this?'

I gave her a brief account of all that had befallen Mr Winchcombe.

'I can't see how that helps my situation.'

'I'm doing my best, Ma.'

'You are not.' Her eyes squinted at me. 'You've been idling your time away with Mr Stanford and Mr Herring instead of earning more money. Unless they paid you to accompany them to Bow Street.'

I was silent.

'And another thing,' she began to bite a nail, 'Amelia's disappeared.'

'Disappeared?' I feigned surprise as best I could.

'She's gone. Left the house. She's taken most of her clothes. I don't know where she's gone – or how she thinks she'll manage on the streets with no money – but she's taken scared and run away.'

I shrugged. 'I suppose you can hardly blame her. It's not a life that anyone wants, is it? And knowing what was about to happen probably made it worse.'

'But Lizzie!' She sounded exasperated. 'Think of the money I'm losing! Never mind the silly little chit: I've got to find more money.'

She fiddled with her rings.

This blackmailer had really got under her skin. She might have been an experienced bawd, but until now she had always been kind-hearted. She had never pressured us for money. Suddenly, she was grasping, and only inter-ested in her own problems.

'Have you been told to make another payment?' I asked.

She nodded. 'Tomorrow. It's to go to the bath house again for Mr Beech.'

This was the chance I needed.

'I'll take the money for you, Ma. I'll have a look around the bath house and ask a few discreet questions. Flutter my eyelashes, that sort of thing.' I grinned.

'Well that would be a very good plan, Lizzie, were it not for one thing: I don't have enough money yet.' Her mouth hardened. 'This was why Amelia was so important. I was going to make a tidy sum from her this evening: enough to pay up and have a little left over for myself.'

Greedy old witch. Still, I could see she was worried.

'How far short are you? Can we help out, do you think?'

She sat back, considering me carefully. Then a thin smile grew on her lips.

'The gentleman calling for Amelia is an older man,' she said slowly. 'Perhaps not so clear-sighted. I wonder whether we can't persuade him that you aren't his little sweetmeat.'

I laughed.

'Don't be ridiculous, Ma. I haven't been a maid for nearly a year and I'm too old to pretend.'

But she was warming to her idea and looked me up and down becoming more enthusiastic as she spoke.

'You're a good little actress, Lizzie, you'll know well enough how to go about it. You're small enough to look sixteen, and you're still the freshest girl in this establishment. I'm sure that in dim light you can pass.'

I didn't like this idea. I might well be able to act like an innocent, I could even sob as noisily as Amelia, but she was suggesting deception. I thought it a dangerous game.

'How will this man react if he discovers I am a fraud? He's paying for a virgin and he's not getting one.'

She waved a hand to dismiss my concern.

'He's paying me half the sum before he meets her – I mean you – and half once the deed is done. If he has any complaint, he'll make it to me. I can always negotiate the final amount. After all, he's getting one of London's finest girls: he can't be too disappointed.'

She leaned forward and gave me a knowing look.

'I have an ointment. Something to make you seem like a maid again. Tighten you up.'

I laid my forehead on the table and closed my eyes. I had heard of such tricks. She would probably expect me to smear pig's blood on my bedsheet, too.

'And what happens when the blackmailer demands more money?'

'The letter says that he'll not trouble me again. I have no reason to trust him; but he says it's his last demand.'

I doubted that. If he knew he could get his hands on Ma's money, then surely, he would try again. I couldn't be a virgin for ever – no matter how good an actress I might be. She wanted to believe, hope, that all would be well once tonight was over.

I groaned into the tablecloth.

'All right. I'll do it. I know I won't get any money for this, so this is a favour to you, Ma.' I raised my head, briefly. 'But after this: no more favours and no more pretence of virginity.'

Even if I were successful in fooling one old man, I didn't want her getting ideas of doing it again, just because it was lucrative.

'What time will he arrive?'

She stroked my hair. I assumed the sudden tenderness was gratitude.

'He'll be here at five o' clock. I have a lovely white muslin for you to wear. I'll bring it up to your room while you make yourself ready.'

She patted my head again and swung out of the room, humming to herself.

It wouldn't be too bad, I thought. I took men to bed all the time, this one would be no different. I wasn't losing my maidenhood – it was long gone. I shivered. I didn't need to act with this man: I only needed to remember.

Chapter Thirty-Nine

I won't dwell on the details.

It was an unpleasant evening and the gentleman who forced himself upon me was not only old, but brutal and bony. The bruises would appear soon enough.

The combination of my kicks and sobs with Mrs Farley's magic ointment were enough to persuade him that he had been dealt with fairly and he paid her the full balance of the money. A carriage collected him and took him back to the House of Lords.

When he went, I curled up into a ball and thanked God that I had, at least, saved Amelia from him. I prayed that she was warm and safe and that she would never have to face a life like mine – or Sallie's.

Ma was delighted and, in a fit of gratitude, even slipped a couple of coins into my hand as she came up with some cold supper. I wanted her to go away and leave me in peace, but her thoughts had turned from making the money to passing it on to the mysterious Mr Beech. I was to be out at midday with the money in a parcel. I needed an extra pair of eyes. Davenport was the man I needed, but he was away. I wondered whether I could persuade Charles. He wouldn't be interested in helping Ma, but he might be sufficiently intrigued by the possibility of catching a man bound up in Reed's murder.

'I want Charles to come with me.' I eased myself up on to an elbow and picked at the bread on the tray.

'I'll send a servant to his lodgings and ask him to call tomorrow.'

Having settled my plans, she took her leave. I wasn't hungry. After slipping the tray outside my door, I rolled back into bed and fell into a deep sleep.

–

I woke with a start. I had been dreaming about Mr Davenport: an odd dream where I was running down a country lane after him. I was trying to call out, but my mouth was full of buttons. Instead I was in my bed. It was morning and I could hear people on the street going about their business. A single gold button lay next to my hairbrush on the table. I thought of Sallie.

There was a tap on the door. It was Meg.

'Mr Stanford is downstairs.'

I sat up, still tired and sore. 'So early?'

'It's not far off midday, Miss.'

I groaned.

'I've brought you fresh hot water, if you want it,' she said. Meg, I had no doubt, knew what I had done for Ma.

Charles had brought a carriage; it was waiting for us. I grabbed a slab of bread to eat, suddenly hungry now, before we left the house.

'I have my own reason for visiting the bath house, you know,' he said as he helped me into the seat. 'Our blackmailer is widening his circle again, it seems.'

'What do you mean?'

'There was a letter waiting for me when I returned yesterday. No one saw who delivered it. It's full of the same sort of bile that I had from Reed. It's even signed from Reed, even though it can't be from him.'

'May I see it?'

He shrank back into the seat. 'I'd rather not show you, if you don't mind. The words are unpleasant…' He glanced out of the window. 'But it tells me to leave money for a Mr Beech. Herring's had a letter too; he's in quite a state.'

I rested my head on his shoulder. 'I'm sorry that you and Herring are caught up in this again, but I'm glad you're coming with me.'

He squeezed my knee. 'You can thank me in so many ways.' He kissed my neck softly, in the way he knows I like, but any hopes he had of a quick grind as the carriage jogged along were, thankfully, dashed when the driver stopped the horses rather abruptly and yelled: 'This is your stop.' Charles' curse, as he fell off the seat, was almost as loud. He was still muttering as we climbed out.

–

The Queen's bath house was on the corner of St Martin's and Long Acre. I wondered whether it was an establishment that Charles knew, but he said not.

Mrs Farley's money was wrapped in a plain packet, but I held it firmly, even in the carriage. Given what I had done to secure it, it felt like my own.

Charles was less anxious. People who have money don't need to worry about it like those of us who work for a living. He was at ease with life, elegantly dressed in a maroon coat and gloves, and sporting a new wig: a gentleman of fashion.

He was at odds with the surroundings. The Queen's bath house was decidedly not a fashionable place. In fact, it looked rather dreary from the outside and inside it was shabby, even squalid. A heavily-spiced perfume that I couldn't identify lingered in the air, very nearly masking the more unmistakable smells of sweat and lust. In the area that might generously have been called a reception, a thin man draped in a silken gown and wearing a small red turban, perched on a stool behind a desk. He was no more a Turk than I, but he was trying his best to look oriental. He smiled a mouthful of black teeth at us.

'Good afternoon,' he said in a heavily-accented voice. 'Welcome to paradise. What is your pleasure?'

Such an introduction would have caused me to giggle, had it not been for the nature our mission.

'We have many pleasures, I can assure you,' Charles said, taking charge of things, 'but today we wish to leave two packages for collection.'

The man nodded solemnly, as if leaving packages were a regular occurrence, or maybe solemn nodding was part of the act.

'And who is to collect these packages?' He maintained his strangely foreign tone as he relieved us of our burdens.

'Mr Beech,' said Charles.

'Ah yes,' the man nodded again. 'Mr Beech will be here this afternoon. Later, perhaps later...' He pushed an open ledger across the desk and dipped a pen into a filthy pot. 'Sign in here, please.' He handed the pen to Charles, who scribbled as best he could, splattering ink, while grumbling about how useless it was.

'I've got ink on my fingers, now,' he complained.

The Turk's eyes took on an almost dreamy look. 'Now, are you ready to sample our delights?'

I shook my head. The moisture in the air was making my clothes stick to my body. I wasn't going to set foot in this stinking hole, even if Charles was. I tugged him away.

'I think that this lovely lady would rather lift her skirts elsewhere. Perhaps I'll come back another time.' Charles said.

The man shrugged. 'Your loss.' His Turkish was abandoned in favour of a more comfortable London twang.

The snigger I had been holding back emerged as we pushed through the door and landed back on to the street.

'Are you ready to sample our delights?' I intoned the words in the same way as the man in the turban.

Charles laughed. 'I'm always pleased to try your delights, sweetheart, but you were right to leave. I suspect that the only thing I'd sample in there is the clap.'

'And you'd leave grubbier than when you arrived – which is no use in a bath house.'

We stood on the pavement. He looked up and down the street.

'What do we do now?' I asked. 'I suppose we just wait for this Mr Beech to call by?'

He frowned.

'I think we have to do just that. At least the weather's kind.'

It was not unkind. A little chilly, but dry at least.

We stood in silence for a time, each of us peering at people passing by, wondering which of them was Beech.

'I'm not cut out to be a guard,' Charles huffed after only a few minutes had passed. 'This is extremely dull.'

'Oh, I don't know,' I said, trying to make the best of it, 'I'm enjoying watching the people, wondering who they are and what they might be up to.'

He shifted from one foot to the other.

'This is what those runners should be doing: waiting here. Where's that Davenport of yours got to, when we need him?'

I laughed and punched his arm. 'He's not my Davenport, Charles, and it won't hurt us to stand here for a while.'

'We don't even know what we're looking for.'

Charles was right. We had no idea whether Beech was a young man, or an older one.

John Groves' comment returned to me. 'I think he might be a servant; even Mr Reed's servant.'

'Why do you say that?'

'It's what Mr Groves said to me,' I said, 'the butcher who let the room to Reed. He told me that he thought Reed was killed by a disgruntled servant.'

Charles snorted. 'People always think that sort of thing. Servants are always out to murder their masters, aren't they? I'm quite sure mine are.'

'I got the impression that Reed had told him something, a story about a servant.'

'Perhaps this Beech is one of Reed's servants,' said Charles. 'It would make some sense for his servant to be collecting the money, especially if he's taken over from his master. We could go and see Mr Groves and ask him if he knows anything.'

I laughed. 'You fancy yourself as a constable, do you Charles? We spent too long in Bow Street yesterday.'

'Certainly not,' he said, shaking out the lace in his cuffs. 'I don't wish to spend my time grappling with footpads and murderers, thank you.'

For a few minutes, we stood side by side, watching the world pass by, everyone with something to sell.

'You know, I wonder,' he said quietly, 'What if "Beech" isn't even this man's name? What if he's just using the name when he collects his money?' He paused. 'I keep coming back to Tommy Bridgewater. Tommy was the name Reed called out that night. Reed obviously knew him, and to call him "Tommy boy" so gracelessly suggests that there was bad blood between them. I only met him once, but he did have the air of a truculent servant.'

I didn't reply. It didn't seem likely that Tommy was involved, and he was more fiery-tempered than truculent.

'You say he's disappeared?' Charles asked.

I shook my head. 'I've not seen him for some days.' Neither had Amelia.

'What about if this is just about Tommy wanting to get his hands on some money? He found Reed's notes and he's making use of them even now?'

It was possible.

'What about the Paris business, though? Has Tommy been in Paris? I doubt it.'

'We don't know,' he said. 'He might have gone with a former employer. Servants do travel, Lizzie. Where is Tommy now, though? Scribbling notes to other victims? Is he our Mr Beech?'

Perhaps he would turn up at the bath house.

Now that Charles was convinced of his own argument, he would hear no counter from me. He sniffed the air, confident. He had solved the crime and would look forward to sharing this with Mr Davenport.

He nodded over to a coffee house across the road.

'Shall we find some coffee? We can keep an eye on the street from inside.'

I was ready to drink a coffee. The sun had disappeared behind clouds and the thought of a warm drink cheered me.

The coffee house was clean and friendly-looking and mostly empty. I settled into a chair at the window and we ordered two coffees from the keen lad who leapt on us for custom as soon as we sat down. The coffee was poor, but it was warm.

'The turban thought Beech would arrive this afternoon, didn't he?' said Charles, looking out of the window.

It was already well into the afternoon.

Chapter Forty

We sat and watched through the window for what must have been an hour, commenting on the passers-by. We saw men saunter into the Queen's bath house looking hopeful and saunter out again shining with moisture and sated lust. The place did a good trade, of that there was no doubt. From time to time we saw a woman, garishly dressed, on her way into work. I recognised the look. They were outwardly cheerful, brightly painted, laughing with people on the street. But when they moved away their faces took on a familiar care-worn expression and the shoulders slouched a little as they passed inside the door.

More people entered the building than left; it would surely become busier as the day progressed.

We scanned the street for anyone who looked as we expected Beech to look.

I saw a man I recognised. Charles was fiddling with a button on his glove, but I saw him as clear as day.

It was Mr Herring.

'Charles!'

'Hmm?' he looked up, his mind on other matters.

'Look – it's Mr Herring!'

He peered through the window.

'Really? Damn it all, it really is Herring.' He made to bang on the window, but I grabbed his arm.

'No, Charles, wait.'

Herring walked past the door of the Queen's bath house, paused, and then walked back towards it. He hung around the entrance for a moment and then slipped inside.

'What the devil would Herring want in a place like that?' said Charles. 'He can find cleaner and fresher beauties at many other establishments we know.'

'Really? *Many* establishments?'

'Oh, sorry, Lizzie, I didn't mean...'

'...didn't mean to tell me what I already know? Never mind that now. Don't you see? Mr Herring has just gone into the bath house. What if he is Mr Beech?'

'Herring? You think he's Beech? Don't be foolish, Lizzie. It's Bridgewater we want.'

'I'm not being foolish.'

'No, I'm sure you're wrong. Herring's had a letter too, don't you recall? He's bringing money, just like us.'

Charles stood up and dropped some coins on the table.

'I'll go over to the bath house to find him.'

I stood up. The coffee was cold in my cup.

'I'll come with you.'

'No, you stay here and look out for Bridgewater. I'll deal with Herring.'

I had no time to argue, as he sped through the door. I sat down and watched him go into the bath house.

The little serving boy removed the cups and gave the table a wipe with a filthy rag. Charles had left enough money for another cup, so I ordered it and kept an eye on the street. The bitter liquid sharpened my mind. Mr

Herring had certainly lied to Mr Davenport in the tavern. He had lied twice.

He had lied when he said that he had met Reed just before Christmas; Winchcombe had told me that he and Herring had met the man in Paris, which was months earlier, even before he was married. Then Davenport had asked whether he and Mr Reed had exchanged words at the party in Berwick Street and he had said not but that he had recognised him, even with the mask. That too was a lie, I was sure, but what was it that made me know this?

I rubbed my temples and tried to remember the evening for myself. Reed had sat next to me at dinner, and I had been asked to remove him to another room by Ma before all the fuss with Amelia.

Outside, it was becoming busy. Street sellers carried their carts to and fro, powdered women swung their hips as they sauntered along, and people passed the time of day with one another, occasionally obscuring my view of the bath house entrance. A pair of young rakes, weaving their way along the road, already full of wine, nearly collided with an elderly man. He said a few words to them and they moved on, bursting into laughter after a few paces. The old man turned and scolded them, waving his stick, and they slunk away like chastened schoolboys.

I remembered.

That night, I had seen Reed speak to Mr Herring and Mr Winchcombe. He had looked, from a distance, to be awkward in the evening's company. He had moved to speak to them and they had walked away, leaving him standing alone. I had, at the time, assumed that he had embarrassed himself, said something foolish, forcing them to abandon him. But what if he had recognised *them* immediately by their conduct – as Mr Herring said he had recognised Reed by his conduct? What if he had gone to them, not seeking companionship in an unfamiliar setting, but deliberately wanting to unnerve them or threaten, even?

Whichever it was, Mr Herring had certainly conversed with Mr Reed at the party. He had lied.

It was beginning to grow dark. I couldn't make my coffee last any longer; and I didn't need another. There was a pie cart out on the street, and the braziers were being lit. I wrapped my cloak tightly across my shoulders, left the coffee house and bought a mutton pie. The pastry was greasy, but the meat tasted good. I licked the juice from my fingers and scowled at the bath house doorway.

They were still inside. There was only one credible explanation for why that would be. Here I was, wanting to be home and comfortable, rather than standing on a street corner, and Charles was inside warming his hands on some poxed piece of flesh who would be pretending to be a water nymph. What was worse, every now and then, a gentleman would approach me, some furtive, some bold, and ask for my price. I kept shaking them away, insisting that I wasn't looking for business – or that they couldn't afford me – all the while trying not to let anyone resembling Mr Beech pass my attention.

Another hour passed, and the tedium was turning into annoyance. I was waiting no longer; it was beneath my dignity. I marched to the door and stood, quietly raging, at the reception. The man in the red turban raised an eyebrow when I enquired after Mr Stanford and Mr Herring. He looked at a surprisingly neat list of the day's visitors, marred only by a few splodges and freckles of ink, and moved his finger down the names. He tapped the paper.

'Here we are, Mr Stanford – who arrived earlier, and Mr Herring. They used their own names.'

Of course, not everyone would.

I sighed, exasperated.

'And where can I find them, please? Where do I go?'

He looked at me, confused.

'I have no idea. You would know that, perhaps?'

The man was an idiot.

'How could I possibly know? I've never been here. Where are they now, which room? Where do I go?'

I saw the comprehension in his eyes. He began nodding. I nodded back, to coax him into revealing their whereabouts in this grimy establishment.

He looked back down at the list and tapped it once more where there were more ink splatters.

'See here. This tells me that they both left two hours ago.'

'Left?' How was that possible? I hadn't taken my eye off the entrance for a moment. 'They have not left this place at all. I have been watching the door for more than two hours.'

That must have sounded rather odd. He started to cackle. The cackle turned into a belly laugh and in a matter of seconds he was wiping tears from his eyes while I stood, almost blind with fury.

'What's so funny?' I stamped my foot.

'Ah, just that you have been waiting all this time by the door for your lover and his friend and they left by the other door!'

'What?'

'We have a door at the back. Come, come in and I'll show you.' He was still laughing.

I followed him through a dimly lit passage way towards a dank room. I could hear splashes and giggles. From large wooden bath tubs, naked men and women watched us, briefly interrupting their pleasures among the rose petals to wonder at a fully clothed woman striding angrily behind the doorman. At the far end of the room, another passageway, leading back to another chamber, where gentlemen customers had left their clothes in neat piles.

Another passage took us out of there and on to the street. They had left from this door and forgotten all about me. For all I knew, Charles, the heartless swine, had taken a woman from here back to his lodgings. She would be pink and warm, not cold and angry, like me.

I nodded politely to the man and thanked him for his time.

'Not at all,' he said. 'It has been very entertaining.'

I ground my teeth. I was about to leave when something occurred to me.

'Has Mr Beech been here this afternoon?'

He laughed again, his rotten stumps of teeth mocking me, and carried on chuckling to himself as he went back inside. I stood, like a fool, on the street, knowing that I had failed. There was nothing to do but walk home.

Chapter Forty-One

They were lighting braziers outside the taverns along the streets. I was in dire need of good food, warmth and cheering company at the end of what had been a dismal and fruitless day. I had left Mrs Farley's money – much of it earned by me – in the hands of a fake Turk with bad teeth and a greasy turban. I hadn't found Mr Beech. I had drunk too much coffee and I was shaking; whether from the coffee, the chilly breeze or my fury at a wasted day, I couldn't tell. I made my way to the White Horse. To rid myself of the filthy temper, I began to imagine that I could smell Anne Bardwell's mutton stew – and Harry Bardwell's tobacco as he embraced me like a long-lost cousin – when I saw something to make me stop abruptly. I pressed my back against a wall, trying to be invisible as I spied.

Ahead of me stood Tommy Bridgewater. I was certain it was him. The collar of his coat was turned up, but his head was bare. His face was serious, dimly lit by the light from a window. He was rubbing the back of his neck with one hand, his hat held in the other. There was another man with him, his back towards me, who looked to be explaining something in detail. He jabbed a finger at Tommy, as if to make a point. Tommy stiffened and then nodded. The other man was smaller, older, I thought, given that he had a slight stoop. I couldn't see much of him except an outline of his shape, black against the shadows of the street. He swept past Tommy, who turned and trailed after him.

I decided to follow.

They turned left, taking me further away from the White Horse, right and then left again down a narrow passageway. It was so deserted that I could almost hear my own heart thumping. We were behind a row of houses in a part of town that I wouldn't choose to walk in, and there was no one who would hear me, or care, if I screamed. Screams were probably common around here. The walls of the passage were high and black and the ground underfoot squelched in a rank and sordid way; even if I had light, I wouldn't want to see what I was walking in. I pulled my cloak to my nose, looking ahead to where the two men had gone, but all the time wanting to turn and run. This was the sort of passage where a woman like me could meet her end. I had no knife, no protection.

A small light bobbed about in the gloom. A third man had joined from the other end of the passage. The pale glow of a lamp lit their heads. They had stopped underneath a window ledge and I saw Tommy pointing up at it. He took the lamp from the other man while the stooping man bent down a little, making a step with his hands. The newcomer, relieved of his lantern, levered himself up to the window and scrambled inside.

They were robbing a house. Tommy Bridgewater was, indeed, a thief. Never mind Joshua Winchcombe, it was Tommy who was involved with Swann's men. Oh God, poor Amelia. This would kill her.

I stepped back and kicked something over. It sounded like a bottle; I couldn't see in the dark. It clinked against a wall; a loud sound in a near-silent place. The lamp ahead was immediately extinguished. I ran back, flailing over the slippery ground in my insubstantial shoes, until I left the passage, turned into a street, and then another, not knowing where I was heading. I stopped running only when I reached a pavement that was full of people and brightly lit with fires.

I glanced behind me, still breathing hard. No one was following me. My shoes were in tatters. And covered in shit.

It was only when I looked up that the flood of relief overwhelmed me. Compton Street. The White Horse was just up ahead. I laughed aloud, drawing a few glances from passers-by, then staggered slowly and heaved myself against the tavern door, nearly falling into the arms of Harry Bardwell who, just as I had imagined, reeked of tobacco.

'Lizzie! My favourite lady of the night!'

'Mr Bardwell!' I gasped as I clung to him. His expression changed immediately, and he helped me to a table near the fire.

'What's happened to you, girl? You been attacked?' Harry was solidly protective of his regulars.

I shook my head.

'I'm fine. Not injured in any way. Well, except for my shoes.'

I pointed to the foul items on my feet. Harry recoiled slightly.

'Holy Mary, where have you been? Wading in the Thames?'

I shrugged. I might as well have been, given the state of them.

'Food, Harry. I need food. Lots of it. And strong beer, please.'

He sent a boy over quickly with a thick stew and bread and I ate, barely looking up.

The White Horse grew busier as the evening drew on, but I wasn't looking for work and flicked away a few culls who tried to approach me. The beer had calmed me a little and, with food in my belly I began to feel nearly myself once more and eased back into my seat, watching people.

There was a musician in the corner, failing to impress a pair of young women with his mandolin playing. He was singing an old familiar ballad – for once, not about John Swann – a tale of hopeless love between a sailor and a mermaid. He wasn't bad at all, but they were unmoved by his playing, most probably because, although he was young, he was odd-looking, with pale eyes, pock-marked skin and bright red hair. The poor man gave up, while they twittered and fawned over a grander gentleman in a richly-decorated waistcoat. The young musician's countenance fell for a moment and then, with an air of theatricality, he snatched up the older man's hat and put it on his head, hiding his hair. He wrapped a thick shawl across his shoulders and pulled it up to his nose, giving him the appearance of a rogue. He took up his instrument again and this time began something more light-hearted. A teasing song about the arousing pleasures of spring.

Now the girls played along, amused by the costume, joining in the words of the chorus and encouraging the older man to sing with them.

Simple things: a hat, a shawl and a witty song, and the red-haired mandolin player was the centre of it all, with two girls hanging on his performance. At the end, they clapped and laughed and pressed some coins into his hand. The older man took back his hat, but bought the musician a beer, and encouraged him to play on, slipping some coin his way.

How foolish we are. How quick to judge a person on their appearance and aspect, when the reality of who and what they are might be so different.

Tommy Bridgewater, for instance. A decent sort of young man, I had thought, who loved sweet innocent Amelia and followed her to Berwick Street. I had assumed he was trying to find honest work to keep them, when all the time he had been out burgling houses with a clutch of thieves, abandoning her to her fate. Had I got it wrong? Had he killed Mr Reed after all? Was he, as Mr Groves had hinted, 'a servant gone bad'? After all, on the night of the party, Reed had recognised him, laughed that he knew who Tommy really was. Had Mr Reed seen what I had failed to see: a dishonest man masquerading as an honest one? Was that why Reed had died?

Chapter Forty-Two

It was Sunday, and the morning was full of bells. The church towers around London rang in different pitches and at different times, meaning one long discordant peal ran from nine until eleven, harassing the population to worship.

I tried not go to church, as a general rule. I think I feared that I would bump into my father: it was unlikely, but enough to make me wary of going. In any case, sermons, when they were not dull and long-winded, served only to remind me of him, charging me with wilfulness and harlotry with all the authority of the Almighty himself.

It was another of Ma's oddities that, in a bid for respectability, she attended St Anne's for the morning service almost every Sunday. We, as her friends and tenants, were expected to join her. This week, however, Polly and Lucy had spent the night elsewhere, and I had decided that attending a funeral had meant I had been to church already. Ma had gone out with Emily and Sarah. Sydney had been dragged along too, still in disgrace and in need of repentance, as far as Ma was concerned.

Ma went to show to everyone that she was an independent woman of business, mistress of a household, and a pious Christian. Emily went to secure her arrangement with the curate, a strange scrap of a man who visited her on Sunday afternoons to be punished for his sins.

I walked over to Marylebone, to catch a glimpse of fields and find some fresher air. I needed to breathe. Mr Reed had been right about the spate of house-building. Even out here, fine new properties were going up. London was a pit, sucking in more of the rogues and fortune-hunters who arrived every week. But the city simply gobbled them up and quietly expanded its girth. Everyone who lived in the belly of the city was on the make; everyone was looking to do better than their neighbours. Mostly that meant moving out – to find better neighbours.

Along the journey to fortune, though, many others got lost, trampled in the scramble. The streets were full of people who hadn't managed to survive in this grasping world; who had been conned, tricked, left out. They were the ones sinking into the mire of oblivion that the gin shops provided, sleeping out under carts or girls like Sallie, selling themselves just to eat.

Out here, in the optimism of a spring morning, with the bells ringing and new houses being built, London looked like a splendid city; a bright, golden, vibrant city. But a few streets away there was enough grime and chaos to swallow it all. And I stood in the breach: for now, I was one of the lucky ones, but all the while I was acutely aware that my future was precarious. My life could descend into Sallie's in the blink of an eye, just as surely as a fortune could be lost on a throw of the dice.

I did not know what to do about Tommy Bridgewater. I had seen him break into a house. I could confront him next time I saw him – which would be stupid and dangerous – or I could share what I had seen with the authorities. Or I could do nothing. It was a fair assumption that he would be caught eventually. Perhaps then, his involvement with Mr Reed's death would come out. All that I could do was lend support to Amelia when that day came. Although, how I would ever get my money back when Tommy was caught and hanged, I had no idea.

I turned back for home.

Chapter Forty-Three

I knew something was wrong as soon as I stepped through the door. Sydney was still at church with Ma – no doubt keen to show himself as respectable as well as loyal for a while – so Meg was at the door. She grabbed at me as soon as I entered, panic in her face.

'I couldn't stop them, miss, I couldn't. They just pushed themselves in and went up to your room.'

'What? Who is in my room?' I thundered up the stairs, without bothering to hear the reply. I should have turned around and left the house. Instead, I reached the door of my room to find Jack Grimshaw and the tall man I'd seen at Bow Street rifling through my wardrobe, throwing hats on to the bed and pulling open drawers. The shriek left my mouth before I could stop it.

'What in the name of heaven are you doing? How dare you come in here without my permission!'

The two men straightened up from their business.

'We dare, Miss Hardwicke, because we heard that you were in possession of a new gold watch and a purse full of money. Mr Reed's money, that is.' Grimshaw snarled at me like a vicious dog. I barked back.

'What? Don't be ridiculous!'

'Not so ridiculous now we're here, is it Snowy?' Grimshaw stood with a look of triumph on his face and pulled a small blue velvet pouch and a watch out of his pocket. He swung the watch to and fro at 'Snowy', who laughed. A wave of panic hit me.

'Where did you find those things?'

Grimshaw gestured at the bed. 'Under your pillow, as well you know.' He spat on the floor. 'Typical whore, sleeping with your true love. I've never known one who didn't care more for gold than anything else.'

'You did not find that watch under my pillow. Nor the purse. There was nothing there.' There was certainly no watch or purse under my pillow last night.

'Are you accusing me of lying now, slut? Mr Snow here saw me turn the pillow over, didn't you, Mr Snow?'

'That I did.' Mr Snow was adamant.

I glanced about my room. They hadn't found my secret hiding place; the rug still covered the uneven floorboard. On the table lay my hairbrush and ribbon box. The gold canary button was missing.

'Where's the button?' I asked. 'The gold button that was on the table.' Their faces were blank. 'There,' I said, pointing to where the button had been.

It was clear that they had no idea what I was talking about, which was interesting. If these runners had found a gold watch under my pillow and Sallie's button had gone, then someone had been in my room before these two ugly brutes had arrived. Someone had planted Reed's things and taken the only piece of evidence I had for Sallie's murder, and my belief that the two deaths were connected. This was not looking good.

'I think you should come to Bow Street with us, miss,' said Snow. 'The magistrate would like a word about what happened to Mr Reed.'

Of course he would. Mr Winchcombe, although tangled up with John Swann's gang, was not a murderer; the magistrate would have worked that out by now. He needed another plausible suspect. And now he had a whore with a gold watch.

'Just a minute,' I said. 'Who told you that I would have Reed's watch? You came and turned this room over before. Why did you come here again?'

'Information,' said Snow.

'We had word come to us,' said Grimshaw.

By a letter, I had no doubt.

'Does Mr Davenport know that you're here?' I asked. 'Has he returned?'

'Oh, he is looking forward to hearing your excuses for this.'

'Are you coming with us like a lamb, Miss Hardwicke,' said Snow, 'or have we got to carry you out?'

Given the choice of exiting the house with my dignity or being man-handled by these two bears, I chose to lift my head and march out in front of them. There was a carriage waiting for us.

Chapter Forty-Four

We travelled in silence until we reached the magistrate's. From time to time, Grimshaw would take out the watch and turn it over in his hand, look up and try to catch my eye, as if expecting a sudden and heartfelt confession to murder. It was undoubtedly Reed's watch; I could see his initials etched on the back, just as they had been embroidered on his handkerchief. Reed had been enamoured of his possessions and his status as a successful man of business. Grimshaw would probably find initials on the purse as well, if he cared to look. The jolting of the carriage only added to my sense of foreboding. Someone had put Reed's watch under my pillow; a person with easy access to my room. Someone had been in possession of the watch in the first place. That could only be the person who had taken it from Reed. The same person had seen the button on my table and recognised it. A murderer had been in my room. A murderer who would be happy to see me convicted in his, or her stead.

I shuddered and began praying that Davenport, at least, would see the truth of the situation.

Instead of taking me straight to the court, as I had expected, they knocked at the door to the house. An elderly housekeeper in a white cap answered the door and ushered us in. I wondered if this was the Mrs Priddy the young boy had told me about, but I didn't have chance to ask, as very quickly I was back in the same room I had visited with Charles and Mr Herring. Immediately, I felt the want of their supportive company as I stood alone in a room of five men, feeling more naked and exposed than ever I did at Berwick Street. Grimshaw and Snow, having escorted me thus far, made their way over to the paper-covered table, where three of their colleagues sat. One of them, Davenport, with his back to me, took the purse and watch from Grimshaw. I saw him turn the watch over. His shoulders dropped, almost imperceptibly, when he saw the initials. He was disappointed, I could tell. He had trusted me, and I had fallen short.

A thudding sensation began to pulse in my body. I was afraid.

Davenport turned, slowly, in his seat and looked at me. I let out a shaky breath. I expected him to be angry, but his face was not angry. It was impassive, and that was almost worse because I couldn't read his expression. He swung the watch on its chain.

'Well?' He was, at least, giving me a chance to explain.

'They said they found the watch and purse under my pillow,' I said, in as calm a voice as I could manage, judging it unwise to accuse the men of ransacking my room. 'I did not put them there. I had never seen these things until they showed them to me.'

He said nothing. The other men glanced up, briefly, but then returned to their papers. Grimshaw and Snow were at the other end of the room, pouring themselves pots of beer from a jug and cutting some cheese. They were listening, but not commenting. They didn't need to – as far as they were concerned, they had done their job.

'Someone has put them in my room,' I said. 'That person has also taken the gold button.'

He raised an eyebrow. 'Gold button?'

'The button Sallie pulled from a man's coat before she was tipped into the Thames. I traced its owner, by the way.'

'Really,' he said flatly. 'Who is this mysterious owner, do you suppose, Miss Hardwicke?'

I did not like the tone of his voice. He sounded like a man humouring a child before setting it straight. But this was my opportunity.

'I think it's someone called Beech.'

That surprised him. I think he was expecting a lame excuse, or a shrug, rather than a name.

'I've not heard of a Beech,' he said.

'Mr Beech is the man who collected the coat from the tailor,' I said, as the suspicious look returned to his face. 'It's what Sallie was trying to tell me. Kitty said that she had heard George Reed arguing with a man about a beach in Paris. That he had missed the beach. But there is no beach in Paris, only a river. He was saying something about a Mister Beech. And Mr Beech is the name of the man with the coat. It all makes sense.'

The men at the table, still with their eyes on the papers, had not turned any pages. They were listening intently.

'Three people have received blackmail letters since Reed died: Mrs Farley, Mr Herring and Mr Stanford,' I said, trying to remain calm.

Davenport rubbed at his forehead and gave me a weary look.

'The letters demanded that money be taken to a bath house on Long Acre and left for a Mr Beech to collect.

I went there with Mrs Farley's money and Mr Stanford came with his, yesterday.' It was frustrating to share the result. I muttered it, still annoyed at my own stupidity. 'We waited, but we didn't see Mr Beech. We have no idea what he looks like.'

He toyed with the watch in his lap, turning it over as he took in my words.

'I think you're lying to me.' His voice was quiet.

'I am not lying!' There was a ripple of excitement at the table. I had, unintentionally, shouted.

'Reed's watch and purse were found in your room. You were always the one most likely to have strangled him for his goods – you told me yourself that you're keeping back some of your money from Mrs Farley.' At that, the men looked up, now cheerfully engaged in the drama.

'How dare you make something of that. I told you my plans in good faith.'

'I didn't know then that you were keeping dead men's watches and purses as well.' His voice was beginning to get louder.

'I've told you, I did not take George Reed's watch and purse, any more than I killed him. Why can't you believe that?'

'Because they were found in your room.'

'I'm telling you the truth, sir. I'll swear on any Bible you have that I never set eyes on them until this morning.'

'Of course you'll swear. You'll say anything to save your neck, I'm sure.'

He was angry now; but so was I.

'Just because someone is a whore, that doesn't make her a liar.'

'Well, experience tells me otherwise,' he said curtly. One of the men at the table sniggered. Davenport threw him a sharp glance before glaring back at me. 'I thought you were different; turns out, you're just like all the others.'

'No. I'm not having that, sir. I have been utterly straight with you, and you know it. If you'd listened to the people on the street, if you'd visited every tailor this side of the river, as I have done, you would be convinced of my innocence – despite what your dogs have brought in.' I folded my arms, mirroring him. 'George Reed was killed by someone who wanted the information he carried, someone he knew in Paris – that's what I learned from the gingerbread seller. The street girls came to me with a story about a beach and then one of them was killed. Her attacker was a man from Norwich, who got his coat from a tailor near Golden Square. The buttons had canaries on them – birds that people from Norwich have a passion for – and the man's name was Beech. Now, I might speak French, sir, but I have never been to Paris, any more than I've been to Rome or Athens. I have no connection with Norwich, and my name, although not Hardwicke, is not Beech...'

There was a great scraping of chairs as the men at the table suddenly stood. My words dwindled into nothing. Davenport was looking over my shoulder to the doorway where, when I turned to see for myself, stood the magistrate.

Chapter Forty-Five

Mr John Fielding was leaning on the door frame, head to one side. As I stopped speaking, he applauded softly.

'Bravo,' he said. 'That's a very pretty speech. But, tell me, what *is* your name?'

He was not a young man, but neither was he especially old; no more than forty. His wig was heavy, rather than fashionable, which made him appear older, and on top of it he wore an ordinary black hat. There was nothing about his person or dress that suggested anything other than gravity, intelligence and sobriety. In fact, the only aspects of him that drew notice were the band around his eyes and the thin stick, currently tucked under his arm.

'Elizabeth Vessey, sir.' The name sounded odd to my ears; it had been months since I had used it. 'But I'm known as Lizzie Hardwicke.'

He eased himself away from the door and pulled off his hat. He was familiar enough in his own surroundings to find his way to the table, where Davenport pulled out a chair. One of the other men poured him a beer and set it in his hand. None of them spoke as he drank. He set down his pot and turned in my direction, a slight frown on his brow.

'Are you related to Sir Francis Vessey, by any chance?'

The question startled me. 'Sir Francis is my uncle, yes; my father's brother.' Davenport shifted his position. Mr Fielding grunted.

'Then no wonder you've changed your name.' He said no more, but I was left with the impression that he had met my uncle at some point and that the meeting had not been favourable.

'You're a long way from home, though, Miss, ah... Hardwicke. And, I think, a long way from the life you are supposed to be leading, if you are standing arguing with my men about stolen property.'

'You are correct, sir. London is not my home; but it is my career now.'

He ran a finger under his cravat to loosen it a little.

'That's a pity,' he said. 'From what I heard when I came in, you sounded like a lawyer – and more intelligent than the one who was wearying me on my walk home from church. But I interrupted you. You were, I think, giving these men a precis of your investigations.'

'Jack and Snowy found George Reed's watch and purse in Miss Hardwicke's room, sir,' Davenport said, cutting across the magistrate.

Mr Fielding smiled to himself. 'They were under her pillow, no doubt.' He didn't wait for an answer. 'Really, Will, does Miss Hardwicke strike you as the sort of woman who would hide treasures under her pillow?'

Davenport glowered at me but said nothing.

'I'm not a man to be swayed by pretty looks, Miss Hardwicke,' Mr Fielding addressed me again. 'Indeed, I can only imagine that you are pretty. If you're playing my men for fools, you're wise enough to know the conse-quences for your games. But I try to be a fair man, and if you have information, or evidence, then we should hear it. I know the matter; Mr Davenport has shared with me the details of your party, who was present, and how Mr Reed was discovered.'

I swallowed hard.

'At the moment, sir, all that I have are pieces of a puzzle. You heard most of it, I think, from the doorway.'

'You'll have to do better, you know,' he said in a soft voice. 'You are still the person most likely to have killed him, at the moment. Try again.'

They were all listening now.

'We are looking for a man called Beech – or perhaps…' it came to me as I was speaking, 'a man who goes by the name of Beech sometimes.' If I could use a different name to escape my past, why couldn't he?

'Go on.'

'When Reed was murdered, I noticed he was missing a packet of papers. I told Mr Davenport about them straight away. When the packet turned up, a day after the death, some of the papers were missing, but the rest were black-mail notes and copies of letters. Several people were being blackmailed. Any of them might have killed him, given the nature of the notes, but none of them, as far as I can see, did kill him. They were all somewhere else at the time.'

He considered this.

'And what do you conclude from that?'

'That if Mr Reed was killed by someone he was black-mailing, and none of the people mentioned in those letters did kill him, then we must be looking for another black-mail victim – one whose name was mentioned only in the missing letters.'

I frowned at him. 'But everyone who was at the party was being blackmailed. Mr Herring, Mr Stanford and Mr Winchcombe were. He was making insinuations to Sydney, our door man, Mrs Farley and a couple of the gentlemen have had letters even since Reed's death. Indeed, there is only Tommy Bridgewater who wasn't mentioned in the letters we found. Tommy was the name Mr Reed shouted as he left our house. "I know who you are, Tommy boy," was what he said.'

'So, the conclusion you reach is that Tommy Bridgewater killed him? Or that Tommy Bridgewater is really Mr Beech?'

'Yes. No. I don't know. Until last night I would have said that Tommy was unlikely to have killed him. He's a hot-headed boy, but I don't think that Reed had any information on him – and I really don't think they had met until that night. But yesterday, I saw Tommy breaking into a house.'

He dismissed the comment with a wave of his hand.

'Leave that for now. If Tommy Bridgewater did not kill Reed, what is your alternative?'

It came to me, even as he asked the question.

'Someone is lying.'

Someone else was, like the red-haired musician in the tavern, dressed up and pretending to be something that he, or she, was not, to fool the crowd.

'So,' Mr Fielding was saying, 'either someone is lying to you, or else Tommy Bridgewater killed Reed.'

There was a racket outside; shouting and jostling in the street. The door flew open with a bang and a man fell into the room, his face bruised and cut. It was the older man I had seen at the table the other day. He saw the magistrate and saluted.

'Mr Fielding! Grimshaw, Snowy, come and help. We've got them!'

Grimshaw and Snow leapt to their feet in a flash and dashed out. Davenport and the others raced to join them. Mr Fielding was slower. He needed no help from me but marched quickly to the street armed with his stick. I ran out too – recognising a chance to escape.

'What's going on?' Mr Fielding was gazing into the street, unable to see what was happening, but assailed, as I was, by the yells and shouts.

Davenport, Grimshaw, Snow and the rest were helping two runners and – how very odd – Tommy Bridgewater, wrestle four other men towards the magistrate's gaol.

'It's Swann's gang,' panted someone. 'We've got them all.'

Mr Fielding clapped his hands with undignified glee. 'Well done men. Another success!'

I flattened myself against the door and watched as the men were marched into the cells. I could hear them shouting and cursing through the thick walls. Mr Fielding was very pleased. Tommy Bridgewater saw me and shrank a little behind the others.

The older man with the bruised face, whose name appeared to be Carter, told Mr Fielding in excited tones how the gang had been discovered in a hovel somewhere between Covent Garden and St Anne's. He dragged Tommy forward and stood him in front of Mr Fielding.

'It's this young man we have to thank, sir. It was his quick thinking and bold courage that led us to them.'

Tommy's cheeks reddened, although Mr Fielding would not have known that.

'Don't be shy, son,' he said – as if he had, indeed, seen the blush. 'Who are you? What manner of man are you?'

'Thomas Bridgewater, sir. I'm a farrier. Well, when I have work I am.'

Mr Fielding cocked his head to one side and looked in my direction, anticipating where I would be.

'Is this your Tommy Bridgewater, Miss Hardwicke?'

'Yes, sir.'

'Well, I think you have the answer to your dilemma, don't you?'

Tommy looked puzzled, but Carter broke in.

'Mr Fielding, but we could do with a man like him with us. He's young, but useful. Not only did he lead us to Swann's gang, having overheard them talking in a tavern, he helped us climb into their room through the window. We waited nearly a day for them to return this afternoon while Tommy here kept watch and then, just as we were giving up hope, they came back from ransacking houses in the west. We sprang on them and brought them here.'

'Indeed. Well, if he's as useful as you say he is, then perhaps I'd better take him on, Mr Carter. I trust your judgement. Come and see me tomorrow, Mr Bridgewater and I'll see what I can offer you.'

Tommy glowed, both at the praise and the prospect of a job. It wasn't what he had looked for, and it would bring its own dangers, but it was work.

'Off with you all, now, please; I have matters to attend to. Go and celebrate your victory in the usual way. Mr Carter—' He reached for a small purse at his waist and found a handful of coins. 'Make sure they don't have sore heads tomorrow.'

While the men were congratulating one another, and while they were still distracted by their good fortune, I slipped away. He did not see me leave, but I guessed that Mr Fielding would know that I had disappeared.

Chapter Forty-Six

The urge to flee had been overwhelming. Now I had to deal with having fled. As I walked back towards Berwick Street the realisation dawned that I had probably just done the most foolish thing in my life — apart from inviting George Reed to our party. I had just given Mr Fielding and Mr Davenport all the evidence they needed that I was mixed up in Reed's death. Why would an innocent woman run away? Escaping while they had been distracted now seemed irredeemably suspicious. And stupid.

I slowed my walk and tried to stem the tide of curses that were flowing in one long mutter from my lips. Ma would have slapped me, had she heard.

I could not return to Berwick Street. That would be the first place Davenport would go, once he realised I had disappeared. I might be welcome at the Groves' — although I would not be able to earn a living from Susan's house, and Davenport would probably search that house too. Thinking of Mrs Groves made me remember Amelia: I ached to tell her about Tommy and his new job. They would, at least, be able to pay their rent. I was sure that Susan would want them both to stay. I was wandering towards Golden Square; I could easily give Amelia the news.

I nearly bumped into Susan Groves as I turned a corner. She had her head down and was scurrying along like a little mouse. She even squeaked when she saw me.

'Oh, Miss Hardwicke. How lovely to see you.' She chattered about several different matters, even before I was able to open my mouth. Amelia was settled, she was eating again, she – Susan – had been baking and the two of them were enjoying each other's company. John had been called out to the butcher to pack a cart which was highly unusual because it was Sunday and it was likely to put him in a bad mood. A note had summoned him that morning and he had been most displeased, and she was fretting about what to cook. Finally, she stopped to draw breath and I told her that I had important news for her.

'I'm so sorry. Here I am telling you everything and you have something special to say. Do go on.' I took her by the arm, to make her cease.

'Would you give Amelia a message for me, please? Tommy has a job at last. He is going to assist at the magistrate's. He helped the runners catch a gang of thieves and now Mr Fielding wants him to work at Bow Street.'

She nearly fainted – whether from surprise, shock or delight I couldn't tell. 'Heavens!' was all she said. I was rather pleased to have made her speechless.

'If she wants to find him, he will be with the runners. They're celebrating at the moment, so she might want to wait until his head has cleared, but he'll be waiting for her. They'll have some money to marry at last.'

'I'll get back to her now,' said Susan. 'I wonder if I can persuade John to make room for them as a married couple. I'd love to keep Amelia with me.' I knew it. 'Will you come home with me?'

As much as the thought of cakes, warmth and charmingly innocent company was attractive, I needed to think about my future. And something was nagging in my mind.

'Another time, Mrs Groves. Give her my love.'

She went on her way with a lighter step, ready to share the news, as I found myself at the tailor's shop. It was closed, as I expected, so I sat on the step and watched people going about their business on the street. It was mid-afternoon and those who had been to church in the morning, were emerging again from their homes to take a walk, or perhaps to find another service. The bells were beginning to ring once more, calling the good and the faithful to prayer.

My father used to begin the afternoon service at three o'clock. He expected us to attend, me and my brothers as well as the servants. He would be walking to church, even as I sat here, a fallen woman with nowhere to go. He would say that my present misfortune was only to be expected – but then, he was unaware of his own brother's part in my fall.

The air was still cool, but I imagined that, at home, there would be crocuses carpeting the church yard. The only spring flowers I saw in London were bought in the market. What was it that Mrs Groves had said? Something had sounded wrong. I couldn't remember. I was, as I had said to Mr Fielding, dealing with puzzles: buttons, beaches, and people from Paris. If Tommy Bridgewater was not the murderer, then who was 'Tommy'? Was there really a man called Mr Beech that I hadn't met, or was someone masquerading?

A small girl was squatting on the ground, a stone's throw away from me. Little more than a baby, she was tipping water from a bucket on to a patch of dirt and stirring it with a stick. She looked as though she was cooking herself a cauldron of soup, thick and muddy. I had done the same sort of thing as a child, to the horror of our housemaid, so I smiled at her. The girl stopped stirring and started to prod her mud soup instead, slamming the stick into the mess and giggling as it splattered and plopped.

'Emmy!' A woman's voice from a nearby doorway, perhaps the child's mother. 'Emmy, stop that, you're splashing mud everywhere. Emily, leave it alone and come here.'

The little girl gave her stick one last reluctant flick and sprayed muddy water across the path in front of her, almost reaching me, before jumping up and running to her mother, in a house just past the tailor's.

'Bye bye, Emily,' I laughed to her as she passed.

Even as I said her name, my skin prickled and I stopped laughing. I knew who it was that was lying, who was playing a part. I knew, because I had, more than once, seen someone make a mess, not with a stick and mud, but with a pen and ink. I had seen ink splashes on paper. And now I realised their significance.

'I know who you are, Tommy boy,' I said softly. A shiver ran, involuntarily, down my back.

Chapter Forty-Seven

The door of the tailor's shop opened abruptly, and a face peeped out from the dark interior. It was the young assistant I had encountered the other day. He had struck me then as an intelligent lad, even though, in looks, he was unremarkable. He was slightly-built, with ordinary brown hair.

'You were here the other day,' he said. It was a statement rather than a question, because he knew he was right. 'You're the lady with the button.'

I stood up and looked him in the eye. 'And you're Jack.' He was surprised that I remembered his name and coloured a little, but then lifted his chin, trying to act like someone in charge.

'What do you want, sitting on the doorstep? Mr Andrews won't be pleased.'

'Mr Andrews isn't here, though, is he?' It was a guess, but I saw immediately that I was right. 'I wonder whether you can help me, Jack. Mr Andrews didn't seem to know as much as you about the canary button. And you, I think, know something about the coat it was attached to.'

He hesitated, torn between showing off to me and keeping a decent silence, like his superior. I leaned towards him a little and stroked his cheek, knowing enough about boys his age to be assured of the effect. 'I'll wager that coat was really special.' The poor lad trembled, just a little, before stepping back into the shop.

'It was a fine coat; not special at all. It was just...'

'Just what, Jack?'

'It was all wrong for the person it was made for.' He was frowning; at the coat, and not at my touch.

'It was made for a Mr Beech, that's what Mr Andrews said.'

He shook his head. 'You'd better come in,' he said, keeping his distance. 'Mr Andrews told you that a Mr Beech collected it, and that he did. But it wasn't made for him.'

The shop was unlit. There was enough afternoon light coming in from the widows, but it was gloomy. The bolts of cloth which, in the brighter light looked rich and warm, now looked dull. We stood in the middle of the serving area, Jack rubbing his sleeve awkwardly.

'So, who was it made for?' I had a feeling that I already knew.

'Charles Stanford.'

Charles Stanford knew Mr Beech, then.

'You said it was all wrong. What did you mean by that?'

He put his head on one side, thoughtfully. He was a young man who took his job seriously, I could tell. He would not have wanted anything to be amiss with a fine coat.

'Because I know Mr Stanford. Or, at least, I knew him when I was a child. I grew up near to Norwich and not far from Stanford House. Mr Stanford lived as a recluse with his old uncle; everyone knew of him.'

Charles had told me the story himself. His uncle had kept him almost like a prisoner until he came into his inheritance.

'Didn't he like his coat?'

'I really don't know, miss. Mr Stanford didn't collect himself. He wouldn't, would he? He never left Stanford House, because of his back.'

'His what?'

'His back. He was bent over, see?' He bent and twisted himself over until he had made himself quite crooked. 'Mr Stanford, the younger man, was a hunchback when I was growing up. The coat we made was paid for by Mr Stanford's account and was supposed to be for Mr Stanford, but it couldn't have been for him, otherwise it would have been measured differently, see?' he said again.

I was beginning to.

'The man who collected the coat, Mr Beech, would the coat have fitted his frame, do you think?'

He thought about it carefully. Then he nodded. 'Yes, I think it would have fitted him perfectly. Perhaps Mr Stanford meant for his footman to have it.'

'His footman?'

'Well, I think that was who he was. He had the air of a servant and was a bit above himself – as footmen can be.' He was a boy who had met a few officious servants in his work, I could tell.

Another thought came to me.

'May I see the ledger again? I didn't quite see Mr Beech's name properly when Mr Andrews showed it to me.'

I hadn't been allowed to see it. Mr Andrews had checked it himself. But Jack didn't know that.

'Of course. I can find it for you.'

He found the page almost immediately and opened out the ledger for my inspection. There was a signature, with, as I expected, the same ink splatters that I had seen in the bath house guest book, and the same marks that I had noticed on the blackmail letter from, as I had assumed at the time, George Reed – the letter about an affair with a girl called Emily, who I now doubted even existed. The same person had mishandled his pen in the same way each time.

The tailor had written the details of the coat and the name of the man collecting it above the signature. Mr Thomas Beech. He had walked in as Thomas Beech and left as Charles Stanford; to be Charles Stanford to the rest of the world.

I didn't know what had become of the real Charles Stanford, the hunch-backed recluse of Stanford House, but George Reed, the man from Norwich, had recognised the imposter immediately, and had sought to capitalise on his knowledge. No wonder he had met his end: such information had been explosive.

Jack was shuffling his feet.

'I ought to close the shop, miss, if you have everything you need. People might think we're open, and we're not. I want to go and find something to eat, if you don't mind, and get some rest. We start early on Monday mornings.'

'Yes of course,' I said, still distracted by my new information. 'Sorry, what did you just say?'

He looked amused. 'I said we start early on Mondays. Mr Andrews likes to check the stock first thing every week.'

Susan Groves had said that her husband had been summoned to the butchers and that this was unusual for a Sunday. The blood began to pound in my head as I tried to remember what I had told Charles about John Groves' belief that a servant had killed his master. I had told him that Mr Groves had been speaking to George Reed.

'Jack, I need you to do something for me, something extremely important, more important than supper. I need you to take a message to Bow Street, to the magistrate's house.'

He looked very anxious. I probably looked anxious myself. That was as nothing compared with how I felt.

'I'll pay you well,' I said, reaching for my purse, hands shaking. 'You must take a carriage and get there as fast as you can. Speak only to Mr Davenport, William Davenport – only him. A man's life is in danger. Have you a piece of paper for a note?'

His eyes began to sparkle at the thought of a wild adventure – the like of which he was unlikely ever to have known in the tailor's – and he nodded vigorously.

I scribbled a note to Davenport, trying to convey as simply and clearly as I could the information I had and what I intended to do. It was the best I could manage, because I needed to hurry. I shovelled several coins into Jack's hand, urging him to keep whatever was left to treat himself to a feast – only once he had delivered the note into Davenport's hands. Then I kissed him, full on the lips, three times; because he had, unwittingly, saved my skin, because I needed him to carry out his task, and because I knew he would like it.

We left together. He waved down a carriage and sped away, hanging out of the window to catch a glimpse of me, even as I made my way to the butcher's.

Chapter Forty-Eight

The butcher's shop was, as I remembered, down a quiet alley. It was almost wide enough to be called a narrow street. There were no other shops in it, and no one was walking up or down the cobbles. The shutters were closed. Tomorrow they would be open wide, displaying the butcher's wares, smoked and preserved for weeks, hanging from the small hooks that, I knew, would be just inside the window. Tomorrow the alley would be busy with servants buying food for their houses. Today it was empty. The wooden door was shut, but I could see it was unlocked.

The cattle were brought to London by the thousands in the autumn, at the beginning of the season, and butchered with gusto by the sort of men who loved hacking at flesh and being up to their armpits in blood. For several weeks, and every day of the week, the roads of the neighbourhood ran red and the drains clogged up with bits of gut and hair and wrecked our shoes.

Once butchered, the meat would be sent out to the fine houses of the city, or packed on to stalls or piled on to carts and hawked about the streets. The heady months that followed would see the butchers selling their wares at inflated prices as the population swelled with incomers from the provinces. Between October and May, all traders pushed up their prices – as did we. Butchers aren't the only ones to trade in flesh.

By the late spring, as the gentlefolk returned to their manor houses and estates in the country, we were out of fresh meat – in the bawdy houses and brothels, as well as the butchers – and life returned to a less-frenzied pace. For the butchers, what had been patiently salted, preserved and hung in ash to smoke, was now taken down when required. We would live on salted ham and beef, or bacon, until the end of the summer. It was better than surviving on turnips and onions – which was the lot of the poor all through the year.

John Groves had been summoned on a Sunday to pack a cart for market. I would have assumed that this would normally be done early on a Monday morning. You wouldn't leave a cart full of meat, salted or not, overnight anywhere in this city. If you did, you would be several hams lighter by the morning.

I banged on the unlocked door for a while, but no one came to answer. I should have waited for the runners to arrive. Instead, I pushed the door open.

The butchery was larger than I was expecting. The shuttered window on the front gave little indication of the vast expanse that lay behind it. I was in a square space that was even higher than it was wide. A stone floor showed the tell-tale signs of its trade. There were black patches where blood had pooled weeks ago, before it had eventually been sluiced out on to the street. In the afternoon light, the stains looked like shadows on the ground.

There was an unmistakable aroma of drying meat. High above me, some twenty feet above, there were dozens of portions of meat, hanging still and silent, waiting to be chosen and bought. They were grouped towards the back of the store, up in the roof space where it was dark and cool. Each leg or shoulder was held on a hook, and then neatly hooked again over the long metal rods that ran horizontally from one side of the room to the other. Access to the meat came via a short wooden bridge that had been constructed underneath them. The butcher's lads would climb the steps to the walkway to hang the meat when it was butchered and then climb up again to fetch it when a customer required it. It was a neat idea and saved using step ladders, which would get in the way when the men were slaughtering. There was still a good amount of meat here to be sold. If John Groves had been here to collect joints for loading, there was little sign of it. The long crook-ended poles, which the lads would use to lift each portion from its place, stood leaning in a corner, untouched at the bottom of the bridge steps.

At the back of the slaughter area was a table, empty, save for a few leaves of paper. A couple of rough chairs stood askew nearby. This was where the business took place, although the money would be safely stored elsewhere.

Beyond the table was a door into what I assumed was the back office. It was ajar, so I walked towards it, my shoes making a light tap on the stones that was almost as loud as the sound my heart was making.

The room was airy, a window looked out over the back of the street and the sun, which was lowering itself towards the horizon shone a reddish haze through the window. The butcher, who had so neatly hung his meats and tidily cleaned the blood and guts from his slaughter floor, had also dusted the window pane recently. Only one or two flies lay crumpled on the sill.

The floor of this room was, by contrast, very untidy.

There was a body on it.

I didn't have to get close to know it was Mr Groves and, as I'd feared, the reason he hadn't started to lift down the meat was because he had been smashed over the head by something heavy. Blood had congealed over the back of his head. It was dull and black, as if it had seeped from his head some time ago.

He had been dragged into the office. The way that he was lying, arms stretched out in front of him, face to the ground, made it look that way. I guessed that he had been hit as he arrived in the larger room, probably even as he opened the door, and then pulled into the back. He wasn't small; it would have been hard work.

The terror of it suddenly struck me. I had to get out, go back to Bow Street, find constables, find Susan, anyone. I heard the front door bang shut. I ran out, and found myself standing under a hundred joints of beef and ham, face to face with Charles Stanford.

He was carrying a bottle of brandy, bought from some-where in the neighbourhood. He checked his step when he saw me. I was supposed to be locked up at Bow Street, I realised.

'Lizzie!' he hailed me with the brandy. 'What an unex-pected joy to see you. Would you care for a drink? My companion doesn't appear to want any more, as you've noticed.'

I watched him carefully, trying to stay calm and working out whether it would be possible to run for the door. He wasn't wearing a sword, but I imagined he would

328

have a knife somewhere. And he was taller and stronger than me.

'So, Charles, it seems you're not Charles Stanford at all, are you?'

He stood staring at me for a moment. Then he laughed, rolling his eyes and waggling the bottle, as if I were making a silly joke.

'Certainly, I'm Charles Stanford. Who on earth else would I be?'

'Thomas Beech.'

As soon as I said the name, everything that had passed between us was altered.

'Who?' There was a sharpness in his voice.

'Thomas Beech. Sometime servant to Charles Stanford. Known to his friends and associates as Tommy.'

My breathing was shorter. I wished that Davenport were here, or even Grimshaw.

'Hmm.' He walked slowly to the table and put the bottle down carefully.

'You have nothing to prove that, of course.'

No outright denial, then.

'I can prove it, Charles… Thomas… I know.'

He undid his coat, sat down on a chair and casually threw an arm over the back. He smiled up at me, as confident and easy in his own skin as he ever was. The coat, middling blue in colour, was sporting gold buttons. I recognised them. One of them had been on my bedroom table until this morning. He was still handsome, still smiling. But his brown eyes were hard; full of spite. He leaned forward and patted the seat of the other chair, inviting me to sit.

'Go on then, sweetheart. I'm all ears.' He grabbed the bottle and took a swig from it, watching me.

I sat down, wondering how many people would hear me if I screamed.

'Charles Stanford had a crooked back. He lived as a recluse with his uncle.'

He paused with the bottle at his lips, before taking another mouthful.

'The coat you are wearing, which, I see, now has all of its buttons again, was made by a tailor who will recognise you as Thomas Beech, the servant who collected it on behalf of Charles Stanford. His assistant, originally from Norwich, will swear that Mr Stanford was deformed from childhood.'

He said nothing, but he did not take his eyes off me. I clasped my hands in my lap to stop them from trembling.

'The ledger in the shop has your signature, Thomas Beech, and a splatter of ink from the pen, similar to the book in the Queen's bath house, and also similar to the blackmail letter you wrote to yourself – that you alleged was from George Reed. That's what I know. That's what I can prove.'

He said nothing, but put the bottle down. He rubbed the edge of the table with one finger. I went on, emboldened.

'I know that the story about Emily is either completely fabricated, or else unimportant. George Reed knew a much bigger and more dangerous secret – one you thought you'd left in Norwich. I would guess that you met Reed in Paris. That's why the gingerbread man said Reed was going to make money from someone he met in Paris. It was you he met in Paris, when you were there.

He, of course, knew the real Charles Stanford. Then he saw you again at the party and recognised you when you were introduced to him. It makes sense now, why he said what he did when you threw him out onto the street. "I know who you are Tommy." He didn't mean Tommy Bridgewater, he meant Tommy Beech.'

'You have no proof. No letters.'

'No, you destroyed those when you took the package. I imagine they exist somewhere because Reed was the sort to keep copies of important documents. If they're not in your lodgings, they'll be at his Norwich home. He had been writing to you for some time, hadn't he? I would hazard that the letters started arriving as soon as he discovered your London address. He would have made enquiries when he was visiting on business.'

He took a swig from the bottle and then slammed it on the table.

'He was a fucking blood sucker. Demanding more money every time to keep silent.'

'He must have been delighted to see you that evening.' The sound of the bottle had made me jump, but I didn't want him to see I was terrified, so carried on regardless – the words pouring out of my mouth in a chatter. 'Here was an opportunity to have you in his power. No wonder you threw him out so firmly when he called you Tommy boy. And then he followed you all to the White Horse to taunt you further. That was when you decided to silence him permanently.'

'The bastard kept calling me Tommy, Tommy boy. He told me that he was expecting to make his fortune in London, what with my secret and others. Then he patted his coat and I realised that all those miserable letters were with him. I couldn't help myself, Lizzie, you must believe me. I followed him out to the back yard. I didn't mean to kill him. It just all became too much, the taunting. I grabbed him, grabbed his handkerchief and pulled so hard until he stopped breathing.'

He looked up at me with pleading eyes.

'I was defending myself, you have to believe me. I didn't mean to kill him.'

Weeks, even days ago, I might have fallen for those soft eyes. Not now.

'What about Charles Stanford? The real Charles?' I needed to know, even though I didn't want to hear it.

The gentle features vanished, and I knew my guess had been horribly correct. It was all an act. All of it. He rolled his eyes.

'Charles had no idea how to live the life he'd been born to. His parents died and left him well-provided for when he was young, and he was sent to live with his old uncle, who was sure to drop dead in a matter of a couple of years. He had stupidly good luck.'

'But he had a crooked back, no parents, and no one to look out for him apart from an old man. He might have attracted your pity rather than your envy.'

He waved the thought away.

'He wasn't the only orphan in the world. He had wealth, breeding and opportunity waiting to be used on adventure. What did he do with it?' He spat out his hatred. 'I'll tell you what he did with it. He sat in his room reading books about philosophy and science. He didn't hunt, nor ride much. He never went to balls or parties; he had no desire to come to town. He wouldn't even play dice or cards. He had all of that wealth and he squandered it on books.'

'Not every man lives for drinking and gambling.' There was a gentleman in my father's parish, I remembered, who devoted his life to collecting insects. My brothers and I had thought him dull, but he was happy in his pursuit.

'But to see it all wasted!' He shook with anger. 'It was more than I could bear. So, I constructed a plan to take him away.'

'You were close to him? I understood that you were a servant in the house.'

His nose wrinkled.

'I was a footman with nothing to do because he never rode out anywhere. But I was lucky to have a smattering of reading, so I asked him if I could read his books and get a bit more learning. I told him I wanted to better myself and he, like a fool, agreed.'

He took another gulp of brandy. I was needing some myself, but he didn't offer.

'It took years. He looked on me as a sort of experiment, I think, little knowing that I was the one in control. I read so many dull books, but my reading improved, and, over time, he was teaching me the manners of a gentleman too. He had me writing as well, but I was never so good with a pen, as you've observed.'

'You didn't become closer to him? Learn to appreciate his scholarship?'

'No. He was a bore; a pompous disfigured bore. I put up with it because I could see that he enjoyed the thought of teaching me. I hoped that when he came into his inheritance, that he would set me up in the world.'

'Give you money enough to pass for a gentleman?'

'Exactly. But his uncle died, and he told me that he intended to give money to the furtherance of science. There was a man in Paris, André, a young chemist, who needed money to develop his work. He was determined to support him, and others like him.'

'And that was how Paris came into it. You must have been upset.'

'I was furious. All those hours spent reading drivel with him and he wasn't going to give me a crown. Why should some equally dull creature get a fortune for glass bottles and tubes when I got nothing?'

I sat as still as I could. This was the man I had given myself to over and over again. A man who had been witty, bright and charming. I had been impressed by his attentions; he had declared himself my darling and everything about his conduct had suggested that he had been besotted with me – even in love. I watched him knocking back the brandy and lolling in the chair opposite me, and the memory of our congress made me feel sick. I had to keep him talking; had to give Davenport time to arrive.

Chapter Forty-Nine

'You took him to Paris?'

'I planted an idea in his mind. It took a while to root –
he was worried about his back – but eventually it did. He
wrote to Monsieur André telling him of his decision to
support his important work and that he desired to travel
to Paris to see it for himself.'

'Wasn't this Monsieur André expecting to see him in
Paris? And receive the money?'

'He was. He sent back a letter saying how honoured
and delighted he was, and that Stanford could visit his
rooms at any time.'

'Monsieur is still waiting for his money, though?'

'Stanford sent another letter a few weeks later saying
that he had changed his mind and would not be travelling
to Paris. His financial situation had altered, and he was
unable to fund the work.'

'You wrote that letter?'

He nodded, an arrogant smile across his face.

'After all, it was a shame to put my studies to waste. My
French is not at all bad, even if my handwriting is poor.'

'Charles set off for Paris expecting to meet Monsieur
André, ready to hand over his fortune, when André was
no longer expecting him,' I said.

'Rather a splendid plan, don't you think?'

'That's one way to describe it.' I thought it vile.

He held the bottle up, shook it a little and squinted at how much liquid was left. He had drunk most of it.

It was getting dark in the back of the slaughterhouse.

'I thought he might even enjoy getting out of the house, find a new lease of life, find some life even, and become a more interesting person,' he said.

'You hoped that he would lavish gifts on you, as well.'

'Of course. It really wouldn't have cost him much to make me a wealthier man. Some decent clothes, gold jewellery, fine women,' he saluted me with the bottle, 'but he was utterly set on getting the money to Monsieur André. I was neglected.'

If he was searching for sympathy I wasn't going to give it. This grasping man had spent years cultivating a friendship with a recluse just to get at his money. And he had killed for it.

'What happened to Charles Stanford?'

He shrugged.

'It was an accident, of course. We reached Paris, and the night before we were due to visit the scientist, he drank something that disagreed with him, fell ill and died in his sleep. You can't trust those French taverns to provide decent ale, you know.'

From what he had said of Charles Stanford, it was unlikely that he would have visited a tavern.

'How did you get rid of his body?'

'It wasn't difficult. I had secured our rooms and the concierge believed that I was Charles Stanford, and he was my servant Thomas. They were nearly as upset as I was when my servant died, and very keen that the authorities didn't find out that he had died in their room. They kindly found an undertaker and the body was taken away.'

I was aghast.

'Charles Stanford lies buried in an unmarked grave in France?'

'I believe so. I was too upset to attend the funeral. But then, I moved to a much better establishment on the livelier side of town, found decent lodging and began to get acquainted with the locals.' He grinned again. 'Especially the ladies.'

'You met Mr Winchcombe and Mr Herring there?'

'Yes, lovely boys they were, both keen to enjoy life to the full. Quite my sort of people.' He frowned. 'And we would have continued to live like kings had Mr Reed not been in Paris at the same time. I had no idea who he was, that odious toad of a man, but he saw me at a gaming house and began threatening me. He knew Charles Stanford too well; knew his uncle. He liked to get acquainted with people of quality, liked to use their names to help his business.' That was the George Reed I had encountered, certainly. 'I made excuses to my companions and left for London immediately. It's a good place to go to ground.'

'It all sounds very easily done,' I said. He had managed to fool everyone except George Reed.

'Oh, people will readily assume you are who you say you are if you carry yourself with sufficient airs. The bank gave me my inheritance, shop keepers sent me their wares, knowing I had means to pay, and once you have the clothes and the gold, everyone is happy to greet you and call you friend.'

He was right. The only thing that separated me from the girls on the streets was my smart address and expensive clothes. I was still a whore – and he, beneath his silk waistcoat, was a murderer.

'Tell me about Sallie.'

'What of her?' he shrugged. 'There's nothing to tell. She saw me taking some letters out of Reed's parcel and putting them in my pocket. I didn't think she had realised what I was doing – she was swaying with the gin – but when those little strumpets told you she had something to say about Paris I couldn't risk it.'

'So, you threw her into the river.'

'She would have died all by herself soon enough.'

She had died because he hit her hard on the head. I had seen the blood.

He fingered one of the buttons on his coat.

'Thank you for looking after this, by the way,' he said, seeing me watching him. 'I wondered where it had gone.'

'You took it from my room when you left Mr Reed's watch and purse,' I said. 'And then you sent a note to Bow Street.'

He said nothing, but his smile had begun to turn sour. He had been quite prepared to let the magistrate believe me a thief, and even a killer. My presence was becoming inconvenient.

Like all the Berwick Street girls, I employed the skills taught by Ma – to sit perfectly still and to exhibit no emotion; to be elegant, refined and ready for anything. Now I sat in fear of my life, but to anyone chancing upon this scene I would have appeared like a polite hostess – back straight, hands neatly folded in my lap, face serene and unmoved by anxiety.

'And Mr Groves?' I asked. 'Do you intend to leave him there on his face?'

He jerked his head over towards the office.

'That fat fool; he's almost as bad as Reed, you know. I swear that he was planning to start blackmailing me, just as Reed did. He knew. That bastard Reed had said something to him – just like you thought he had.'

I didn't want Mr Groves' death on my conscience. I would never be able to look Susan in the face again.

'But it wasn't John Groves who sent blackmail letters, was it? It was you. You sent a fresh letter to yourself. You sent letters to Mr Herring and Mrs Farley.'

He chuckled.

'Oh, she's been a very naughty girl, you know. I was delighted to read Reed's comments about her. Even that scratchy writing couldn't hide her sins from me.' He sniggered into the brandy.

A new sensation prickled behind my eyes. Not fear, but fury. Ma had been distraught. She had turned to drink, bled us all dry for money and forced me into bed with a monster. Memories of that night would haunt me for years. The hurt Charles had so casually caused made me want to scream.

I still sat, silent on the outside.

'What did you hit him with?'

He sighed, as if this were a dull question.

'It's a butchery, Lizzie, there are mallets and cleavers in the back. They keep them in a cupboard.'

I hadn't noticed the cupboard; the dead man on the floor had rather put me off examining the furniture.

'And what will you do, Charles? Where will you go?'

He rubbed an eyebrow idly, as if he were pondering a holiday.

'I rather fancied going back to Paris, you know. I liked it there.' He leaned forward and proffered the brandy bottle which, by now, had only a few fingers of liquid left. 'You could come with me.'

I took the bottle and had a small sip, just enough to let it touch my tongue and give me courage. I forced a laugh.

'Be a rogue like you? Living on the road as your doxy? You might want to make it sound more attractive.'

He smiled at me again, almost fondly this time.

'Well, you're either coming with me or staying with Mr Groves.'

He didn't need to make the meaning plainer. I steadied the bottle on the table and smoothed my skirt, careful not to glance at the door even as I readied myself to run.

I smiled back.

'Then I suppose I'd better brush up my French,' I said, sounding as bright as I could.

I leaped to my feet, catching him off guard and flinging myself towards the door. But even as I pushed my own chair back, I heard his scrape and clatter to the floor. He was faster, and he didn't have skirts clinging about his calves. I didn't make it more than a couple of yards.

His hand dug into my upper arm as he grabbed me and spun me around to face him. There was rage in his eyes.

'Stupid bitch!' He smacked me hard across the cheek and I crumpled to the ground at the force of the blow. The pain tore through my face somewhere between my mouth and eye and I wondered whether he had broken bone as well as skin.

Before I had chance to put a hand to it he was on me. On top of me. His fingers pressed into my neck until I was fighting for breath. Then he stopped squeezing my throat, sat back and let me gasp for air. I tried to scream but only a gurgling noise came out.

He tugged my skirts up and kicked my legs apart. He laughed, one hand pressing me to the hard floor.

'One last fuck, eh Lizzie, for old times? You were always such a willing little slut.'

I had been willing enough before; I was not willing now. He was strong, but he was also unsteady, and his breath reeked of brandy. He fumbled at the buttons on his breeches. There was a split second when he lost the focus of his intended course, and his eyes strayed briefly from my face to his own crotch. I was sober, and I was anticipating it, and it was just enough. With all my strength, I jolted him off balance and thrust him to one side.

Face throbbing with pain, throat sore, I ran for the door, only to find that, again, he was faster. He reached the door, slammed it and stood glaring at me.

He pulled a short knife from inside his coat and began to walk slowly towards me. I inched back in step with him, as if we were engaged in some sort of horrific courtly dance. Then I turned and ran for the steps of the wooden bridge.

There was a hard laugh behind me as I ran up the steps. I saw why he was laughing. The bridge was not symmetrical. There were steps only up one side. The other end of the bridge, to which I was running, ended in the wall. I was trapped.

Chapter Fifty

He climbed the steps after me, taking his time. He had the knife in one hand and, in the other, a long pole. I could make out the curved metal crook at the end of the pole, even in the dark of the ceiling. The slaughterhouse floor looked a long way below me; I couldn't land without breaking a limb, at least.

'I'm sorry it's got to end this way,' he said, advancing like a knight, lance tucked under his arm. 'You know too much, my darling.'

'I'm sure that we can come to some sort of arrangement,' I said, trying to work out a way of getting down from the bridge. 'After all, we're both people of business, in our different ways.' I took another step back, conscious that my back was now only inches from the wall.

He lunged at me with the pole. I dodged it, only to find he was coming now with the blade. Again, I swung away to avoid it, but there was no way that I was going to pass him on the narrow walkway. He frowned at his clumsy attempt, knowing that he had downed too much brandy for precision. I knew that he would only have to strike once to wound me fatally.

The pole was hampering him. Eyes on me, he propped it up against the handrail and gripped the knife again.

'Let's finish this now,' he said, to himself more than to me, wiping his hand across his mouth. 'I need to get going.'

'Charles, don't!' My cry was enough to catch him off guard as he lurched into me. The knife caught the inside of my arm and a sharp pain sliced through me, but it was he who staggered. I seized my chance, grabbed the pole, cracked it hard on his foot and whacked it up into his groin.

He howled – whether in anger or pain, I couldn't tell.

'Damned fucking whore!'

I still couldn't pass him. He was bent double, but I was trapped up against the wall.

He pitched towards me again with the knife. Without thinking, I swung the pole up, hooked it on to a metal rod full of hams and leaped over the handrail, clinging on to the pole for dear life. I had jumped off the bridge – but was now swinging in mid-air like a piece of meat.

Charles leaned over the rail and tried to grab me, but I was just too far out of reach. He threw a leg over and sat astride the rail to try again. As he reached for me I swung on the pole to escape his hands. He lost his balance and, with a yelp, crashed to the stone floor, landing badly.

His right leg was splayed at a horrible angle. From his cries, he was still very much alive, and in pain.

I was swaying on the pole, but my hands were starting to lose their grip, my arm was stinging with the pain of the knife wound, blood beginning to colour the sleeve of my gown. The sight of it made me feel sick. I would be joining him on the floor unless I could swing myself back on to the bridge.

There was a commotion below. Half a dozen men burst through the door. Tommy Bridgewater, Grimshaw and Carter flung themselves at the prone figure of Charles, while the others sprinted up the steps to the bridge, one ahead of the rest.

'Do you think you can swing yourself towards the rail, Miss Hardwicke? I don't think any of us wants to lean too far over it.' It was William Davenport.

'I'll do my best. My hands are slipping.'

I began to rock my legs, like a child on a swing, increasing the angle with each effort, trying not to panic about my sweating palms and the pain screaming in my arm and in my face.

With another man holding him secure, Davenport reached for me. He clung tightly to my skirts and with a grunt tugged me over the bar. I fell on him and knocked him over.

'Thank you for coming,' I said, lying awkwardly on top of him.

'Not a moment too soon, it appears,' he said, voice muffled by a greater expanse of my chest than either of us might have wished.

We lay like that for a moment, each of us getting our breath back. I eased myself off him and stood to survey the scene below. Thomas Beech was being half-carried, half-shoved towards the door by Fielding's men.

'He told me everything, you know,' I said to Davenport, as I tugged the top of my gown back to a more modest location.

'I'm pleased to hear it,' he said, dusting off his breeches, 'it'll add to what's been found at Norwich.'

I must have looked surprised, because he added, 'I sent a man to Reed's house, you remember that I said I might? He brought back a pile of letters and notes this afternoon – just before your messenger arrived. They make for interesting reading.'

There were men milling around on the floor below us, gathering themselves to deal with a dead body. I started to feel light-headed and put a hand out to Davenport to steady myself.

'May I escort you home, Miss Hardwicke? You look as though you need some rest.'

I nodded.

'Thank you, Mr Davenport. I'd like that.' Suddenly I was shaking. My legs wobbled uncontrollably, and I crumpled to the floor. He came to me, picked me up as if I were a child and, slowly, carried me down the steps, out of the butchery door and into the evening sun.

Chapter Fifty-One

It was daylight. I had a thumping headache, a sore arm and a throat like sand. For a moment, I had no idea where I was or what day it was. All I knew was that most of me hurt. Polly was sitting by my bed; I was home. I grunted at her, unable to form words properly.

She kissed the top of my head and said gently, 'Shh. Lie still. Try not to speak.'

'Where's Mr Davenport?' I croaked.

She laughed at me.

'He's downstairs. He asked me to fetch him when you woke up. He's been here all night, you know.'

'Really?'

'He told us what happened. Charles nearly killed you.' Her eyes began to water.

'Don't cry,' I rasped, my throat on fire. I patted her hand. 'I'm not dead. But tell Ma that I'm only attractive to gentlemen with very unusual tastes.'

She sniffed and nodded.

'I'll go and find Mr Davenport. And I'll bring you some brandy.'

'Not brandy.' I couldn't face that. 'Tea. Sugar. Lots.'

I turned over and let quiet tears seep into my pillow.

He tapped at the door and entered with a tray.

'Polly says you're awake, but you've lost your voice,' he said as he laid the tea on the table. 'That sounds like a perfect outcome.'

I rubbed a hand over my face, brushing the tears away, and sat up. His face fell.

'I'm sorry, I shouldn't joke about it. Forgive me.'

I shook my head.

'Nothing to forgive. I'm only glad you helped me down from among the hams.'

He started pouring the tea, then put the pot down suddenly and snapped. 'Why did you have to tackle Beech on your own? Why didn't you wait for us to reach you? He could have killed you, you know.'

I closed my eyes. I didn't like being scolded, especially given how much pain I was in. I had, after all, just caught a murderer for him. When I opened my eyes, I saw he was concerned, rather than cross.

'If I'd waited, then he might have got away; he was leaving for France. I didn't know how long the tailor's lad would take to reach you and I thought I could keep him at the butcher's. Besides,' and this was the truth of it, 'I needed to know, for myself, what he had done. I just needed to know.'

I took a gulp of tea and let it warm my throat, unwilling to admit that I also had a tendency to rashness.

He sat in the chair next to my bed and sipped from his own cup, nodding at my bandaged arm.

'Are you still in much pain?'

'Thank you, doctor, I'm sure I'll survive.'

He muttered something to himself that I didn't hear and then gave me a half-hearted smile. 'Yes, I understand from young Sam at Bow Street that you've been asking about me.'

'It seemed unfair for you to know about my past and for me not to know a little of yours.'

'Touché, Elizabeth Vessey.'

The sound of my own name made me nervous.

'Lizzie,' I said. 'Lizzie Hardwicke, always.'

He caught enough of my meaning to let the subject drop. He bent forward and untied the bandage before taking a careful look at the wound Charles had scored with his knife. He reached into a large bag that I hadn't noticed was on the floor and spread a thin layer of some sort of ointment onto my skin. It stung, and I yelped.

'This will help it heal faster.'

'It seems to be making things worse at the moment.'

He snorted as he found fresh cloth and wrapped my arm again.

'You can have more laudanum if you want.' He nodded to the bottle on the table. I dimly remembered him forcing me to drink a glass of something last night when he brought me home. No wonder I had slept. 'You're lucky. He's made a bit of a mess of your skin, but, beyond a scar, there'll be no lasting damage.'

My eyes dropped to my old wounds, those criss-crossing my left hand and arm. Davenport noticed and picked up my hand to look more closely.

'This looks a lot worse to me. You were cut, badly – a while ago. It wasn't properly treated at the time.' He touched one of the scars very gently. 'Your uncle did this, I think.'

I took a breath. 'It was my fault. I made a mistake. One day I told him that I wanted nothing more to do with him.

He took a knife, held my arm, and cut my skin. There was a lot of blood and I passed out at the sight of it. I think he just kept cutting. He told the servants I had broken a glass in a fit of temper.'

He told me that if refused him again he would put a scar on my face.

'It doesn't hurt so much anymore. It itches sometimes; just an ugly reminder of my past.'

He ran a finger over the marks. 'I'm not sure I can heal these.'

'Lots of us carry scars, Mr Davenport; not all of them are visible,' I said, touching my hand to his chest. 'Some pains we simply have to live with.'

We were both quiet for a while. I went back to my tea.

'What's happened to Charles – Thomas Beech, I mean?'

He straightened up and shook his shoulders. His face assumed its usual serious expression.

'Mr Fielding has sent him to Newgate. The men took him this morning, first light. He'll be tried very soon and hanged before the month ends.' He tilted his head to look out of the window. 'He's likely to go out with John Swann, although the irony will probably be lost on him on the day.'

It wasn't lost on me, but the pretty poetry of it paled alongside the reality of what he had done to deserve his death. 'He killed four people: George Reed, Sallie, Mr Groves and the real Charles Stanford.'

'He tried to kill you too, of course, but I'm afraid that will be forgotten in the light of his greater crimes.'

'At least Sallie will have her justice.'

349

He smiled a little. 'Only because you refused to give up on her. It was Sallie's button that led you to the tailor's.'

The tailor's shop made me think of Susan Groves.

'Mrs Groves!' I nearly sent the tea flying. 'Is she still waiting for her husband? She won't know he's dead.'

'Calm down, she knows. We're not monsters at Bow Street. Mr Fielding sent a man round to speak to her.'

'Not Mr Grimshaw, I hope?' I couldn't bear the thought of that man breaking bad news to such a fragile person.

'No, not Jack. Subtlety is not Jack's finest quality – although he has many admirable traits when you get to know him, really he does.' I must have looked doubtful at this, because he kept repeating it.

'At least she has Amelia to care for her, and I think she was hoping Tommy Bridgewater might stay too,' I said. 'Amelia can marry now and be respectable. She doesn't have to linger in this pit of vice, this house of sin at least.' Recalling our earlier conversations, I gave him the most lascivious wink my sore face could manage.

He ignored the wink; it can't have looked alluring.

'Mr Fielding sends his regards to you, by the way.'

'Really?'

'He asked me to invite you to Bow Street – when Beech's trial is over. He would like to discuss how much he might pay you for the information that led us to Beech. And how he'll pay you in future.'

'I don't understand.'

He smiled. It was a warm and open expression. I could genuinely like him when he smiled.

'He was most impressed by you. We could do with someone in Soho, watching, listening to what's going on behind these elegant doorways.'

'Be like John Reading, you mean?' I raised my eyebrows at him.

'Like John Reading. But in better clothes.'

'Working with you?'

He nodded. 'Sometimes.'

'And I'll be paid?'

'Not much, but yes – by results.'

I stuck out a hand.

'I'll do it.'

He took my hand and shook it firmly. It wasn't only Mr Fielding who had been impressed, I was sure of it.

'You've got your retirement fund to think of, after all,' he said.

I didn't know whether it was the money or the adventure that was uppermost in my mind. Or even the possibility that we might work together again.

'Thank you.' I put my hand over Davenport's. I had nothing else to say.

He stood up. 'I really must go,' he said. He hesitated, '...ah, but I have something of interest for you. I nearly forgot. This will take your mind off your pain.'

'What is it?' I sat up, intrigued.

'Among Reed's papers we found the letters to Mrs Farley. I thought that you might return them to her for me. Of course, they are addressed to her, so really ought to be private—'

He handed me a small packet of papers with a knowing look. I smiled back and tucked them under my pillow to enjoy later. Whatever was in them, such knowledge would be enough to keep Ma off my back for a long time.

Historical Note

This is a work of fiction. However, as someone who has spent a lot of my life studying and writing about history, I feel duty-bound to offer some comments and disclaimers on the places where I have taken liberties.

Firstly, this is a twenty-first century take on the mid-eighteenth century and not historical pastiche. Although I have tried to make sure that my characters don't speak too much in twenty-first century idiom, I have written for readers who do. Likewise, I have avoided too many eighteenth-century-isms that no one uses any more. I've sneaked a couple in, when the meaning is obvious, just because. I've held back on the swearing. They cursed fulsomely in those days and were much ruder than I have dared to be.

Secondly, a word about John Fielding. He was a real person (1721–1780), knighted in 1761 (two years after this story takes place). Along with his half-brother, the writer Henry Fielding, he began what became England's police force. Most people who have heard of John Fielding know him as the founder of the 'Bow Street Runners'. They were not called 'runners' until the 1770s, and the term was a nickname, rather than a proper name, but I like it — especially when it's used by the more cynical characters in this book – so I have unashamedly allowed this anachronism.

Thirdly, John Fielding's clerical staff kept meticulous and detailed reports. These would have been extremely useful to historians and novelists alike. Sadly, they were destroyed by fire in 1780 and what is known of them comes via the records of the Old Bailey. It means that a full and thorough account of Fielding's work can never really be written. It also means that a novelist can take a good deal of licence, using her imagination.

Here are some of the books that I have found useful in my research for this novel. If you want to discover more about London, Britain and the eighteenth century, you might like to have a look at them.

Beattie, J. M., *The First English Detectives. The Bow Street Runners and the Policing of London*, 1750–1840.

Beaumont, Matthew, *Night Walking. A Nocturnal History of London*.

Buck, Anne, *Dress in Eighteenth Century England*.

Cruickshank, Dan, *The Secret History of Georgian London*.

Gatrell, Vic, *The First Bohemians*.

McLynn, Frank, *1759. The Year Britain became Master of the World*.

Picard, Liza, *Dr Johnson's London. Life in London 1740-1770*.

Porter, Roy, *English Society in the 18th Century*.

Pringle, Patrick, *Hue and Cry. The Birth of the British Police*.

Rubenhold, Hallie, *The Covent Garden Ladies. The Extraordinary Story of Harris's List*.

Vickery, Amanda, *Behind Closed Doors. At Home in Georgian England.*

White, Jerry, *London in the Eighteenth Century. A Great and Monstrous Thing.*

Acknowledgements

Thank you to Laura Macdougall at United Agents for being such a brilliant agent and fabulous person. I am grateful beyond words for her encouragement, attention to detail, and good humour.

Thanks to my editor, Laura McCallen, and the team at Canelo, for their imagination, expertise and enthusiasm for this book – and for their excitement at the prospect of more Lizzie Hardwicke novels.

The members of the Worcester Writers' Circle were the first to hear me read chapter one of this novel and they giggled in all the right places and advised me to get on with it. Cheers, you lovely bunch.

Thanks to Hannah Persaud for her support, especially over the summer of 2018. It is possible, it seems, to meet someone on Twitter and click. And, in real life, we can talk for hours.

Thanks to fellow writers on Twitter for all the retweets and GIFs. You know who you are.

Only a few friends knew I was writing a novel. Their gentle encouragement kept me going more than they will know. I'm looking at you, Yvonne Pollitt, Elaine Willmore, Robert Jones, Amanda Woodd, Jenny Floyd, Mark Pryce, Charmian Manship and Sarah Henderson. Thanks also to my colleagues, Peter Atkinson and Michael

Brierley, for showing entirely appropriate levels of interest and amusement – as always, chaps.

I'd like to thank my brother, John Byrne, for bearing with his odd sister and her need for lots of words. It's such a pleasure to have a brother I can talk to for hours and connect with at such a deep level, and, from my heart, I thank him for encouraging me.

Thank you to Kay Garlick, who is gracious, good-humoured and wise, and who offers sound advice.

Thanks in abundance to my soul-sisters, Faith Claringbull and Jane Tillier, who know what makes my heart sing, and who join their voices in such wonderful encouragement. Together, we've walked the good times and bad, and I could not have made this journey without them.

Finally, the boys. My son Sebastian: I have written around the school run, his social life and his bed time. This novel has only appeared on my laptop when he has not appeared in front of it. One day he will realise that his mother knows four-letter words. That day is not yet.

Thank you to Tim: husband, friend, confidante, lover. He has had my heart for eighteen years – long enough for me to know that he won't appreciate me gushing in public. Instead, I am dedicating this novel to him, as a small token of my love and gratitude – for all the sticky toffee pudding, for the one word he contributed, and for everything else.

Lizzie Hardwicke

Death and the Harlot
The Corpse Played Dead